The Staveley Suspect

By Rebecca Tope

The Staveley Suspect

REBECCA TOPE

Allison & Busby Limited
12 Fitzroy Mews
London W1T 6DW
allisonandbusby.com

First published in Great Britain by Allison & Busby in 2018.

Copyright © 2018 by REBECCA TOPE

A CIP catalogue record for this book is available from the British Library.

First Edition

ISBN 978-0-7490-2239-6

Typeset in 11/16 pt Sabon by
Allison & Busby Ltd

The paper used for this Allison & Busby publication
has been produced from trees that have been legally sourced
from well-managed and credibly certified forests.

Printed and bound by
CPI Group (UK) Ltd, Croydon, CR0 4YY

*This one's for Gary – a very welcome
new member of the family*

Author's Note

As in previous stories, the village settings are authentic, but individual properties have been invented.

Chapter One

Bonnie had a cold, which turned her eyes and nose bright pink. 'You look like a white rabbit,' said Simmy. 'A very poorly white rabbit at that.'

'Urggh,' said the girl. 'Am I going to put the customers off, do you think?'

'Very likely. They'll think I'm a cruel employer, forcing you to work when you're ill. You ought to go home for a couple of days.'

'The house is freezing. It'll make me worse. Corinne let the oil tank run dry and a man has to come and do something complicated to get the boiler working again.'

'It can't be worse than here.' The florist shop was never very warm, since the blooms lasted much better in cool temperatures. The humidity caused by the watering increased the feeling of being in a rather inhospitable northern forest.

'It's all right,' said Bonnie with a sniff. Before Simmy could reply, the phone pealed imperiously, and she was distracted.

'Hello – is that the flower shop?' The voice was female, and instantly likeable.

'That's right.'

'Good. I've got a commission for you, if you're interested.'

Simmy picked up a pen, and swept through a mess of junk mail and delivery notes for the notepad she used for taking telephone orders. The system still hadn't reached the level of efficiency that she had aimed for when she first opened the shop. The fact that the majority of orders came through the computer reduced the urgency. 'Right,' she said. 'What can we do for you?'

'It's a party. A retirement party. I want to make it a bit special, with lots of flowers everywhere.'

'When?' asked Simmy, having written *retirement party* on the pad.

'Rather short notice, I'm afraid. We were hoping for the weekend after next.'

'Shouldn't be a problem,' said Simmy confidently. 'Though it's a bit close to Mother's Day.' Her silent inward sigh marked her customary reaction to that particular cultural atrocity. However she looked at it, she could only see it as cynical, commercial and sometimes even cruel.

'Oh, God, Mother's Day,' said the woman on the phone, with a heartfelt groan that more than echoed Simmy's little sigh. 'It seems to come round every few weeks. I suppose it's a big day for a florist.'

'Right,' said Simmy.

'Anyway. The party. It's going to be in Staveley.'

Simmy wrote *Staveley* on her pad. 'Can I take your name?' she said.

'Oh – sorry. Yes, I'm Gillian Townsend. It's my colleague who's retiring. We're solicitors. Things have been so busy lately, we didn't get around to organising the do until now.'

'Is it in a hall, or somebody's house?'

'That's been quite a burning question. We did think of using the party barn at Askham Hall, but it's a long way away, and somehow it doesn't strike the right note. So now we've finally decided to have it at my mother's house here in Staveley.'

Gillian Townsend sounded to be at least sixty, which gave Simmy a startled moment to think she had a mother living. But this was a regular experience in recent times. People in their seventies quite often had an ancient parent still surviving.

'Is the party to be a surprise?'

'God, no. What a horrible thought! Anita is quite central to the whole business. She's right here beside me now, listening to us on the speakerphone. She has the final say on everything. But she's a good delegator, so I get to do flowers, food and invitations.'

Simmy gave a polite laugh, while wondering what else was required. Drink; car parking; music, she supposed. 'How many rooms do you want decorated? With flowers, I mean.'

'Oh, gosh. Only two or three, I suppose. There's a big hallway, two reception rooms, the kitchen . . . we won't do the kitchen. And we'll be using the conservatory, so we should do that as well. Can you come and look at it with me, do you think? We can plan it together, then.' The voice had become breathless towards the end of this little speech, causing Simmy to wonder whether it was due to excitement or defective lungs.

11

Simmy was thinking about money, and lessons learnt over the past year or two. Charge for your time. Charge for wastage. Charge for use of containers and clearing up afterwards, if required. She was entitled to make a decent profit from the job, she reminded herself. Solicitors were generally well-heeled, after all. 'Yes, of course. When?'

'Well, the sooner the better.'

'This evening? I could come on the way home, after I've taken some flowers to someone in Crook.' Only then did Simmy notice that Bonnie wasn't listening in with her usual avidity. Her young assistant had a habit of standing two feet away and mouthing comments on the conversation. Instead, she was drooping at the front of the shop, like a melting wax statue. Her head was bowed and shoulders slumped. Simmy took the phone away from her ear. 'Bonnie? What's the matter?'

'I feel funny. My head hurts.'

Simmy went back to the phone. 'Sorry. Did you say something? I was distracted for a minute. Can you tell me where to come, and I'll see you at about a quarter to six.' Her eyes were on Bonnie, who had straightened up slightly.

'If you're coming from Crook, you can most easily meet us at the lay-by by the bus stop in the middle of the village and we can lead you to the house. It's a bit difficult to find, especially in the dark.' It got dark by six, Simmy remembered, with her persistent nervousness about roaming the Cumbrian wilderness at night. Just a mile or two off the main roads, you could be lost forever if you took a careless turn somewhere, either on foot or in a car.

'Actually, I'm not sure I can find the lay-by. Is there an obvious landmark?'

'It's across the road from the fish and chip shop, and the bus stop is part of the public lavatories. You can't really miss it, when you come out from the Crook road. It's just across from the turning to Kentmere.'

'It sounds fairly foolproof. I'm sure I'll find it. Thanks. I'll see you later.'

'Take my phone number, in case you get delayed – or lost.' The last words were added with a laugh that sounded mildly scornful to Simmy. She had delivered flowers to addresses in Staveley perhaps half a dozen times in the past year, but had no recollection of a bus stop. She remembered a network of small streets, many of them cul-de-sacs, a defunct bridge that was slowly being rebuilt and a beautiful winding road out to Kentmere, running alongside a cheerful little river.

With a flicker of resentment, she jotted down the digits and hoped she would remember to put them into her mobile. The need to attend to Bonnie was the prime concern of the moment. 'Hey,' she said, as soon as the phone call ended. 'Come and sit down. You must have got flu.'

'I hope not,' said Bonnie waveringly. 'That would be a real pain.'

'I'd better take you home. You look rather awful.'

'Oh, no. You can't close the shop on a Friday. Mrs Hyacinth hasn't been in yet. And isn't that man coming for his roses at eleven?'

Mrs Hyacinth was in fact an affluent local businesswoman who had, the previous Christmas, ordered eight bowls of hyacinths on the brink of bursting into flower. Simmy and Bonnie had agonised over the things and cast many slanderous aspersions on the woman. In the event it worked perfectly, and earned a surprising gratuity on top of the inflated price Simmy had permitted herself to charge.

Now Mrs Hyacinth materialised every Friday lunchtime for more highly scented weekend flowers.

'I'll be back in time for both of them if we go now.'

'No,' Bonnie almost whined. 'I don't want to go home. I'll make myself a Lemsip and I'll be okay. It's not flu. Corinne would tell you that flu's a lot more serious than this.'

Outside the weather was dithering between winter and spring. The fells had snow on their heads, and the becks had fringes of ice. Snowdrops nodded cheerily in gardens and on mossy banks, but most of the trees were still playing dead. Nobody had very high expectations of March, with its tendency towards biting easterly winds. The majority of customers coming into the shops had the same pink noses and clogged throats as Bonnie had.

'I bet Spike would be glad to see you,' Simmy cajoled. Spike was Bonnie's dog, whose welfare and general happiness had suffered some neglect over the past half-year or so. Not only had his beloved young mistress taken a job, causing her wholesale removal from his life during the day, but she had also taken a swain, who occupied her during evenings and Sundays.

'Spike's fine,' said the girl defensively. 'Corinne takes him everywhere with her these days.'

'All right, then. But try to avoid fainting on me, will you? You look awfully cold to me. That jumper's not much use, is it?' Bonnie was wearing a thin garment with a low neck, leaving her bronchial region exposed to the cool air. 'There's a fleece in the back room that might fit you. Put it on.'

14

The fact that the girl didn't argue was proof enough of her illness. 'And Lemsip's a good idea,' Simmy added.

Fridays had, in recent months, acquired new levels of significance. Since the rekindling of a relationship from her teenage years, Simmy had begun to expect more of weekends than hitherto. But because both she and Christopher were often busier on Saturdays than any other day, the expectations had to be modified. It was worse for her, with every Saturday morning relatively hectic in the shop, while her boyfriend only worked every other weekend. He was the auctioneer at an operation near Keswick. For six or seven hours on sale days he sold antiques, collectables and general items to dealers and housewives and auction junkies of all kinds.

The arrival of the man for the roses meant leaving Bonnie to wrestle with her germs unassisted. The order had been for two dozen mixed blooms, scented, still in bud, and embellished with wispy ferns and other greenery. An anniversary, he said, without any further explanation. When he'd gone, the usual speculations as to the length of the marriage, the ages of the parties involved and the nature of their celebration did not take place. Bonnie sat down in front of the shop computer, and started making notes on the prices of various flowers, in a half-hearted attempt to educate herself. In the process, she tidied Simmy's messy heap on the table. 'Retirement in Staveley?' she said, looking at the notes on the pad. 'That's a bit different. You haven't put the date.'

Simmy was picking out faded blooms from the displays at the front of the shop. 'It's the weekend before Mother's Day. I've got to go and meet the woman this evening.

She's taking me to see the house where the party's going to be. Oh, and I should put her number into my phone. I nearly forgot.'

'I'll do it if you like,' Bonnie offered. 'Is this it here?'

'Thanks.' Simmy willingly handed over her mobile, grateful for the skill of the young.

Bonnie changed the subject as she handed back the phone. 'Has Chris got a sale tomorrow?'

'He has. I won't see him until Sunday. I'll go over to Beck View after we close up tomorrow and give my mum a hand. Last time I was there, the place was looking very grubby. There'll be complaints if she's not careful.'

'Is she bothered?'

'Not very. But she's got to stick to at least some of the rules. They'll close her down if they think she's a health hazard.'

Bonnie gave a choked little laugh. 'That's not going to happen, is it? What does a bit of dust matter?'

'It's more than that. The bathrooms have to be spotless, for a start.'

'Was that your dad's job before he – you know?'

'Before his wits started to go. Don't worry, you can say it.' They exchanged smiles. 'He did quite a lot of that sort of thing, yes. He still polishes all the mirrors every week. That's always been his speciality. And some people do leave the loos in a pretty bad state. My mother hates anything like that. Always leaves it till last and then it doesn't get done.'

'Yuck,' said Bonnie.

The demands of the Lakeland B&B run by Simmy's parents were quickly becoming more than they could easily cope with. Her father's sudden plunge into a mild variety of dementia had thrown the entire operation into confusion. His chief symptom was anxiety, causing him to lock doors and make excessive demands on the guests' patience. While his memory and general capacity to function remained unimpaired, he was unpredictable and increasingly uninhibited in what he said.

'Are you feeling better now?' Simmy asked, at lunchtime. 'Have you got plenty to eat? They say you should feed a cold, you know.'

'I'm okay. Mrs Hyacinth's late. I might have another Lemsip.' Bonnie was distracted by the warbling of her phone. Simmy had no doubt that it denoted a text from Ben Harkness. He invariably phoned or texted in the middle of the day. Still at school, he was in the final stretch of his A-level studies, trying to make light of an almost intolerable workload.

'You have to wait four hours,' said Simmy. 'It says on the box.'

'Duh,' said Bonnie.

They were diverted by the arrival of a small fistful of post coming through the door. The general procedure was for the postman to come in, and put the letters on whatever clear surface he could find, if Simmy didn't rush forward to take them from him. But this was a different man, and he simply threw them down without taking a step off the pavement outside. The absence of a letter box was clearly an annoyance to him. A long way down Simmy's to-do list was to attach a box of some sort to the outside wall for the purpose.

Bonnie went to collect the scattered envelopes. The mere

fact of old-fashioned letters intrigued her. People paid their bills with cheques to a surprising extent. Once in a while they included handwritten letters of appreciation. Two or three had enclosed photos of the wedding or birthday party showing how handsomely the flowers had enhanced the occasion. 'This one looks like it's from a satisfied customer,' Bonnie observed, pulling out a white envelope with a handwritten address on the front.

Simmy took it. 'Not likely. The postmark's Birmingham, look.'

Bonnie peered at it. 'Postmark?' she said with a frown.

'Good God, girl. Don't you know about postmarks?'

Bonnie grimaced. 'Not really,' she admitted.

'I'll report you to Ben. He'll be disgusted with you. Postmarks are often crucial clues in a criminal investigation. Agatha Christie must be full of them.'

The letter was giving Simmy some early pangs of apprehension. She knew the handwriting, but could not believe her own eyes. Surely it wasn't from the woman who made large capital letters and then bunched the rest of the word together after it? 'Windermere' followed this familiar pattern. And the person in question lived in Birmingham.

She opened it, took out the single page, and turned it over to see the signature. 'Bloody hell. It is her.' She looked at Bonnie, as if for an explanation. 'It's from my mother-in-law.'

Chapter Two

'Who?' said Bonnie.

'My husband's mother. She's called Pamela.'

'Oh. Did you get along okay with her?'

'Pretty well,' said Simmy vaguely, having begun to read the letter. 'This is incredible.'

Dear Simmy,

I hope you will forgive this intrusion, but I feel you should know what has been happening to Tony. You will have perhaps been aware that he suffered a violent attack last year, and spent several days in hospital. Although I realise that you might well not have known about that, because neither he nor I have told you. I suppose we just assumed that somebody in authority would have sent notification, since there is at least an indirect connection with you, and the loss of your baby.

Anyway, be that as it may, I must tell you that your former husband is now under prosecution for the crime (if crime it be) of stalking the woman who delivered your little girl. It is a sorry tale, I'm afraid. The woman claims that Tony developed an irrational feeling for her, and would not accept her refusal to reciprocate. Eventually she felt forced to take extreme action, and she stabbed him in the back. When the police investigated, she said it was self-defence, and she made a counter-accusation against him. Needless to say, there have been months of rather low-level legal wrangling, while the woman lost her job, and Tony recovered from a punctured lung. But now it is due shortly to come to trial, and there will be unsavoury publicity, which might even reach the wilderness where you currently live. And given that this whole business began at the time of your distressing experience in the Worcester hospital, I fear you will be drawn into it – if you haven't been already.

I have no way of knowing whether or not any of this has already been conveyed to you. The trial is to be in April. Tony is very much reduced, and it is a source of great sadness to the whole family. He has never even begun to recover from the loss of the baby, and his defence will focus very much on that. I cannot say for sure whether you will be asked to give testimony to the effect that his very sanity was disturbed by it.

I hope that you are well and happy in your new life. I remember you fondly, and am very much the

poorer for the cessation of our relationship – the
reasons for which I shall never fully understand.
  In friendship,
  Pamela Brown

'Can I see it?' asked Bonnie, having jigged impatiently throughout Simmy's perusal of the letter.

'I suppose so.' Simmy handed the paper over. Before the girl could finish, the shop doorbell pinged and the woman they had nicknamed Mrs Hyacinth came in, brisk as ever.

'Are those freesias in?' she asked, less than a second after the door closed behind her. 'And the jasmine you were going to get for me?'

'All ready and waiting,' said Simmy. 'As well as some very nice winter honeysuckle. I thought we could get some forsythia next week, and possibly mahonia.'

'No, not mahonia. I hate their smell. I've got one in the garden, and every year I remember how vile it is.'

'Okay,' said Simmy, thinking the woman must have a defective nose, if that was what she thought. 'Well, the choice is going to get wider from here on, of course.'

'I can't *wait* for sweetpeas,' said the customer, with wide-eyed enthusiasm. 'I'm growing my own, but I'm still hoping you can get me some special ones as well.'

'I'll try.' Simmy was watching Bonnie as she put Pamela's letter down on the table beside the computer. 'Let me get this week's offerings.'

She wrapped the flowers that had been sitting in the cool back room, and took the woman's money with a smile. 'Have a good weekend,' she said. 'See you next week?'

'Oh, yes. I must say you've improved our lives

tremendously. The house is always so full of wonderful scents now. And freesias are so marvellous, aren't they? Whatever you find for me next week, I still want plenty of freesias.'

'Right,' said Simmy.

'Wow!' said Bonnie, almost before the door had closed. 'Your ex is quite a case, from the sound of it. Did you know anything about all this – him being a stalker or whatever?'

'Not a hint. I haven't heard from him for a year or more. Once the divorce came through, I assumed that was the end of it. We'd got no reason to bother with each other ever again. I do miss Pamela sometimes, though. She was always quite nice to me.'

'Was she very upset about the baby?'

'I don't really know. Isn't that awful? She's got five grandchildren already, so I suppose it wasn't a huge loss for her. She was sorry for us, of course, but kept saying we could try again and these things happen. She's very old-fashioned.'

'Yeah. That letter – it sounds like something Wordsworth could have written.'

Simmy laughed. 'She must be eighty-five by now, and she was a civil servant much of her life. I think she was old-fashioned even as a girl.'

'She was pretty old when she had Tony, then?'

'Not a lot older than I am now,' said Simmy, with a pang. 'He was an after-thought, as they called it then. He's got two older brothers – much older. She'd been back at work for ages when she got pregnant again with Tony. She got a nanny for him and went right back to the Department of Trade, or whatever it was called.'

'How old is he, then?'

'Forty-four, I suppose, or thereabouts. Old enough to

know better than to go stalking some wretched nurse.' She picked up the letter. 'It's a strange sort of story, don't you think? I had no idea he'd been in hospital. Why would anybody tell me, anyway? They won't want me to be a witness at the trial, surely?'

'We can ask Ben. I expect he'll know. You might be able to send them something in writing, or get old Moxon to ask you some questions and send the answers. It's *miles* to Birmingham.'

'I don't think it'll be in Birmingham. That's just where his mother lives. He still lives in Worcester, so it's most likely to be there.' The strangeness of the whole business was increasing, the more she thought about it. The Tony she knew had been as sane as the next man, albeit undemonstrative and unreflective. The shock of the stillborn child had rendered him silent for weeks, dividing him from his wife to the point of no return. She suspected that it was the first time anything had gone wrong for him, and his lack of preparedness had been catastrophic. He had also refused to hold or even really look at the dead baby, while Simmy had cradled her for twenty minutes of acute but cathartic agony.

She could barely remember a midwife. Women had come and gone. Some had held her hand, some had looked away. They had known from before the labour began that the baby had died, which gave the whole experience an unearthly sort of futility. Afterwards, countless people had queried the lack of intervention. 'Couldn't they have saved her with a Caesarian?' they all asked.

The reply was never entirely satisfactory. 'By the time I got to the hospital, it was too late. There was no trace of a heartbeat. She probably died a day or two before I went into labour.' The truth was that Simmy could not reliably recall the series of events, the people who spoke to her, coloured as they were by the grey of Tony's face, and the endless waves of pain and panic that accompanied her contractions.

With an effort she did remember a woman leading Tony into another room. A large buxom nurse or midwife, who put an arm around his shoulders and said something about a cup of tea. Could he have somehow insanely fallen for her, as a kind of rescuing angel? There had been another encounter with her later in the day, as Simmy was waiting to go home. Papers had to be filled in, reports made, counselling offered. Somewhere on the ward Tony had also waited, sitting beside this woman who apparently had nothing else to do for a while but console the shattered father.

It all felt long ago and far away. She was a new person now – a florist, with a house and a boyfriend and increasingly dependent parents. She didn't have time for Tony any more. And if he had provoked that kind professional woman into attacking him with a knife, he probably didn't deserve any assistance she might be able to provide. Not that she could see the slightest chance of doing that. 'Yes, there was a kind midwife,' was the most she could say. That was the sum total of any testimony she could produce.

'That's a clever idea,' she told Bonnie. 'Using Moxon as a go-between might be all it needs.'

There ensued a Friday flurry of customers, including a pair of teenagers wanting to place advance orders for Mother's Day. Simmy sighed at the prospect of the busiest day in the florist's year, which had distressing personal associations, and which she passionately wished did not exist.

'Three new orders on the computer,' Bonnie reported at half past one.

'Great,' said Simmy, with more sincerity than it sounded. 'How's your cold now?'

'I'll survive. Time for another Lemsip. It's been four hours now.'

'You don't sound quite so bunged up. Has Ben got it as well?' It had been three days since Ben had visited the shop, thanks to his packed schedule. Course work, revision, additional subjects to those provided by the school, and his own personal pursuits – it all kept him fully occupied. Simmy sometimes wondered when he managed to give Bonnie any attention.

'No, he's okay so far. He said he'd come in today, after he's finished the biochemistry test.'

'Biochemistry? Surely that's not one of his A-levels, is it?'

'Biology is. He's applied for an aptitude test, to see if he can fit biochem into his first year at uni.'

Simmy shook her head. The complexities of the boy's studies were impossible to keep track of. His central ambition was to become a forensic archaeologist, which apparently called for Latin, geology, criminology and half a dozen other subjects. The local comprehensive was doing its best to fuel his needs, but inevitably left him to a certain amount of private study of subjects they didn't cover. In particular, he was teaching himself Latin, as well as instructing Bonnie in the basics.

'I'm hoping to close a bit early, so I can get to Staveley in good time,' she said.

'We've been busy, haven't we?' said Bonnie. 'New orders, plenty of customers. You must be pleased.'

'No deliveries today, though. That's unusual.'

'They'll be saving themselves for Mother's Day.' Bonnie was almost as hostile to the whole idea as Simmy was, for very different reasons. Her own mother had been damagingly deficient in her relations with her daughter, with Bonnie taken into care at the age of nine. Quickly scooped up by a foster mother named Corinne, she had endured many rocky years of dysfunction before attaining something resembling normality. The idea of sending cards or flowers to the woman who gave birth to her made her tense and rancorous.

Simmy had been raised to sneer at the blatant commercial cynicism of the whole business. Her mother refused any observance of the day intended to celebrate her unselfishness in producing a child and keeping it alive. 'The whole thing stinks,' said Angie reliably every year.

Now, not only could Simmy not ignore it, but a large portion of her annual income was derived from that single day, all on its own. Advance planning meant filling the storeroom with ribbons and cellophane, cards and wires, before the actual flowers could be acquired. It was exhausting, but undeniably exhilarating as well. This would be her second year of it, and she was determined to increase turnover, range and reputation, ignoring the emotional fallout.

'Here he is,' called Bonnie, ten seconds before her beloved came through the door. The repeat dose of Lemsip had already begun to take effect, her colour improved and nose less stuffed.

Ben actually looked rather worse than his girlfriend. Dark rings under his eyes, lank hair and chewed lips betrayed the weight of work he was carrying. Three more months of this, worried Simmy, would surely see him crumble under the strain. At eighteen, it seemed very hard to be devoting so much time and effort to his studies. 'Couldn't you spread it over an extra year?' she'd asked him. 'Instead of doing everything at once.'

The answer hadn't been entirely clear, but it seemed the idea was ludicrous.

Bonnie brought mugs of tea and a bucketful of tender female sympathy. 'Simmy's got to go to Staveley,' she told him. 'So we're closing up a bit early. I'll come back with you for a bit. I can carry some of the books.'

In fact, the bag of books was of modest proportions, since much of his study material existed in cyberspace and weighed nothing at all. 'Is your cold better?' he asked.

'Pretty much,' Bonnie lied.

'Good. There was something about Staveley last night.' He thumbed his phone-cum-computer and nodded. 'That's right. Man found dead, possible foul play. That was this morning. Nothing else since then, that I can see.'

His careless words struck alarm through Simmy's upper body. If somebody was unaccountably dead in Staveley, she very much didn't want to go there, for any reason, until the matter was safely resolved. Past experience had taught her that apparently irrelevant murders had a very nasty habit of turning out to be all too unpleasantly close to her and those she loved.

'Oh no,' she said. 'Not another one.'

Chapter Three

The delivery of a bouquet to a large house in Crook was a mild adventure in itself. The village comprised little more than a pub and a church, and was approached along an undulating road that carried as many tractors as other vehicles – at least on this particular afternoon. Overtaking was compromised not only by frequent blind bends, but dips and rises that concealed oncoming traffic. Simmy opted to wait patiently, enjoying the ancient fields on either side, with granite outcrops and moorland heathers here and there. One sheep she noticed had a lamb already. Spring must definitely be on its way, she thought gladly.

The road was wide enough for two vehicles, but there was no pavement, and the grass verge looked muddy in places. A pedestrian was barely visible in the fading light and Simmy had to swerve around her at the last moment. An oncoming car was going much too fast. It was all successfully negotiated, but Simmy's heart rate took a while to return to normal.

The flowers were for a pleasant woman with a small brown dog, living in a handsome property standing well back from the road. Simmy had some trouble finding its entrance, overshooting it and having to turn around in a gateway and go back. But it was all well within a normal day's work, and she forgot most of it as she carried on to Staveley, emerging almost like magic at the precise spot where Gillian Townsend had arranged to meet her.

Two women were awaiting her, standing in clear view on the pavement. One was unusually tall and the other noticeably short. There had to be ten or eleven inches difference in height, and the tableau they presented made Simmy smile. She drew up beside them, leaving the engine running. The shorter one twirled a hand to indicate that she should turn it off, which she did. Simmy opened the car door and the woman leant in.

'Hello. I'm Gillian. This is Anita. We thought I could drive ahead and you and Anita could follow on foot. You can leave your car here. Is that all right?'

Simmy could see no grounds for objection, despite the slightly peculiar arrangement. 'Fine,' she said.

'It sounds worse than it is,' said the taller woman. 'It's only two minutes away. Gillian doesn't walk if she can help it, that's all.' She had a musical voice and the immobile face that had become familiar on women in late middle age.

Botox, thought Simmy as she hesitated, looking from one face to the other. 'No problem,' she smiled. They set off as arranged, and after a few moments Simmy asked Anita whether she lived in Staveley.

'Just a little way over there,' she said, waving back towards the main road. A large area of green was ringed by substantial houses, and Simmy assumed one of those was the woman's home.

'Nice,' she said.

'Staveley's an oasis of normality, all the better for its lack of fame amongst visitors.' Anita took them only a very short way along the unassuming main street with a scattering of very ordinary shops, before turning right into the residential part of the village. Two more turns, and Simmy had no idea where they were when they stopped in front of a large stone house with a splendid garden between itself and the road. The light had almost gone during the past few minutes, and Simmy had to peer at the carpet of scilla and miniature cyclamen that replaced the usual lawn. A large mahonia reminded her of Mrs Hyacinth and her perverse dislike of it. She paused for a sniff of its yellow flowers that were just starting to fade and fall. The scent was perhaps a trifle sickly, she conceded.

'Taking a professional interest?' laughed Gillian Townsend, who was waiting for them by the front door.

'You could say that.'

'Well, you'll get plenty more chances, if this works out as we hope. Now come in and meet my mother. She's expecting us.'

They trooped up the path and through the front door, which Gillian opened with a loud 'Hello! We're here!' She led them across a good-sized hallway and into a front room where an elderly woman was standing beside an oak settle.

'You're very prompt,' she said. 'I haven't got the kettle on yet.'

Simmy was already envisaging swags of honeysuckle slung between the pictures, and large displays of spiky delphiniums on either side of the window. 'What a fabulous room!' she sighed.

Anita made a sound that suggested agreement, while her face carried a rueful expression.

Gillian made the introduction. 'Mrs Brown, this is my mother, Barbara Percival. Mum, this is the lady who runs Persimmon Petals in Windermere.'

'Yes, dear, I know,' smiled their hostess. 'Pleased to meet you.' She held out a hand for Simmy to shake. Her grip was firm and muscular. All that gardening, Simmy thought. 'I'm so glad you like the house. It is rather splendid, I must admit.' She looked up into Simmy's face with a mixture of admiration and friendliness. 'I really am very glad to meet you,' she said again.

'Have you always lived here?' Simmy asked, unsure as to how to respond to such obvious liking.

'Oh, no. Not at all. It came to my husband from his older brother, through a series of very sad events. That was sixteen years ago now. Then poor Stuart died only a year later, and here I am, rattling around in it all on my own.'

Simmy was still gazing around in rapture. 'But you've made it so lovely.'

'Thank you, dear. I felt I owed it to the place to keep it nice. And I turned out to be surprisingly good at it.' She laughed. 'Silly to waste one's time on a house, I suppose, but there it is.'

'It's perfect for a party,' Simmy went on with enthusiasm.

'Yes. Well, let's have some tea, shall we?' said Gillian briskly. 'I know it's officially cocktail time, but . . .'

'Don't be silly, Gill,' said Anita. 'Can we get on with it?'

It wasn't until they were seated around the room with

31

cups of tea that there was any chance of assessing at least the basics of the three new characters before her. Gillian was cheerfully breathless, a natural organiser and problem-solver. But there was something amiss with her, Simmy realised. Poor skin, restricted movement, and the difficulty with breathing all pointed to some kind of chronic physical malaise. But it evidently did not impede her competence. She produced a notepad from her bag, as well as a phone that she consulted at frequent intervals. As they started to discuss specific flowers, she would bring up an image, which she showed to the rather silent Anita.

Mrs Percival bustled about, equally focused as her daughter, but more gracious, as if aware of her status as senior person as well as owner of the party venue. She repeatedly smiled warmly at Simmy, treating her as the most important person present. She also inserted routine remarks concerning the safety of her porcelain and carpets. 'It won't be that sort of party,' said Gillian.

But it was Anita who drew Simmy's attention, time and again. The subtle power of silence was making itself felt across the whole room. Gillian and her mother both glanced repeatedly at the woman, who smiled bravely every time she met a pair of eyes. After twenty minutes or so, Gillian had had enough. 'Oh, Neet, come on. I know you're worried, but honestly, there's nothing more you can do about it now. This party's for you, remember. You need to tell us what you'd like.'

Simmy looked at Mrs Percival, wondering whether she knew what her daughter was talking about. Apparently she did, since she looked less bemused than Simmy felt. 'Darling, poor Mrs Brown doesn't want to hear all that sort of thing, now does she? She has no idea what's been going on. Keep it for later.'

'Sorry.' Gillian adopted an expression of deep contrition. 'The thing is, you see, Anita's son-in-law has been causing some concern, and now there's been some sort of discovery and the police won't tell the family anything. You can understand how worrying it is for everybody.'

With a sense of the inevitable, Simmy instantly connected this disclosure with Ben's report of a body found in Staveley. She looked round at the three women, marvelling at the realisation that somehow she had once again been dropped into the middle of a family catastrophe.

'Oh, *Gillian*,' snapped the old lady.

'What?'

'I asked you not to talk about that sort of thing. Never mind, my dear,' she said to Simmy. 'There's no need for you to bother yourself over it. Once we've given you the order for the flowers, there'll be no going back on it, whatever happens.'

Simmy was impressed, insulted and alarmed all at the same time. Impressed that the implications of the situation for the florist were so clear to the old lady; insulted because there was an assumption that all she cared about was her commission; alarmed because she actually was fearful of cancellation. If the son-in-law turned up dead, there was scant chance of a carefree party only a week or two later.

Anita finally spoke. 'That's not really true, Mrs Percival,' she said in a low voice. 'In fact, I think it's a mistake to be ploughing on with it as if everything was going to be all right. Debbie would see it as heartless and use it as further ammunition against me. Matthew would be just as angry,

33

too. I can't bear to risk that for something so frivolous.'

She had a pleasant accent, sounding the 'r's like an American and the 't's like a BBC announcer. It made her sound definite and unambiguous. Her height added further authority. Gillian looked at her with something close to sycophancy. 'Well, I suppose that's true,' she sighed. 'But we have to assume that Declan is perfectly all right. I know it's awful for poor Debbie – and it probably isn't anything good – but he can't possibly be *dead*.'

The word echoed ominously. Simmy experienced a fleeting moment of scorn towards the woman. Wasn't it deeply foolish to say such a thing? The others appeared to feel something similar.

'You can't know that,' said Anita. 'Unless you're not telling us something, of course.'

Gillian laughed so wildly that Simmy wondered if the accusation might be true, or close to the truth. At the same time, there was a lightness to the conversation, as if everyone liked everyone else and wished no harm or hurt whatever.

'Girls, girls,' said Mrs Percival, with deliberate humour that increased the sense of goodwill. 'Settle down now. I suggest we proceed on the assumption that the party will take place as planned, but make no secret of the fact that there's a provisional element to it. Mrs Brown – is that acceptable to you? We'd obviously pay you for any inconvenience. We're very aware that this is a busy time of year for you.'

Nobody had to say the words *Mother's Day*; the meaning was plain. 'Well . . .' Simmy was reluctant to give any firm commitment. An irritation was developing as she considered her options. 'I think we'd have to agree a deadline. I mean, a date for a final decision.' She knew there were rules and protocols for cancellations. Weddings were aborted, celebrations abandoned, minds changed, but she had never suffered such a disruption personally. In this case, if she was reading the situation correctly, the chances of the party going ahead were worryingly slim. How many candidates could there be for turning out to be the mysterious body found by the police? It seemed to her almost inevitable that it would prove to be the unfortunate Declan, given that his family already had the idea that it must be, and arrangements for his funeral would obliterate all thoughts of a retirement party.

'She's right,' said Anita, as if reading Simmy's mind. 'And realistically that moment is now, not sometime next week.' Simmy gave her a grateful smile, which was returned threefold.

'No, no,' wailed Gillian. 'We're being much too pessimistic. By tomorrow the police are sure to know who it is they've found, and then we'll know exactly what we have to do. One more day won't hurt, will it? Oh, and before we forget, can you give me your mobile number? Then I can send you a text if there's any news.'

There was something peculiar about this little woman, Simmy concluded. The lack of sensitivity towards her colleague was remarkable. And yet Anita did not appear to mind. Perhaps they knew each other so well that it was not even noticeable. Perhaps it revealed a genuine friendship, so deep that there was no need for caution or evasion. And, she remembered, they were solicitors. They knew about crime and evidence and law and extremely bad behaviour.

They had to be pragmatic and businesslike and decisive. If Gillian was peculiar, it could be because she wasn't in good health. There was nothing malign about her and she seemed intensely fond of Anita.

Barbara Percival was listening intently, but remained silent. One of the privileges of old age was that you could be excused from awkward or complicated judgements if you so chose. Perhaps rightly, she seemed to think that anything she said would be overruled in any case. Despite being the hostess for the proposed party in her highly desirable house, she was not the prime mover, and little was being demanded of her. Simmy almost envied her. She was sitting regally above the fray, paying attention and making suggestions, but not viscerally involved. Everything she said focused minds and forced good sense onto the others. *Clever*, thought Simmy. All she has to do now is sit there and wait.

'Tomorrow is fine,' she said. 'I wouldn't do anything before Monday, anyway. Now I've seen the house, I've got a few ideas as to what I could do. The colours in this room, for example, will work well with pinks and the paler yellows. Some mauve as well. And the hall needs some whites, I think. If I could have a look at any other rooms . . . ?'

'I'd like some red in here,' said Gillian. 'That won't clash, will it?'

Two walls of the room were papered with a William Morris design in green and pink, depicting fruit that Simmy suspected were pomegranates. If she could pick up the tones, and then add some rich reds, she might make something quite spectacular, she realised. 'It would be great,' she told Gillian. 'Red instead of yellow – much better.'

All three women laughed indulgently, refraining from any hint that Gillian might be doing Simmy's job for her.

'Oh, I do hope we can go ahead,' Gillian said. 'Anita deserves a good send-off. She's worked in the business for thirty-five years, all told.' She gave her colleague a fond smile. 'I couldn't have asked for a better partner.'

'It's no good, Gillie. You can't change things by wishing – you know that.'

'Trust Declan,' sighed Gillian. 'He's been a trouble to you from the start, one way or another.'

Anita forced a smile, and then sighed. 'But Debbie has always loved him, despite everything. She'll be desperately worried, poor girl.'

'Yes, well . . .' Even Gillian seemed at a loss for something to say to that. She glanced at her mother, as if waiting for her to speak. Simmy's instinct was to leave them all to it, and make no further investment in the uncertain commission. If the son-in-law was dead, that would be an end to it. She wouldn't have any reason to see these people again.

Not until she was driving away at seven-fifteen did she allow herself to fully consider the fact that Ben had heard or read that foul play was suspected, and would therefore be drawn as if magnetically to every detail of the story. She had repressed any awareness of that aspect of the business during her visit to Staveley, but now it returned with spikes on. And yet, she still saw no reason to involve herself with whatever had been going on. Gillian Townsend would phone and tell her the party was at best postponed, that there would be a period of recovery for the shattered family of her friend, and no more need be said.

Ben was too busy anyway to pay attention to even the

most compelling crime. Bonnie had a cold, and Simmy had to give some consideration to the unwelcome re-emergence of her one-time husband. Staveley could get along perfectly well without any of them.

She went home on a road she seldom used, aware of a recently increased level of confidence when it came to driving after dark on the deserted little lanes that connected the various settlements. This time, she was happy to turn off the main road to follow Moorhowe Road as it climbed up to Troutbeck. It was half the distance she would otherwise have to travel, and in the dark it had a pleasing romance to it. Clumps of late snowdrops gleamed luminously in the headlights. Not a single vehicle could be seen, leaving her to imagine herself alone in the world. Where once that would have terrified her, she now found it almost enjoyable. She knew where she was, and that her home was barely three miles away. If her car broke down, she could walk, without any ill effects. There was a new sense of being where she belonged, amongst people of great friendliness and goodwill, in a landscape of utter beauty. She dismissed all thoughts of the missing Declan, as well as the beleaguered Tony, and gave herself up to the mysterious evening shadows of South Cumbria.

Back in her little house, she found herself humming gently as she prepared a modest meal. She had taken more interest in cooking since Christopher had started coming over regularly. Although they often ate at the local pub, she was eager to demonstrate a level of competence that she hoped she still possessed. She had cooked for herself and Tony as a matter of course – real food from fresh ingredients. Christopher appeared to find this a highly entertaining novelty, acting up accordingly. 'What's for supper?' he would demand, the moment he was in the house.

But without him, she reverted to the much more boring scrambled eggs, sausages, baked potatoes and cheese on toast. As she ate, she made a phone call.

'Busy?' she asked him. 'Any treasures in the sale tomorrow?'

'Of course. Spring cleaning seems to be upon us, and there's a woman from Penrith getting rid of an attic full of stuff. Lovely things, most of them. I was up there with her two weeks ago, and we've been valuing and cataloguing it all right up to three days ago.'

'Anything I might like?'

'Practically all of it – but if you want it, you've got to bid properly like everybody else.'

'Maybe I'll get Bonnie to do it online from work.'

'Oh, yes. I can see that working when she's trying to serve a customer. I bet you've got to do some deliveries tomorrow, so she'll be in the shop by herself.'

'I wish your sales weren't on a Saturday. Any other day, and I could probably get away once in a while.'

It was nothing she hadn't said before. In fact, during the winter, she had closed the shop one Saturday and gone to Christopher's auction near Keswick with her father. Russell had bought a china dish and Simmy had enjoyed every moment.

'Actually,' she said, taking a mouthful of egg, 'I should probably tell you about a letter I got today.'

Chapter Four

It had been a mistake to try to explain the unsavoury story about Tony over the phone. Just as she had yet to hear the details of Christopher's marriage, he had not been given the full account of hers. It was only four months since they had rediscovered each other, and the logistics of their work and respective homes meant they spent less time together than they would have liked. He managed one or two nights a week, disappearing early in the morning, and most Sundays. But they both had other obligations, including Simmy's parents.

They talked about their teenage years, when they first had feelings for each other. They looked to the future and tried to establish a viable pattern in which they could become a proper couple. Each one placed high value on their work. Christopher was soon to become part-owner of the auction house, anticipating a move to sole proprietor when Oliver retired. It had been a rapid progression, full of excitement and challenge. He had been forced to learn about porcelain and glass, furniture and textiles, art and old postcards, and all the history that went with them. 'I know about two per cent of what I need,' he said gloomily. 'Every day I'm confronted by the limitations of my own ignorance. Did you know,' he went on, eyes wide, 'that women used to hang a little china pot on the wall beside their dressing table, and put the hair from their brushes into it? A hair pot. When there was enough of it, they sold it to wig makers, or stuffed cushions with it. Sometimes they plaited it into little threads and made pictures with it. Don't you love that!'

Simmy countered by sharing her own new discoveries about flowers, their origins and quirks, but she could never make them sound nearly so thrilling as Christopher's antiques. He was more intrigued by the string of violent crimes she had become embroiled in repeatedly, thanks to her role as florist. 'Let me get this straight,' he said. 'You turn up on a doorstep with a lovely bouquet of roses, and find a body waiting for you.'

'Not quite. No, not even close. But somehow or other I get to be a link in a chain. And then DI Moxon chases after me, and Ben gets to work in finding the solution, and it's always very nasty.' She had grossly oversimplified, of course. No two cases were remotely the same. There had been people exploiting Valentine's Day; people using flowers to send a threatening message; people using Simmy as a witness. Every time it was different, and every time she strove in vain to remove herself from the whole business.

So now there was a new element to talk about – one that neither of them found appealing. As Simmy haltingly gave the bones of the story about Tony and the midwife, admitting that she barely understood it herself, Christopher went quieter and quieter. In the end, she said, 'Are you still there?'

'Uh-huh. I don't see why they would need you, though. The facts are pretty clear already. All you can say is, yes, I had a stillborn baby and yes, this woman was one of the midwives. All that's a matter of record anyway, isn't it?'

She admired his courage in uttering the word *stillborn*. She could tell that he'd had to make an effort to say it. When they had first got together, back in November, he had made a fairly bad mess of accommodating this inescapable fact about her, and since then it had not been mentioned. With her outspoken mother in mind, Simmy had worried about the development of a taboo between them, but had lacked the strength to tackle it. It would lead to a second no-go area, which was the question of whether they should deliberately try to have a baby or two of their own. Time was against them, which only made it more difficult.

'They might want my impressions of her. Was she kind or not – did I notice how my husband was reacting to her? That sort of thing.'

'They each did something criminal, then. But her crime is a lot worse than his. So she needs to prove provocation, and that's where you come in. Right?'

'Right.'

'Hmm. Well, all we can do is wait and see what happens. Things okay other than that, are they?'

She kept back the Staveley story, for reasons she didn't quite grasp. It was unfinished, something and nothing – and she had a superstitious feeling that the less said about it the better. Christopher was easily diverted into further descriptions of the following day's lots. The contents of the Penrith attic were to be accompanied by the results of two substantial house clearances, and there was a new dealer to the area, who was eager to buy stock. 'Pictures are his thing. I have a feeling he'll be driving some of the prices up, which is always good. It kills me sometimes, the way perfectly good oil paintings go for ten quid.'

They ended by arranging what they would do on Sunday. Brunch, they decided. And a walk, if it wasn't raining. 'And I should go to Grasmere sometime soon,' he added. 'Maybe we could go there for the walk?'

'What's at Grasmere?'

'It's an old family friend. He came to my mother's funeral, actually, but I only had a couple of words with him. Now he's phoned to say he's got to move to a sheltered housing place, and can I look at the contents of his house. Happens all the time.' His sigh was one of sheer satisfaction, and Simmy laughed.

'Grasmere it is, then,' she said.

Saturday morning was cloudy and damp, but not actually raining. Bonnie's cold was no worse, and she sported a warm long-sleeved jacket that came up to her chin. 'That's much better,' said Simmy. Bonnie was nearly eighteen and everyone would probably always treat her as if she were twelve. Concern for her welfare followed her around; her efforts to shrug it off were more automatic than genuine. The morning was busy with orders coming through and people calling in. Simmy had to go to Newby Bridge with an anniversary tribute, and then Troutbeck Bridge with another. Bonnie was left to handle the shop, which she did with no difficulty.

They closed at two-thirty, later than the 2 p.m. announced on the door. Feeling under pressure, Simmy went directly to her parents' home on the edge of Windermere. Her mother immediately set her to work ironing sheets and pillowcases, and then cleaning the porcelain and china items in the dining room, which was used exclusively for the guests' breakfasts. These were mainly decorative jugs and teapots that ranged along a shelf, never actually used, but valued as having belonged to Angie's grandmother. Simmy had to concede that they looked delightful when the sun caught them – although that was almost always a moment that went unwitnessed. The dining room window faced west, the sun paying a fleeting evening visit before sinking behind trees and buildings.

She went home at seven, after supper with Angie and Russell. There had been almost no meaningful conversation, with Simmy oddly reluctant to reveal the reappearance of her former husband. Until she knew more about the story, it felt ill-advised to talk about it. There would be too many old memories, questions and painful emotion. Her parents had been unusually forbearing over the separation and subsequent divorce, offering support and sympathy, and making very little by way of judgemental comment. The sadness of the lost baby made them quiet.

The drive up to Troutbeck saw all Simmy's thoughts redirected to her increasingly significant new relationship. Christopher's auction would have finished by five, but he would be too tired to trek down to Troutbeck for the night. His voice would be hoarse, throat dry and head whirling. There had been one occasion when his ardour overcame exhaustion, but it had been a poor business. 'I should have pushed that Russian icon higher. I was too quick to bring the hammer down. The vendor's going to be furious.' And with many similar worries arising from a prolonged post-mortem on the day, Simmy had come close to sending him home again.

She was content to end the day alone. There was a double lump inside somewhere, caused by her mother-in-law's letter, and the absence of any message from Staveley. Insoluble worries that required her to simply wait for what happened next. Another lump lurked deeper, due to the imminence of Mother's Day. How many times had she kicked herself for failing to anticipate the pain and resentment that this was going to inflict on her in her capacity as a florist? She'd been fine with Valentine's, and weddings and funerals and even christenings. In her plans for the business, all these had been a natural part of her thinking. But her foolish mind had simply blanked the big one. She found herself half expecting that some understanding deity would cancel the whole thing, just for her. She witnessed the endless stream of dutiful adult sons and embarrassed teenaged ones going through the motions of buying flowers for a mother with whom they had their own unique relationship. A relationship that worked well enough without following a script imposed from outside. A collective idiocy was lying just beneath the surface, despite a wholesale pretence that all was sincere and enjoyable. The mothers themselves pretended hardest of all. Yes, they'd endured the pangs of childbirth, and done years of dirty work on bottoms and snotty noses, and worried over the late homecomings. But they'd done it willingly, taken pleasure from it, and now had at least the hope of a safety net in old age.

Melanie Todd, Simmy's first assistant in the shop, had taken her to task over this sort of thinking. 'You've got it all wrong,' she said. 'They need this special day to shore up the whole business. The mothers have to be convinced that their kids aren't going to abandon them to an old folks' home. They have to be told they didn't waste the best years of their lives. I can see that it's horrible for you, because of your baby, but it's *nice* for most people, Simmy. Like Christmas and birthdays. People like to feel special, and loved. Don't be such a curmudgeon about it.'

Simmy did try, that first year, with Melanie keeping her on track. She smiled and gushed and listened to the stories of maternal heroism, before taking her own mother a modest bouquet, and a rueful smile. 'I could hardly not,' she said.

Angie had been equally rueful, and not at all gracious. 'Thanks. But don't do it again, okay? Just take the money and try not to think about it.'

All of which led to agonisingly complicated feelings this year. If she could simply follow Angie's line, hating the whole silly business, it would be easier. But she could not sustain such a level of cynicism. Persimmon Straw had been born with most of the softer virtues, and only the constant exposure to her mother's world view had shown her that you sometimes had to be hard or selfish in order to survive. She sometimes thought this made her a moral coward; all her instincts being to withdraw and ignore the harsher side of life.

Christopher was even more exhausted than usual when

46

she put in her nightly phone call. 'We didn't finish till nearly six,' he moaned.

They could find little to say, twenty-four hours after their last exchange. Plans were made for the Grasmere trip, with hopes for the weather buoyed by a favourable forecast. Logistics occupied a few minutes – should they go separately, or should he come to Troutbeck and collect her? Was he going to stay over on Sunday night?

All was decided, and Simmy began to prepare for bed. Then the landline trilled.

'Simmy? Did you get my letter? I thought I should follow it up with a call, now I've finally found your number. I'm sorry it's a bit late, but you were engaged when I tried before.'

'Pam,' said Simmy weakly. 'Yes, I got your letter.'

Chapter Five

It was unwelcome and weird to hear the woman's voice again. They had been close for ten years, pleased with the way they managed the relationship. Sometimes Tony complained that he was just an incidental element. His father, present in the flesh, but hopelessly distracted by his passion for old cars and the history of the Second World War, was nobody's best friend or significant other. He had begun to slide into premature old age, reaching the age of seventy as if it was ninety.

Pamela had two other sons, having always wanted girls. She had seized on Simmy as a gift from heaven. Another daughter-in-law had taken against her from the outset, remaining hostile and spiky for the rather brief duration of her marriage to Daniel. Richard, the middle son, never once presented a girlfriend to the family, leaving them to slowly conclude that there was no place for women in his life.

'I want to make it very clear that I'm not blaming you in

the least,' said Pamela Brown now. 'I'm not defending Tony for his behaviour. At least, I suppose I *am* in a way, because I think it's down to his mental state. He would never have done such stupid things if he'd been in his right mind.'

Simmy had heard similar sentiments before. The umbrella excuse for a large proportion of criminal acts – he wasn't responsible. His reason had deserted him. He didn't know what he was doing.

'It came as a shock,' she said. 'I had no idea he'd even been injured.'

'I'm sorry. It never occurred to me that you wouldn't know about it, until I realised there might not be anyone still in touch with you both. Foolish of me.' The voice tailed away and Simmy had to acknowledge that the woman had good reason to be distressed. 'I suppose I hoped that there would be at least some contact between the two of you. After all, you were a close couple for a long time.'

Simmy made no attempt to explain her marriage breakdown. She had barely managed to explain it to herself, and any words she found to summarise what had happened always felt inadequate. It was all about failure and cowardice and the bottom falling out. 'I can't see why I should be involved with the trial or whatever it is,' she said. 'What do they want me to say?'

'I know. It was all the idea of his defence barrister. Human interest, gaining sympathy and that sort of thing. It's probably clutching at straws, but, well . . .'

'It must be awful for you. They're not keeping him in custody or anything, are they?'

'No, no, not at all. For months, he was absolutely the victim. The woman *stabbed* him. Then everything turned around, and she accused him of aggravated harassment, or whatever they call it, and he had to defend himself. She's gone public on how he ruined her life for years, until she couldn't take any more.'

'Is she allowed to do that? Isn't it *sub judice*?'

'I'm not sure any of that works any more. People seem to be able to say anything they like on Facebook and all that sort of thing.'

'What a mess,' sighed Simmy. 'But as you say, she caused him actual injury. That must be far more serious than anything Tony did. Is he completely recovered now? How bad was it?'

She couldn't avoid a mental image of her former husband's naked body: his smooth pale skin with a ragged scar on it, vulnerable and spoilt. Tony had always been slim, hairless, his muscles soft and inconspicuous. His weakness, previously accepted as part of his nature, had forced itself unpleasantly onto her when Edith died, and now, apparently, it had afflicted another woman, who surely had not deserved it.

'His lung won't ever be the same, but it's not life-threatening. Do you remember this woman at all?'

'Well, sort of. There were three or four of them, all silent and sympathetic, and I didn't really focus on one in particular. I could hear another woman giving birth in the next room, everybody shouting at her to push, but with me they just let it happen at its own pace. No worries about getting the baby breathing, you see. And I had the feeling they were hanging back from me, because they didn't quite know what to say. I didn't blame them.'

'Tony says she held his hand. Do you remember that?'

'Not really. He cried a lot. Somebody rubbed his back.

That was probably her. She was quite big and solid. A nice soft bosom. But most of them are like that, aren't they?'

Pamela gave a little laugh. 'They do seem to be, yes. It's nice to talk to you, after all this time. I've missed you, you know.'

'I'm sorry,' said Simmy, thinking at that moment that it really was all her fault. Then something more assertive kicked in, and she physically drew back, pulling the phone away from her head. She had moved past that phase of her life. Tony and the baby were firmly in the past. 'But I've got things pretty well organised here now. The business suits me very nicely. My parents are glad to have me close by. And, actually, I'm in a new relationship, which feels very right. I've moved on, as they say.'

'Good. That's good. I wouldn't wish anything less for you.'

'Thank you, Pamela. You're a good person. I wish . . .'

'Yes. We all wish that. I'll tell the legal people what you said, anyway. If it was down to me, I'd leave you alone, but knowing the way these things work, I'm afraid you're quite likely to be bothered again. They're hoping to get Tony cleared completely, you see.'

'That's their job, I suppose,' said Simmy. 'I'll do what I can, but I don't think it'll be very much.'

'We'll see. Thank you for listening, anyway.'

The memories haunted her for the rest of the evening, and made it difficult to get to sleep. When she dreamt, it was about the fells between Troutbeck and Kentmere, with a dog finding a fresh grave, and the flowers intended for the funeral thrown into a dustbin. Her first thought when she woke on Sunday was that the Staveley people had failed in their promise to update her on Anita's party.

* * *

51

She and Christopher spent the whole of Sunday together, slipping into their customary topics of conversation, rather than anything more sensitive. The auctions, the flowers, his family and her friends were enough to occupy them until well into the afternoon. The long-standing family friend in Grasmere turned out to be a wispy old man called Philip who said little as Christopher did a rapid tour of his house. His possessions amounted to little of any commercial interest, except for a handful of old model aeroplanes and an even older Persian rug. 'I can get you a good price for them,' said Christopher.

The old man showed no sign of offering them lunch, so they headed for a pub that neither of them had visited before. It was after one o'clock, and they were offered no alternative to a traditional roast dinner. Across the room from them was a couple with two babies. 'Twins?' asked a passing customer.

'Right,' said the father. 'A bit more than we bargained for.' All those in earshot laughed sympathetically.

Christopher and Simmy could not evade the domesticity all around them. This was an English Sunday – people eating roast beef and Yorkshire pudding, a woman with her dog in a corner, chatter and muted music forming the background ambience. 'How are your mum and dad?' he asked her.

'Same as usual, pretty much. They're worried about the busy season, I think. My mother's going to have to change the way she does it, which she's not happy about. I think it'll spoil it for her, actually. I wouldn't be surprised if this is their last year.'

'And then what? Would they sell the house and downsize?'

'I have no idea. That never crossed my mind.' Her

breathing grew faster and more shallow. 'It panics me to think of it,' she admitted.

'Why? They can't go on indefinitely, can they?'

'She's not even sixty-five yet. I've been to B&Bs where the people are in their eighties.'

'Really?' He gave her a sceptical look. 'They must have had some help, if so. And you said it yourself – that this might be their last year.'

'I know I did. But I—never mind. Let's talk about something else.'

But they seemed stuck on families, the future, passing time and fading youth. By increments they shifted from the general to the particular, leaving gaps and diverting into safer waters, but Simmy knew it was coming. When it did, she almost missed it.

'What're we going to do, then?' said Christopher.

'We could stop in Ambleside and watch the boats on the lake,' she said, in all innocence.

'No – I mean us. What're *we* going to do?'

'Oh.' She looked around the bar, nervous about being overheard. 'Not here. Not now.' Didn't he understand that such conversations were supposed to happen in bed, or cuddled on a sofa? It had been dawning on her for a few weeks that Christopher wasn't very good at timing. He spoke before thinking of the likely reaction. Having known him all her early life, literally, she was gradually coming to realise that in the years since their teenage romance they had both changed considerably.

'Sorry,' he said, with a little frown. 'Did I get it wrong again?'

'A bit. I'm not fobbing you off, but we need to be somewhere private, okay?'

'Sorry,' he said again. 'You're absolutely right. I do *blurt* things, don't I? Oliver told me off last week for doing the same thing. I've got to learn discretion, he says.'

The antiques business was, of course, notorious for secret deals, dishonest valuations, shady transactions. When Ben Harkness had become aware of Simmy's new boyfriend's line of work, he had been hugely excited. 'A hotbed of crime – that's what an auction house is,' he cried. 'Can I go and watch? Can I spend a day behind the scenes? Will you ask him?'

'You haven't got time,' Simmy had said. 'And I'm sure Christopher's not involved in any sort of crime.'

But when her mother had made a similar remark, invoking the *Lovejoy* television series as evidence, Simmy had begun to wonder. There had to be temptations to hold back the true value of an object, or to inflate the desirability of another. She tried to suggest some of this to Christopher, half expecting him to fly into a defensive rage.

'Not if you want to keep a good reputation,' he told her seriously. 'The slightest whiff of dirty dealing, and you're sunk. However dishonest the buyers and sellers might be, the auctioneer himself has to stay right above it. We go to a lot of trouble to make sure nothing sticks to us. Obviously, there are loads of games going on. The specialists all know the precise value of every item, and make sure they don't pay a penny over that. They all know each other, as well. But then you get somebody new turning up, and that throws everything into confusion. Is it a novice, an amateur who has no idea what's what? Or is it someone from the other end of the country, looking for fresh pastures? New people tend to drive the prices up, and that makes the regulars cross.'

'But not you. You want the prices as high as possible, for the commission.'

'More or less, yes. But in the long run, it can put people off. And really, we just want everything sold.'

She had asked about ivory, and old oil paintings, and with every reply she'd found the whole business more and more fascinating. 'You know what,' said Ben astutely. 'I think you'd really like to go up to Keswick and get him to give you a job. Forget flowers – antiques are loads more fun.'

That had been two weeks ago, and she had buried the comment as deeply as she could. The thought of selling her Troutbeck cottage, abandoning her parents, closing the florist business, all sent her blood running cold. And yet . . . Might she not bitterly regret missing such a chance, if Christopher lost patience with the geographical distance between them and the dithering about what happened next?

They finished their meal and wandered back to the cars. In the end, they'd decided to drive separately to Grasmere, and then both go back to Troutbeck for the evening and night. There was a spiteful east wind blowing that made the fells uninviting. 'We could go to Ambleside for a bit,' said Christopher with a little laugh. 'And watch the boats on the lake.'

'Too cold,' she protested, shamelessly contradicting herself. 'We need to be indoors on a day like this. Don't forget I'm a soft southerner. It'll take a few more years before I properly acclimatise to these winters.'

'Wimp,' he accused. 'Besides, it's not cold over here. Wet, though, I grant you, and that looks like a very purposeful black cloud over there.'

It felt strange to be driving alone, despite seeing his big

Volvo in the rear mirror, following her all the way back to Troutbeck. The sense of a new chapter, an imminent decision, was sending all kinds of electricity around her frame. 'There's no need to be scared,' she muttered to herself. 'Be happy. This is what you've wanted for ages. This, Persimmon Straw, is what your mother always said was your destiny. Goodbye, Simmy Brown.' She waved foolishly at the following car, unsure whether Christopher could see her, and wondering what he was thinking. Did he assume they'd get married, or was the very idea horrifying to him? Was this sudden reappearance of Tony and his mother going to taint or impede whatever it was that had developed between her and Christopher?

His surname was Henderson. Like an obsessed teenager, she played with the sound of it as she drove. It had a perfectly good rhythm to it, although her full 'Persimmon' was rather too close to 'Henderson' for a perfect fit. The whole name was cumbersome. But then, nobody but her mother ever called her 'Persimmon' anyway.

And all the time she knew that none of that mattered. Even the quality of their relationship, the chances of it succeeding for the next fifty years, the details of how they would organise work, house and money came second to the single big question: would they ever manage to become parents?

Chapter Six

In the end they talked much less than expected. Each had an instinctive resistance to dragging delicate emotions out into the daylight, where they might shrivel and die. 'Let's just go on as we are until after Easter,' he said. 'We're both going to be dreadfully busy until then, anyway. I can get a week off over the holiday, but I don't suppose you can. Isn't Easter hugely important, flower-wise?'

'Not desperately. I could give myself a week's break from Easter Monday onwards.'

'Great! Let's go away somewhere. France or Spain. Somewhere we can rely on some sunshine.'

Simmy had never closed the shop completely, since starting the business. She had missed some days, but Melanie had always kept it going. Bonnie, however, was not equal to managing all on her own for a whole week. It was scary to think of hanging a sign on the door saying 'CLOSED FOR HOLIDAY. BACK NEXT WEEK'. But it was not impossible, and everybody deserved to get away occasionally. 'I've always fancied going back to Lanzarote,' she said. 'Do you think we could go there?'

'Blimey! I don't even know for sure where it is.'

She told him, along with the fact that one of Tony's cousins had owned property there, and early in their marriage they'd spent a few days in a beautiful apartment, free of charge, thanks to the cousin's generosity. 'It's always a perfect temperature, all the year round. There's an open area on the roof, where you can just slob about and look at the view. Or you can go for boat trips to the other islands. It's lovely.'

'I believe you. But we can't use Tony's cousin's place, can we? It's probably pretty pricy to rent somewhere.'

'Let's find out, then. We can google it.'

But they didn't, because they were too cosily entwined on the couch.

Monday morning was a scramble, with a very early start and a feeling of resentment at the violence of the separation after a thoroughly blissful night. 'We can't go on like this,' Simmy found herself saying. 'It's horrible.'

'It's pretty normal. All across the land, people are heaving themselves out of bed and preparing for a long drive to work.'

'You wouldn't want to do it every day, though. It'll take you at least an hour to get to Keswick.'

'It'd be worth it,' he said fondly. His grey eyes looked intently into hers. 'Why on earth did I let you go when I had you, twenty years ago? What a stupid waste of time.'

'We let each other go. We weren't sure enough then.'

'And are we now?'

He was literally on the doorstep. He was doing it again, and she gave him a little push. 'I'm not answering that now,' she said.

'I know the answer anyway,' he said airily. 'After that night, who could doubt it?' He pulled her to him and squeezed her tight. 'Have a good day, my sweet.'

The goodbye kiss was witnessed by at least three drivers, hurrying through the village on the way to their own workplaces.

Bonnie still had her cold, but looked much better. 'I've found this stuff called Sudafed,' she said. 'It dries up all the snot like magic. You'd never know you'd got a cold at all.'

'Great,' said Simmy doubtfully. The girl's prediliction for non-prescription medicines appeared to be increasing. But, she reminded herself, that was perfectly normal. It was only the Straw family who regarded any medication as a personal insult, so that taking it was a sign of failure. It went back to Angie's own mother, a latter-day Edwardian who believed firmly in the power of positive thinking. Her descendants had yet to shake off this attitude to life.

'Three new orders, not counting the Mother's Day ones. You've got to go to Bowness for two of them, and Brant Fell for the other. All nice and close together.'

'When?'

'First thing tomorrow, preferably. You might see Ninian.' Bonnie had a soft spot for Simmy's one-time boyfriend, who lived on the slopes of Brant Fell. Her foster mother was a friend of his, and everyone had felt mildly let down when Simmy transferred her affections to Christopher Henderson.

'I won't see Ninian,' said Simmy firmly. 'How many are there for Mother's Day so far?'

'Nine. And it's still weeks away yet. I bet there'll be at least thirty by the time the day comes.'

'Last year there were twenty-eight. That felt like too many, at the time.'

'People buy pot plants as well, don't they? You should check there's enough in stock.'

'I should, you're right.'

'Melanie called me yesterday. She sends her love. She told me how much you hate the whole Mother's Day thing. Obvious, really. I should have worked it out for myself, when you started being funny about it last month.'

'Melanie was very sensible. She gave me a talking to. I am trying harder to keep my own feelings out of it.'

'Think about the money,' Bonnie advised.

'I'll try.'

The morning passed much as usual, with the mixture of preparing for the following day's deliveries, checking stocks of potted plants, tidying up, and dealing with the overflowing compost bin in the little yard at the back. Dead flowers and foliage were an inevitable by-product of the business, and disposing of them was complicated. 'You should have an allotment,' her mother told her. 'That'd be a constructive solution.' Simmy didn't want an allotment, but she did sometimes take a smelly black sack of detritus to her father for his struggling vegetable plot. His efforts at gardening had never been very consistent, and now he neglected it all for a lot of the time. Simmy tried to encourage him, and had a plan to get some seed potatoes and help him put them in.

Bonnie had taken her last Sudafed early in the day, and it had worn off by noon. She had got through half a box of tissues by the time Ben came in at half past three. He was all solicitude over the streaming nose. 'I thought you were better,' he accused.

'I thought I was as well,' she nodded. 'It's been nearly a week now. Lucky you didn't catch it.'

'A miracle,' he grinned. 'Lucky old me.'

'How's the work going?' Simmy asked him.

He shrugged away the predictable question, and replied with one of his own. 'What happened in Staveley, then? I've been wondering all weekend. There wasn't anything else on the news last time I looked. That must have been Saturday.'

Simmy blinked. 'I'd forgotten all about it. They said they'd tell me by now for sure whether or not the party was on. And I haven't heard a thing. I suppose it's off, and they're too preoccupied to think about telling me.'

'So – tell me the whole thing. And that business with your ex, as well. Those are the only two crime stories going on just now and I'm getting withdrawal symptoms.'

Bonnie giggled, and Simmy sighed. 'Not much to tell,' she said. 'There's a woman called Anita, who's retiring from her job as a solicitor and her friend Gillian wants to give her a big party at her mother's house. Gillian's mother, that is. Anita and Gillian's mother both live in Staveley, and I suppose Gillian's in Kendal. At least that's where the solicitors' office is. Anita's daughter has a husband called Declan, and he's the one they're worried about. When the police found a body last week, they must have known it was him, but they wouldn't say for sure. If it is, they can't have a party. It's a fabulous house,' she finished, feeling wistful at the lost commission.

'Okay,' said Ben slowly. 'So Declan's not very old. Was he sick? Or suicidal? Did anybody hate him?'

'Shut up. How would I know any of that?'

'Observation,' he told her severely. 'At least some of it should have been mentioned.'

'Not sick,' she ventured. 'The wife is called Debbie, and there's a Matthew.' She had to strain to recall as much as that. A lot had happened since Friday evening. 'Anita was obviously very worried. She hardly spoke at all, and when she did she was a bit snappy. She's nice, though. They all are. I liked the old lady, and Gillian's sweet. Very short and dumpy and always smiling. I don't think she's well, though. She's breathless, and seems rather stiff.'

Ben made a long sound of frustration. 'You're a hopeless detective,' he moaned.

'That's because it's the last thing I *want* to be. I just sell flowers. Why won't people leave it at that?'

'Yeah, yeah. Let's check then.' He devoted a minute's attention to his device. 'Well, as far as I can work out, the body they found was an old man who'd been dead in his garden shed for a week. And there was also a chap knocked off his bike in Crook.' He looked up. 'So what about this other thing? Your stalker husband.' He gave an apologetic grimace, which carried little sincerity.

'His mother phoned me on Saturday. She's still very friendly towards me, which is a bit of a surprise. I'd forgotten how much we always liked each other. She's remarkably realistic about Tony, and what he might be capable of. I think we both feel sorrier for the midwife than we do for him. Anyway, I told her I didn't think there was much I could say that would help. I got the impression it had been her idea in the first place, to try and get me to provide some of the background. But I can't remember very much. Tony wasn't there when they gave me the baby to hold. He might have been in another room, crying on this woman. Something like that must have happened, to make him think there was anything between them.'

'Like a baby duck imprinting on the first thing it sees when it hatches,' said Bonnie.

'No. Nothing like that at all,' said Simmy crossly. 'Much more complicated and embarrassing than that.' She tried to ignore the pang of remorse she felt at the sight of Bonnie's drooping response

'Embarrassing,' Ben repeated. 'It is, isn't it? Stalking is really very pathetic. Being caught doing it has to be embarrassing. And Bonnie's right, actually. It must be a bit like imprinting. A powerful instinct that overrides common sense.'

'Or a stray dog that follows you home and sits outside your door whining for days.' Bonnie had bounced back at her boyfriend's approving words. 'In the end, you'd have to kick it or shout at it, to make it go away.'

'But she *stabbed* him,' said Simmy. 'That's going rather too far, surely? She must have taken a knife with her deliberately, as well.'

'Where did this happen?' asked Ben.

'Um . . . I don't actually know. It could have been at her house, I suppose, although she probably wouldn't have let him in if he'd gone to the door. I haven't been told anything much.'

Ben was activating his all-purpose phone. 'Anthony

Brown? Worcestershire . . . stabbing . . . last year. Let's see . . .'
He stroked and prodded the screen for a whole minute, before
proffering an item from the *Gloucestershire Echo*. 'It was in
Chedworth, in the Cotswolds. Look, it's all here.'

Overcoming a mild resistance, Simmy took the phone
and read the piece. 'Okay,' she said when she'd finished. 'So
I was right – she *did* take a knife with her. She must have
been expecting him to follow her.'

'She says she was trying to have a quiet day in the
countryside, thinking he'd never find her there,' Ben
pointed out.

'Oh. So she does. Well, it looks bad for her, doesn't it?'

'She's bound to argue that it was self-defence. Some
stalkers get very violent.'

'There's a wonderful book,' Bonnie enthused. 'It's called
Into the Darkest Corner. Really scary. Made you feel you
were right there, with the poor woman who was being
stalked.'

'Stop it,' begged Simmy. A residual loyalty to Tony
was stirring inside her. 'I was *married* to the man. He was
nothing like a baby duck or a stray dog then.' But she paused,
remembering moments when Tony had indeed seemed less
than competent, even less than rational when faced with
difficulties. His attitude to work colleagues had sometimes
been extreme, whether positive or negative. He still harboured
bitter feelings towards a boy at school who had bullied him.
Some of this came back to her now. 'Poor old Tony,' she
breathed. 'What a mess he must have been in.' Another wave
of remorse flooded through her. Perhaps she should have
tried harder to stay with him and keep the marriage alive.
Perhaps, indeed, this was at least partly her fault.

But Pamela had assured her this was not the case. 'His mother was really nice to me. She said it wasn't my fault.'

'How could it be *your* fault?' Bonnie looked genuinely blank.

'Don't do the guilt-tripping again,' Ben warned her. 'It's not big and it's not clever.'

A customer broke up the darkening atmosphere with a request for a large spray of the biggest spring flowers Simmy could provide. She disappeared into the storeroom to fashion something suitable. 'Give me ten minutes,' she said.

The man eyed the two youngsters carefully, and then mooched off to examine the stand offering greetings cards to go with flowers. Simmy was back sooner than predicted and the customer went off looking as if he'd escaped some unpleasant fate. 'What a plonker,' said Bonnie. 'What did he think we were going to do to him?'

'Talk to him, presumably,' said Ben. 'Some people think kids are a different species from themselves.'

'We're not *kids*,' Bonnie protested. 'You're eighteen, and I nearly am.'

'You know what I mean.'

Simmy went back to the storeroom and made three mugs of tea. She was still thinking about Tony, and how he had become so distant and alien to her since she'd left him back in Worcestershire. But even at a distance, he was interrupting her relationship with Christopher. The past and present were getting mixed up and that was uncomfortable.

When she took the tea into the shop, Bonnie was lavishly filling another tissue. 'It just won't stop,' she said thickly.

'It might be something allergic,' said Ben, looking closely

at her. 'Have you got new plants in here?' he asked Simmy. 'Something you haven't had since Bonnie started.'

'Can't think of anything.' The idea of her assistant becoming sensitive to plants was alarming. 'More likely to be that Sudafed stuff she's been taking.'

'Doubtful. What does it say about side effects?'

Bonnie shrugged. 'No idea,' she said.

Ben was already tapping busily on his phone, his eyebrows rising dramatically as he read the screen. 'This is an American website,' he realised. 'They really go overboard on this sort of thing. If this is anything to go by, the stuff's lethal. Seizures, sweating, quivering . . . but they're all rare. Nothing about excessive mucus, though.'

'That would be ridiculous, when the pills are designed to dry you up,' said Simmy. 'It's probably just the tail end of the cold, and she'll be fine by bedtime.'

'Side effects was your suggestion,' Ben reminded her.

'A silly one.'

They drank their tea in silence. Outside there was enough sunshine to cast shadows, which were lengthening as the afternoon went on. 'You can go early, if you like,' Simmy told Bonnie. 'On the grounds that you're sick.'

'Okay. Thanks.' It was as if both youngsters had been waiting for those very words, and within sixty seconds they'd gone.

'They really are a different species,' Simmy murmured to herself. More like puppies than people, much of the time. Or skittish colts. She wasn't sorry to be left on her own. There were things she wanted to think about and get straight in her head.

But she had little time for her musing. Five minutes after

Ben and Bonnie had gone, the door opened, admitting the person who had so very often come through that door with trouble and confusion in his wake. Meeting his eyes, she knew she'd been expecting him all day. The sense of him had been hovering on her shoulder, his face clear in her mind's eye.

'Hello,' she said.

'And hello again to you,' said Detective Inspector Nolan Moxon.

Chapter Seven

'I thought you might be coming in sometime this week,' she told him. 'My mother-in-law warned me.'

He looked at her in astonishment, as if she had said something in Swahili or sworn at him. 'Mother-in-law?' he repeated. '*Mother-in-law?*'

'Yes. Pamela Brown, who lives in Halesowen, near Birmingham. She wrote to me, and then phoned. I know what you're going to ask me.'

'I don't think you do. This has no connection to Birmingham, or anyone called Brown. It's about an incident in Staveley.'

'Oh.' She leant against her worktable, where the computer and till were sitting. 'I'd forgotten about that. Again.'

'You know what I'm talking about, then?' He gave her another wary look. 'People by the name of Kennedy?'

'Not really.' She recovered her balance, and with it an

energetic resistance to whatever he wanted of her. 'This honestly can't have anything whatsoever to do with me. Just because I went there on Friday is no reason to try and pull me in to whatever it is that's happened. Besides – Ben says it was an old man who died, presumably of natural causes, in a shed.'

'I'm sorry.' He seemed to really mean it, she had to acknowledge to herself. 'This is another matter, concerning a Mr Kennedy. We've been given your name as somebody who can confirm the whereabouts of Mrs Anita Olsen on Friday evening.'

She had to take a deep breath, quelling indignation and apprehension. 'There were two other people with her. How can I tell you any more than they can?'

'Let me explain, then.' He looked round for somewhere to sit, as he very often did, leaving Simmy to reproach herself for the hundredth time for not adding a chair at the back of the shop. As it was, only one person could seat themselves at a time, on a wobbly stool in front of the computer.

She waved at the stool. 'Go on, then. Sit here, while I get on with tomorrow's orders. I can do some of it in here, just about.' There really wasn't any space for creative expression in the main shop, but she could assemble a decent bouquet of flowers, tied, wrapped and labelled, with her eyes shut. This she did, except for keeping her eyes open, as the detective gave an account of events in Staveley.

'For a start, Mrs Olsen's son-in-law, Declan Kennedy, was found dead on Friday evening, at about half past eight.'

She wished she'd kept the stool for herself. Implications were making her feel weak. 'Oh, no. They were worrying about him when I was there. They weren't sure whether they could go ahead with the party they were planning. You can't have found him on Friday, right after I'd been talking to them.'

'I promise you we did. The incident you're thinking about was nothing to do with these people.'

'So there were two dead people in Staveley on the same day? Surely not.'

'The first one was a confused elderly man, who probably died of exposure because he was out all night in a cold shed. It looks as if he collapsed out there several days ago and nobody found him until Friday.'

'So why did Anita and the others think it might be their Declan?'

Moxon sighed. 'Because nobody told them otherwise until late on Friday. There was a degree of confusion, actually. They'd reported Declan missing on Thursday, then when the news mentioned the discovery of a body, they rightly feared it might be him, but we weren't in a position to reassure them until after we'd found Declan. And then we took a while to identify *him*. It all takes time,' he concluded with a sigh.

'So—'

He interrupted her. 'Just listen for a minute. Declan Kennedy was killed on the road not far from Staveley. A car must have hit him and knocked him into a ditch. We think it happened sometime during the late afternoon or early evening on Friday.'

'Poor man.'

'Yes. But it's not that simple. He had words with his wife, about a personal issue, and then stormed off.

70

Apparently that was something he did rather a lot. But he's always come back next morning, with everything forgiven. This is different. Nobody in the family had seen him since Wednesday afternoon – or so they say.'

She kept her lips together, suppressing the many questions she was bursting to ask him. He would know what they were, anyway.

'All right, I'm getting to the point. The main thing is that more than one person has told us that Mrs Olsen had a particular animosity towards him. She regarded him as a very undesirable husband for her daughter. She's retiring from her job this month – or rather, selling her share in a successful business to her partner, and there are disagreements about the money. And a few other things.'

'They're solicitors,' said Simmy.

'That's right. And now they need somebody new to replace Mrs Olsen, and Declan has – had – his own ideas about that. You don't want to hear the whole story. We got most of it from Mr Kennedy senior. Declan's father. He's incandescent – convinced that the Olsen woman killed his son.'

'But why does anyone have to have killed him? I mean deliberately. Why can't it just be an accident?'

'There are indications that support the hypothesis that it was deliberate,' he said stiffly.

She made a face that she hoped conveyed her need for him to explain why she, Simmy Brown, should have anything to contribute to his investigations.

Moxon continued, 'So Mrs Olsen is a person of interest, and we're hoping to get a full picture of her movements for the whole of Friday. That's all. We interviewed her, and her business partner, Mrs Townsend, and they both told us of the visit to the home of Mrs Townsend's mother. When they said you were there as well, that added weight, you see.'

'Not really. Surely two witnesses are enough? I think you've been very mean to drag me into it. You *know* how I hate all this sort of thing.'

He gave her an injured look. 'You're a useful outsider. Your verification will – as I say – add weight. And you could tell me something about how they all seemed.'

'I can't. I never met them before. I have no idea how they usually seem.'

'Stop it,' he said, more shortly than she could remember him ever having been with her. 'I've got good reason to come here and ask for your help. An objective eye, at a time like this, can give extremely useful pointers. A man's dead, and at the very least it's a hit-and-run, which is a serious crime. Given the circumstances, and the way Mrs Kennedy and her father-in-law are talking, we have perfectly good reasons for thinking it was a deliberate act. When she reported her husband's absence on Thursday, Debbie Kennedy clearly believed him to be in danger. We owe it to her to establish the facts as quickly and completely as we can.'

'All right,' she capitulated. 'I'll try.'

'Thank you. So, can you tell me everything you can remember, from the first contact? Was that a phone call?'

'Yes, Gillian Townsend called, and explained about the party. I met her and Anita at the bus stop and they took me to Mrs Percival's house. And then they said there was some doubt as to whether the party would actually take place, because of Declan being missing, and possibly dead. They obviously did think the body you found first was probably him. Anita was very quiet the whole time. She seemed worried.'

'They wanted you to provide flowers for the party that was in celebration of Mrs Olsen's retirement – is that right?'

'Yes. They'd been stuck for a venue, until someone suggested that house. It *is* gorgeous,' she added wistfully. 'I'd have loved to decorate it.'

He was making notes on a pad. 'Mrs Olsen seemed worried?'

'I think so. It felt as if she was resisting her colleague's headlong party plans, as if she knew they were premature. The old lady didn't seem to know what to think.'

'But they all looked as if they knew each other well, and were easy together?'

'Gillian's the sort of person who's easy with everybody. Very cheerful and enthusiastic. Not at all a typical solicitor, actually. But I don't think she's very well. She looked as if she might be in pain.'

'I gather she's got Crohn's disease, which is fairly serious. But she's very popular, by all accounts. And a lot more clever than first appears.'

'Poor thing. But doesn't that make you terribly thin? She's quite . . . well-covered. And she's short of breath. Does it do that?'

'It causes a lot of pain, and that catches at your breath. And she's not really fat, you know. I think most of it is abdominal swelling, from the condition. I had an uncle with it. It's a ghastly business, with no proper cure.'

Simmy had no reply to that. She was thinking about Anita Olsen. 'Well, I can confirm that they were all in Staveley from six o'clock to just past seven, if that's any help. I can't say much more than that, except they looked as if they were all going to stay there after I left. They were very nice to me. Although they promised to let me know about the party, one way or the other, and they never did. I thought they'd forgotten about me.'

'They haven't. They were impressed by you, actually. But we asked them not to contact you until we'd had a chance to ask you some questions.'

'Really? Why?' She tried to think. 'In case they told me what I should say? Gosh! Well, they didn't.' She put down the flowers she'd been fiddling with. 'You really think Anita might have killed her daughter's husband, do you? That would be an awful thing, if so.'

'She's a person of interest,' he said again. 'And I think you know exactly what that means.'

'If I don't I can ask Ben,' she smiled. Then, 'Oh Lord – he's going to love this, isn't he! Except he hasn't got time for anything else on top of his A-levels. His workload is terrifying.'

Moxon's expression was a complicated mix of admiration and ruefulness. Ben Harkness had made the detective look foolish more than once, despite a mutual liking. 'I wish I knew where he'll be in ten years' time,' he said. 'People as clever as he is often burn themselves out by the time they're thirty.'

'I know. I worry about him as well. He's so bright-eyed and confident at the moment. Some of that's sure to be knocked out of him when he gets out there in the big bad world.'

'It's a lot badder than any of us really knows.'

Simmy was moved to contradict herself. 'I hope you're wrong about that, even if we've seen some horrible things right here. They're a tiny part of the whole picture. Most people are perfectly decent. I can't help feeling the whole world is more or less the same, at least in the basics. Don't you think?'

'I doubt whether the people of Mexico would agree with you, for a start. Or Pakistan, the Philippines, Venezuela . . . it's a long list. We're very sheltered and spoilt here, by comparison.'

'Anyway . . . is that all you wanted? It's time to close up and go home.' Then she remembered her original assumption as to the reason for his visit. 'No – wait. Haven't you got something else to talk to me about?'

He frowned. 'I don't think so.'

'No word from the police or courts or whatever they are, in Worcestershire?'

He had gone completely blank. She pressed on. 'My ex-husband was attacked by a woman he was stalking. That's the story, anyway. There's a trial coming up, and my mother-in-law thinks I might make a useful witness.'

'This is totally new to me. Can you explain where I might come in?'

'I just thought – hoped – that I could send some sort of written statement, which maybe you could take charge of, with confirmation of who I am. Isn't there a procedure like that?' She was floundering, aware of her own abiding ignorance of how the police operated. She knew even less about courts and trials.

'Well . . . possibly. You know this woman who attacked him, do you? They want you as a character witness, is that right?'

'I'm not sure. Pamela – that's Tony's mother – suggested

that I could give some background as to why Tony went off the rails. The shock of our baby dying was what did it. But I barely remember the midwife they're talking about. There were quite a few of them, and I wasn't in any state to notice which was which. They were nice enough, but nothing special.'

'I'm not sure I'm getting this. Your husband developed feelings for one of the midwives? Is that right?'

'Apparently, yes. I didn't have any idea until last week. It does explain a few things, I suppose. It never crossed my mind that he might be talking to another woman about what happened. From what Pamela said, it could have been going on for ages without me realising. I don't know for sure what he did. The woman might have refused to have anything to do with him – but I suppose he must have had some sort of encouragement. Stalkers think the other person feels the same as they do – don't they?'

Moxon pursed his lips. 'It varies,' he said. 'But it sounds very messy. She turned the tables on him, did she?'

'Stabbed him. He was in hospital. Nobody told me anything about it. No reason why they should, of course.'

'So whose character do they want you to defend?'

'Tony's. The loss of the baby is the mitigating factor. But I feel sorry for the woman. I don't want to make it harder for her.'

'Did she report the harassment to the police, do you know?'

'I've got no idea. But I would guess she must have done. She sounds fairly tough.'

'Don't you remember her at all?'

'Vaguely. She was big, if it's the one I think it must be. She took Tony off for some tea and sympathy when he fell

76

apart and wouldn't look at Edith.' Already she was feeling she'd been required to tell the story too many times. It was getting easier to talk about it without the acute pain there'd been at the start, but it still wasn't pleasant. Edith and Tony had both been packed away several months ago, and it was time to start a new phase. The timing was worse than frustrating. 'I really don't want to have to dredge it all up again now,' she finished.

'I can imagine,' he said.

'So do you think I'll have to show up in person? I don't even know for sure where I'd have to go.'

'I'll see what I can find out,' he promised, with a reassuring smile.

'Thank you,' she said. There was gratitude in her heart, and a sense of good fortune that this man was such a decent person. Moxon's decency never failed to make itself apparent, and she only now realised how much she had come to depend on it.

She went home to the rumpled bed that she and Christopher had rolled out of in such a hurry that morning. The day had been unsatisfactory, over all. The Staveley party wasn't going to happen. The death of a close relative of the retiring Anita, possibly deliberately inflicted, was an uncomfortable reality that Simmy feared would involve her more directly than she would like. There was no resolution of the business of Tony, and Bonnie's streaming nose might be a warning that she could no longer work with flowers. There were threats on all sides, compounded by her father's declining mental state adding a claim on her attention that might conflict with her plans concerning Christopher. Nothing was straightforward.

The coming months of spring and summer looked like a tangled maze of frustrations and complexities.

And she had to make three deliveries of flowers the next day, only one of which was complete and ready to go. She would have to go in early and construct the others before nine o'clock. If Bonnie didn't appear, the shop would have to stay closed until Simmy got back from Brant Fell. The logistics occupied most of her thoughts, as she made another unappetising little meal for herself.

Chapter Eight

When the alarm went off at seven, it woke her from a very enjoyable dream. All her worries had been smoothed away, and she was gliding along a country lane, with wild flowers burgeoning on either side. Christopher had his arm around her, keeping pace with her smooth progress, and they were laughing at patterns made by the clouds above their heads.

Despite the long list of worries from the previous evening, the happiness in the dream sustained her for the next half-hour or so. She opted to see it as an omen, predicting all kinds of positive outcomes over the next few weeks. She did at least have a clear conscience, after all. Unlike Tony, and perhaps Anita Olsen, who were under suspicion of behaving very badly.

But the mood was short-lived. There was Bonnie to worry about first. And the orders to be filled. She had to scramble to get everything done, leaving the house just after seven-thirty. At least the sun had started to rise at a more congenial hour, so she wasn't driving in the dark. It was already hard to recall the horrible dark mornings of early January, where icy patches on the road could be treacherously invisible until too late. And in another month, with the clocks put onto Summer Time, it would be light by six, and the evenings would be blessedly lengthening. Simmy's natural inclination was to look to the future with optimism, anticipating the next season of flowers and making plans. But this habit of anticipation had been tainted by the knowledge that she was getting older, her reproductive organs drying up, her chances of motherhood receding with every passing day.

Many of her years with Tony had been spent in a cycle of hope and disappointment as they tried for a baby. It had become almost routine, never exactly painful, because they were happy enough as they were, most of the time. But then, when conception finally did occur, when Simmy was in her mid-thirties, excitement had overwhelmed them. They both finally acknowledged how desperately they had wanted this to happen. They felt renewed as a couple, and almost sanctified by the miracle of pregnancy. The extreme high had made the crashing horror of the stillbirth worse than anything either of them could ever have imagined. Simmy still sometimes found herself shaking with the traumatic memory of it.

And now they wanted her to relive it all, because Tony's insane and unacceptable reaction had brought him to a trial in which he was both victim and perpetrator. Poor pathetic, exasperating Tony, she thought, with a great sigh.

The shop was chilly when she went in through the back,

but she did nothing to warm it. If Bonnie arrived at nine, she knew how to work the heating. Otherwise, Simmy would be back from her deliveries soon after, and could get everything more welcoming. Until then, she preferred to be frugal, the bills always just too high for comfort, leaving only a narrow margin for her own living costs.

Given that Bonnie had sent no message about absence it seemed probable that she would report for work as usual. It was like a game, guessing what symptoms she might be manifesting on this new day of her everlasting cold. Initially, the girl's health had caused Simmy quite some concern, but over the months she had realised there was a toughness beneath the fragile surface. Bonnie had come through a short life of trouble and misery, still smiling. Her elfin looks made people think she'd emerged from another realm altogether, where bad things routinely happened, but nonetheless life was good. A confusing mixture of wisdom and ignorance, guile and trustfulness, she was loved by everyone. Except for a succession of semi-human men brought into the house by her impossible mother, who had seen her as a plaything to abuse as they liked.

The bouquets all constructed, Simmy left the shop at eight-thirty, crawled through traffic down to Bowness, then back via Brant Fell to an address just north of Windermere. It was all familiar territory, and with her gain in confidence, she blithely parked on pavements or double lines while making the deliveries. In her first months of business, she had timidly stuck to the rules, using official car parks with their inflated prices, despite being told repeatedly by other business people that the regulations did not apply to her, and besides, the chances of being apprehended were minimal. In the end, the impossibility of even finding an authorised spot during the summer forced her to have more courage. Now she just drew up outside people's doors with the hazard lights flashing, and performed most deliveries in a fraction of the time they had once taken.

She got back five minutes after opening time, congratulating herself on a performance that outstripped her own expected schedule. It was going to be a good day, she promised herself. Spring was coming, and flowers were sure to sell spectacularly.

There were already two people in the shop, which brought both relief and surprise. Bonnie was still in her coat, facing a woman even smaller than herself – at least by a vertical measurement. Simmy's surprise turned to apprehension as her startled memory finally identified who it was. 'Mrs Townsend,' she said, with a nod. Then to Bonnie, 'How's your cold?'

'About the same,' said the girl. 'It's freezing in here.'

'Yes, I know. Go and put the heating on. I've done all those deliveries,' she added proudly.

'That was quick,' said Bonnie without much expression. 'You'll be bored all day now.'

'No I won't.' Simmy threw an embarrassed glance at Gillian Townsend, who seemed eager to have her say about something, but was unsure as to Bonnie's role. Simmy could read the thoughts: was this a daughter, customer, passing stray, or what? 'This is my assistant, Bonnie Lawson. She works here,' Simmy explained. 'So, what can we do for you?' She felt brisk almost to the point of impatience. There was nothing this woman could say that would be agreeable.

Gillian took a breath, and Simmy was reminded of her illness, and the perpetual discomfort she was likely to be suffering as a result. 'I came to apologise, mainly. I know we promised to let you know on Saturday whether or not Anita's party would be going ahead, and then we just left it hanging. Did that police detective give you the message? He said he would, but I wasn't sure he'd remember.'

'He did, thanks. I'm sorry about your friend's son-in-law. It must have been awful for all of you when they found him.'

'How much do you know?' The question was bald, and Simmy became instantly defensive.

'Not much. But given that I was questioned by a police officer, I suppose I deserve a bit of an explanation.'

'When?' Bonnie interposed. 'When were you questioned?'

'After you'd gone yesterday, if you must know. Moxon turned up here.'

'I'm really sorry,' Gillian said again. 'It was mean of us to drag you into it, I know. But they were so insistent that Anita give an account of her movements that we thought it would help if we could give an independent witness to confirm where she was on Friday.'

'What?' Bonnie's inquisitiveness was verging on the outrageous. She was bouncing on her toes like a five-year-old. 'What's happened?'

'Stop it,' Simmy ordered her. 'Behave yourself. Go and get the heating on, and make some tea or something. This is none of your business.'

'I know, but . . .' The girl rolled her eyes to express how earnestly she wanted to be involved. Just as earnestly as Simmy wanted *not* to be. The irony was evident to them both.

'Go,' said Simmy. 'You're being rude.'

'It's all right,' said Gillian. 'It's not secret, after all. I mean, there's absolutely nothing for us to hide. Anita hasn't done anything and I'm determined to prove it.'

This sounded odd to both Simmy and Bonnie. 'Oh?' said Simmy.

'You can't prove a negative,' said Bonnie. 'At least, you *can*, but it's difficult.'

'Fortunately, the law understands that, which is why the onus is on the prosecution to make a convincing case. But there are such things as alibis and witnesses, who can testify to the effect that the suspect could not possibly have committed the crime.'

Simmy reminded herself that this woman was a solicitor, and as far as she was aware solicitors did not participate in trials, either as prosecution or defence. But she supposed they knew people who did, and could act as part of a team, if necessary.

Bonnie had nodded impatiently through the little lecture. 'Yes, I know,' she said. 'My boyfriend is interested in all that sort of thing.'

'Oh? He's a law student, is he?' Gillian smiled to soften her words. 'I mean – he sounds very impressive,' she added.

The girl lifted her delicate chin and met the woman's eye. 'He's got a place at Newcastle to do a first degree in forensic science,' she said grandly. 'And he plans to go to America after that, as a postgraduate. He's going to be a forensic archaeologist.'

'Well, bully for him. That's the next five years or so all mapped out, then.'

For the first time, Simmy wondered what the effect of

separation would be on the young couple, if indeed they allowed themselves to be parted. Ben would go off to university in October – which suddenly didn't seem so very far away – and Bonnie might easily insist on going with him. She could find work close by, and stick by his side for the duration of his course.

'He's very clever,' Simmy said. 'It's almost frightening at times.'

'You know him, then?'

Simmy smiled. 'Yes, I do. You could say that he and Bonnie got together through me – although they were at school together before that.'

Gillian Townsend was clearly not very interested in young love. She had a hand pressed to her lower abdomen, and her face looked damp. 'Anyway,' she said. 'I hope you won't be troubled any more about this business in Anita's family. The police have got completely the wrong idea about it all.' She shook her head. 'I can't imagine what they think they can achieve. As if it wasn't bad enough that Declan's dead, without all this suspicion and accusation flying about. It's absolute nonsense to treat it as deliberate murder. Far more likely to have been an accident. It's ruined everything.'

'The party,' Simmy said.

'That's the least of it. Poor Anita feels terrible about it all. Her daughter's distraught, and blaming her. But you don't want to hear all the sordid details. When it's all over, we'll have that party, just as planned. I'll let you know.'

'Thanks,' said Simmy, speaking over Bonnie's attempt to ask another question. The girl had ignored the order to go and switch the heating on, glued to the conversation.

Simmy knew she was avid to glean every detail she could, in order to pass the whole story on to Ben. And, in spite of herself, she would have liked to know a bit more. 'So you're saying the police really do think Anita might have been involved in Declan's death? And you're acting on her behalf – professionally?' Quite why she couldn't simply let it go was obscure to her. Afterwards, she realised that this had been the pivotal moment when she might have escaped from the whole thing, once and for all.

'Involved!' Gillian shot back. 'The fools think she *killed* him. They listened to Debbie and Declan's idiot father, and now they think she cold-bloodedly crashed into his bike and sent him flying into a ditch.'

Of course, the implication had been there since the previous afternoon, but nobody had said the words outright. Anita Olsen was under suspicion of having deliberately killed her son-in-law and then concealing the fact. The woman Simmy had experienced as perfectly pleasant and civilised, if a trifle detached and silent, was thought to be capable of murder. A retiring solicitor in her mid sixties, helping to plan her own celebratory party, had instead attracted the attentions of a criminal investigation.

'That's ridiculous,' said Simmy. 'You must have got it wrong. I hadn't realised he was on a bike,' she added as an afterthought. It made the whole idea of an accidental killing more likely – didn't cyclists get slaughtered all the time?

'I'm afraid you don't understand. Why should you? It all goes back a long way. I don't remember quite what was said on Friday, but you will have been aware that Declan was missing, and everybody was worried about him –

86

including Anita. Prior to that, Debbie, Anita's daughter, had fallen out with her mother because of her behaviour towards Declan.'

'Yes,' said Simmy, as much of what Moxon had told her began to fit into the picture. 'And Debbie has a brother as well. What does he think about it all?'

'He was the first to accuse Anita – his own mother – of having at least had something to do with Declan's death. Honestly, it's been the most ghastly weekend. Anita's been in tears for most of it. She's staying with me for the time being. I can't let her be on her own, she's in such a state. I live in Kendal, not far from our office. I thought it would help her to stay away from Staveley for a bit.'

'Well, I'm glad to have helped, even if only slightly. After all, I was with you for barely an hour. I can't imagine what else I can do or say that would be of the slightest use.' She had intended to say *and we know how hard it is to pinpoint the time a person dies* when she thought better of it. For all she knew, there were indications other than a physical examination of the body to account for the moment of Declan's demise. Someone hearing a cry, or a squeal of brakes, perhaps.

Gillian was inattentive, moving towards the door, having glanced at her watch. 'Sorry,' she muttered. 'I've got a client due soon, and it'll take me nearly half an hour from here.'

'Well . . .' said Simmy vaguely, unsure of where she stood.

'I do wish we could have a bit longer. You're so easy to talk to, and I honestly think you'd be able to help us.' She turned a beseeching face up at Simmy. 'It's all such a strain, you see. I've known Anita for thirty years and more. This has come completely out of the blue. It's terribly unfair.'

Simmy said nothing more than 'Mmm', her own thoughts straying elsewhere. However certain the police might be, she found it hard to credit that there had in fact been a murder at all. Was it not much more likely to have been an accident, with the driver oblivious to what he or she had done? Or too panicked to stop and do the right thing, having realised they'd hit a person? The car would be dented and bloodied, most likely, and easy for the police to find and examine.

'If I could just use your toilet before I go . . .' Gillian said suddenly. 'I'm really sorry, but . . .'

'No problem,' said Simmy. 'It's just off the room at the back. I'll show you.' She led the way into the tiny lavatory with its sliding door that stuck halfway, and the threadbare bit of carpet underfoot. 'Sorry it's a bit tatty.'

Gillian barely waited for the door to close before yanking at her clothes, and Simmy made a tactful retreat. It was some time before the woman emerged again, her face even damper than before. 'Thank you,' she said. 'I'm so sorry about that.'

'No problem,' said Simmy again, thinking it would ease the embarrassment if she told the woman she knew about her illness. But before she could find the words, Gillian was gone.

She was hardly out of sight before Bonnie began dancing again. 'Oh, wow!' she yodelled. 'Another murder. Ben's going to be so frustrated. I'll have to do everything for him – gathering facts, and making a flow chart. He showed me how to do that, you know. I *love* flow charts.'

Simmy was not entirely certain of what a flow chart was, but it did sound efficient. Perhaps she could do with one herself. 'In your own time, then,' she said. She almost regretted the passing of the girl's cold, which had served to at least slightly quell her exuberance. 'Looks as if your cold's almost better, anyway,' she said.

Bonnie stopped bouncing and gave her a penetrating look. 'What's the matter with you? Why have you been so off lately? Corinne thinks you're turning into your mother – which wouldn't be a good thing. You're much nicer than her. It can't be because of Christopher, can it? That should be making you all happy and moony, not bad-tempered and impatient.'

Simmy's instant reaction was to snarl at the girl and put her in her place. But her better nature prevented her. 'Impatient?' she repeated. 'Have I been impatient?'

'A bit. Rushing about and moaning about Mother's Day. And apart from your dad losing his marbles, I can't see what you've got to complain about. Everything's going pretty nicely as far as I can see.'

'I wouldn't say that. This business with Tony, for a start, is nagging at me. And now there's been something horrible in Staveley, and they're trying to involve me in it. It's all worrying and stressful.'

'Okay – but you were stressed before that. A month ago, even. All this stuff is just making it worse.'

'Oh.' Simmy thought about it, crediting Bonnie with good intentions as well as courage in confronting the situation. 'I guess it's to do with my age. I'll be forty before I know it, and it scares me. Silly, I know, but it doesn't seem to be something I can control.'

'You want a baby,' said Bonnie flatly. 'That's what it is. Simple.'

To her horror and shame, Simmy started crying. As the tears erupted, she understood that they had been pent up for a long time. So much had happened in the past four or five years, piling distress upon loss, fear upon anxiety until she felt pummelled on all sides. All she could do was to remain upright and get through the daily tasks.

Bonnie did not panic, as might have been expected. She acted as if she'd spent a lifetime dealing with weeping women – which perhaps she had. 'It's okay,' she said. 'Go out the back for a minute. I'll see to any customers.'

A lesser girl might have apologised for breaching the floodgates, but Bonnie evidently saw no such need. Simmy meekly did as instructed, barely capable of rational thought. She still wasn't clear as to why she was crying anyway. Where was her self-control? What was the matter with her? A noxious smell wafted from the little toilet, reminding her that other people had much worse trouble to cope with.

It took less than five minutes to recover her balance and return to business. 'Gosh, that came out of nowhere,' she said with a feeble grin.

'Yeah,' said Bonnie. 'And you know what? We've both been sent to the back room this morning. But when you tried to make me go out there, I ignored you. And you did what you were told.'

'Maybe we should change places, then. You might make a better boss than me.'

'Yeah,' said Bonnie again, with a flash of mischief. 'That might not be a bad idea.'

* * *

The day turned out to be busier than for many weeks. Buckets of daffodils still in bud were emptied as fast as they could replenish them. 'We should charge more for them, if they're in such demand,' said Simmy. 'I thought the supermarkets would take all that business.'

'People buy them on impulse,' said Bonnie. 'Just passing by, and they think – "Ooh, they look nice. Better get a few."'

'Most of them must have their own daffs in the garden. And the woods are full of them.'

'Yes, but they don't want to pick them, do they? And it makes them feel all Wordsworthy to have a houseful.'

Simmy laughed. Since her unscheduled descent into a weeping fit, she had felt strangely light-hearted, as if some kind of blockage had been washed away. It also made her feel very foolish, and she hoped Bonnie would refrain from telling anybody about it.

They made no reference to it, anyway, which was a relief. Nor did Bonnie ask questions or form theories about the death of the man in Staveley. Simmy supposed that the girl was waiting for Ben to appear, at which point another pair of floodgates would probably burst and there'd be a spate of talk about it. There might even be a flow chart, she thought wearily. Ben would want to know names, dates and other details, not that he had time to take the matter on as a project.

But Ben never materialised. There was a text sent to Bonnie's phone at three o'clock to tell her he was staying late at school and then going straight home. 'Some sort of experiment he can't leave,' said the girl ruefully. 'Never mind. We knew it would be like this until the middle of June. Only three and a half months to go.'

Instead of Ben, there was another arrival; another person coming for conversation rather than plants or flowers. A woman came through the shop door, looking around herself as if expecting to be accosted. She wore a woolly hat that had a very obvious hole in it, and her face was smudged with greyish marks. But it was a pretty face, just the same, on a woman in her thirties, above average height with strands of fair hair escaping the impossible hat. The smudges showed every sign of being caused by tears, not unlike Simmy's own cheeks had been when she'd checked in the mirror earlier that day.

'Hello? Are you Persimmon Brown?' The voice was sweet and soft and halting.

'That's right. What can I do for you?' Simmy was never going to say *How can I help you?* if she could possibly avoid it. Nor *What do you need?*

'I'm Debbie Kennedy. I think you met my mother last week, in Staveley? She's called Anita Olsen.'

'Oh! Gosh. Yes. Your husband . . .'

'Declan. He died on Friday.'

Simmy knew better than to think the widow had come about funeral flowers. It was too soon, for one thing, and her complete lack of interest in the displays on all sides confirmed the fact that she was here for something else. 'I heard,' she said. 'I'm really sorry.'

Bonnie was on her knees amongst a collection of tall grasses, not immediately visible. Now she got up, making a deliberate noise, and Mrs Kennedy whirled round. Why was she so nervy, Simmy wondered. Bonnie gave a little smile of apology, and said, 'Only me,' in a light little voice.

'I know who you are,' said the woman. 'You were in the papers over that trouble in Hawkshead last summer. They said you were a hero. Really brave. I wanted to meet you then, to see what you were like.'

'I *was* brave,' said Bonnie, to whom false modesty was very much like dishonesty. 'You don't know the half of it.'

'I wish I was. Brave, I mean. I seem to be permanently scared of one thing or another. And now . . .' Her blue eyes filled with tears. 'Now I've really got reason to be.'

'Oh?' Bonnie came closer, with an intrigued expression. 'Why?'

'Because my husband's been murdered, of course. And because I know who did it.' The pretty chin lifted defiantly, and the words emerged clear and certain.

'But why have you come here?' asked Simmy, not thinking nearly as fast as she ought to. 'We don't know anything about it. It's got nothing at all to do with us. You ought to be talking to the police.'

'I know. I'm sorry.' Debbie Kennedy wilted, the tears still in evidence. 'We have told the police what we think. It was Matthew's idea that I should come and see you. He's my brother. He knows Corinne vaguely, and has kept track of things that have happened over the last year or two. All those horrible crimes, and you two always seem to be helping the police and being brave. And that boy, of course.' Again she looked round, as if expecting Ben to emerge from behind the potted bay tree near the door.

'Everybody knows Corinne,' said Bonnie. 'It's a curse. And the boy is my boyfriend.'

'Yes, I know. So – Matthew thinks you, between you,

might help. The thing is, my mother's got a powerful ally in the shape of Gillian Townsend. You met her as well, I assume. They're both solicitors, with an office in Kendal.'

'Hang on,' said Bonnie. 'You've missed a step somewhere. How do you know that Simmy went to Staveley on Friday?'

'Mrs Percival told me. We call her Auntie Barbara. She's Gillian Townsend's mother. She came to see me when she heard about Declan. She's always been ever so kind to me and Matthew. I think she wanted to compensate us for . . . well, for the way we've always been so let down. She's a really nice lady.'

Simmy was trying to imagine how the conversation must have gone. 'But why did my name come up?'

'Oh, she told me about the retirement party and flowers and how Declan dying meant it would have to be postponed. As if I care about *that*,' she added venomously.

'You and your mother don't get along, then?' said Simmy slowly and far from surely. 'I think I'm starting to get the picture, even though it adds up to something very nasty. As far as I'm aware, the police suspect your mother of killing your husband, and that means she's going to need help from Mrs Townsend. So, you think there's something wrong with that? You think an ordinary country solicitor isn't adequate to the task of defending Anita? Is that it?'

The younger woman's face clenched with a furious frustration. 'No, no, of course that's not it, you idiot. I don't care if nobody defends my mother at all. I *know* she did it. But she'll get her defender, of course. Gillian is more than adequate for the job. If anybody can defend her, it's Gillian.'

'But . . .' Simmy floundered, knowing more than she

94

was able to admit to herself, cringing away from what was bound to come next.

'But nothing.' Debbie's voice was suddenly much stronger. 'My mother killed Declan and I won't rest until I've found someone who'll help me prove it.'

Chapter Nine

'Well, don't look at me.' Simmy was horrified at the implication that she might commit herself to anything like the extent that was being suggested. 'It's your family's trouble. It has absolutely nothing to do with me.'

'That's true, I know. And I was thinking more of Bonnie and her boyfriend. What's his name? Tom, is it?'

'Ben. Ben Harkness,' said Bonnie. 'But he won't have time. He's doing his A-levels and hasn't a minute to spare.'

'I still don't understand what you think we could do. Even Ben doesn't have any kind of qualifications for getting into legal matters.' Simmy was increasingly resistant to the apparent suggestion that she, Ben and Bonnie become some sort of unofficial investigators.

'I suppose we're clutching at straws. We seem to be so isolated, you see. Everybody's convinced that my mother would never do such a thing.'

'But she's your *mother*,' Simmy burst out, not caring

that she was stating the obvious. 'How can you even think such a thing?'

'It would take me quite a time to explain. And I can't stay now. I've got my girls in the car. They'll be getting impatient.'

'Girls?' said Bonnie. 'How old are they?'

'Eight and eleven. They're shell-shocked, obviously. I've had to keep them off school and take them round with me. It's a comfort to have their company. They're very good on the whole.' Her gaze became distant, as she visualised her daughters. 'I'm lucky to have them,' she concluded.

Yes you are, thought Simmy. *You have no idea how lucky.*

'Do *they* think their granny killed their father?' Bonnie demanded starkly.

'You don't believe me,' said Debbie with a sigh. 'See what I mean?' she addressed Simmy. 'See what I'm up against?'

'I'm not sure I see anything very clearly. Nor do I think I want to. I'm a florist, not a private detective. I'm really very sorry about your husband, and I can't say much more than that. It's only been a few days, and you must still be very shocked. I only met your mother briefly, and she hardly said anything. Gillian was here this morning – I'm not quite sure why. All I know is that you're all trying to drag me and my friends into a real mess that doesn't concern any of us at all.'

'Gillian was here?' Debbie frowned. 'She must be trying to get you onto her side. That would be typical. Well, it doesn't matter. It's the boy, Ben Harkness, we really want to talk to. Matthew's seen his Facebook page, and thinks he'd have plenty to offer us.'

Simmy felt foolishly offended at the implication that she

was essentially useless. Hadn't that been exactly what she wanted to hear? And yet it rankled to be so belittled.

'Your brother thinks his mother's a murderer as well, then?' Bonnie was clearly stuck on the idea of a homicidal mother-in-law.

'Even more so than me. He knows what she's like,' she said darkly.

The next they knew two young women had come in wanting to buy flowers to take to a party. The conversation was broken up with no resolution. Simmy watched with a welter of mixed feelings as the unhappy woman departed. The hat alone made her look mentally disturbed. The story was still skeletally thin, with no background information or reasons for suspecting Anita Olsen of murder, other than Moxon's mutterings about the financial affairs of the Kendal business. The demands being made on all sides were all the more unreasonable for the lack of any persuasive explanations. When the customers had gone, she looked at Bonnie. 'What am I meant to do, then?' she demanded, feeling a burgeoning exasperation. 'It's actually incredibly *rude* to come and accost me like that.'

'Well . . .' Bonnie began, with uncharacteristic hesitation. 'I don't think it really was you she wanted, was it?'

Simmy blinked. 'Don't you start as well. It's one thing not to want to get dragged into all this, and quite another to be made to feel ignorant and useless.'

Bonnie gave her a very grown-up look. 'That's not what she said. Weren't you listening? She said it was Ben and me she thought could help, I know, but she would have been quite happy to include you until you made such a thing about not wanting to be involved.'

'Oh.' Simmy thought about it. 'Yes, but . . . no, but . . . no, she *did* want to tell me about it. At first she did. After all, I've met her mother and you haven't. Ben doesn't know any of them.'

Bonnie gave her a carefully considering look. 'This is what Ben would call mixed messages,' she said. 'One minute you're cross at being asked to help, and the next you're cross because I said you don't have to be involved if you don't want to.'

'What is it with you today?' Simmy burst out. 'I feel as if I'm being interrogated all the time. First you make me cry and now you make me feel I don't know my own mind.'

'Sorry. I didn't mean to be annoying.'

'Oh, it's all right. It's not you, really. You're just forcing me to face things I'd rather not. I'm sure it's good for me, in the long run. And I can see I'm being inconsistent about this Staveley thing.'

'I'm guessing maybe you think Ben and I are too young to go investigating on our own. Except we won't because he's too busy. And I'm not doing anything without him. So, you don't have to worry. Besides, that woman, whatever her name is, didn't say anything definite, did she? Nothing at all. She wasn't being rational. I don't even know exactly how the husband died. Do you?'

'He was knocked off his bike by a car – or some sort of vehicle – in a side road somewhere. That's all I know. It might easily have been an accident, although Moxon said they were sure it wasn't. He didn't give any details, thank goodness. But it's hardly the sort of thing you could plan in advance, is it? How would you know where he'd be at any given time? And how would you know you'd killed him? He could just have been injured, and then told the police who did it.' She paused, trying to keep pace with her own logic. 'So there'd be a strong incentive to make sure he was dead, I suppose,' she concluded unhappily.

'Right. I knew that much, actually. But there's a lot more to find out. Like exactly where was it? Did he die instantly? What time of day? Who found him? How long had he been missing from home? Why hasn't it been on the news? All that stuff that Ben always wants to know.'

'Moxon told me some of it yesterday.'

'Ah! I forgot he'd been to see you. That means he thinks you're involved, doesn't it?'

'I'm involved in backing up Anita Olsen's alibi for Friday, that's all.'

Bonnie frowned. 'But that's quite silly, isn't it – when you think about it? How many people were there, not counting you?'

'Three. Anita, Gillian and Gillian's mother.'

'Hm. And there'd been something on the news about a man going missing in Staveley, hadn't there? And then they found a body?'

'Yes. And Anita was worrying that it might be Declan. But Moxon said that body was an old man, a vagrant or something in a shed, and not Declan at all.'

'Isn't that rather weird? Two dead men in Staveley on the same day? It's not a very big place, after all.'

'Weird but true,' shrugged Simmy, thinking much stranger things had happened.

'There was something in the news about a man being

100

knocked off his bike,' Bonnie remembered. 'But they never said his name was Declan Kennedy.'

'All this politics and economic chaos is drowning out practically all the other news, at the moment. There'll probably be something in the paper this week. And why does that matter, anyway?'

'It makes me think the police are hushing it up for some reason.'

'They could be, if they're not sure whether or not it was an accident. The whole thing feels terribly murky.'

Bonnie gave her another narrow look. 'You're hooked, aren't you?' she said, sounding more sympathetic than accusatory. 'Anybody would be.'

'I live and work here, just a few miles from Staveley. I've learnt by now that I can't just cover my head and try to ignore this sort of thing, however much I might want to. It'll come back to bite me, sooner or later.'

She wasn't entirely sure what she meant by that, but all her instincts, both personally and professionally, were to keep as many people happy as she could, however difficult that might sometimes be. But this time, it seemed she would have to take sides. 'But I can't please Gillian Townsend *and* Debbie Kennedy, can I?' she wailed. 'They're on opposite sides.'

'They are. And they both want us to help them. How did that happen?' Bonnie went into a near-trance as she tried to think it through. 'Well, I hate to say it again, but Debbie really wants Ben, not you. And Gillian's already used you for an alibi, so she might leave you alone now. I suppose the next thing'll be the brother, Matthew, coming in to nag at us. Have you met him?'

101

Simmy shook her head. 'They all talk about him, though. He must live somewhere local.'

'We don't know anything about them, do we?' Bonnie looked irritated. 'Unless you got a whole lot from Moxon that you haven't told me.'

'Not really,' said Simmy absently. 'They're very different, aren't they?'

'What are?'

'These women. Anita's tall and serious, probably clever. I rather liked her. Gillian's so short and bouncy, like a little dog and I imagine *everybody* likes her. She's the sort of person you trust instinctively. Her mother's very old-fashioned, elegant and civilised. Her house is gorgeous. And now this Debbie, completely different again. She seems absolutely genuine, coming in that awful hat and being so intense. I don't think she'd thought at all about what she was going to say, before she got here. She just had an idea that Ben might be able to help her somehow. If you met them at a Women's Institute or in an evening class, you'd be happy to have any of them as your friend. And yet there must be something really dreadful going on between them, for them to accuse each other of murder.'

'They're not accusing each other,' Bonnie corrected her. 'It's only Anita who's being accused. By her own daughter,' she added miserably.

'Why does that get to you so much? It's not as if your own mother is any great shakes.'

Bonnie snorted. '"Any great shakes"? Who says that? What does it even mean?'

'My mother says it sometimes. You know what it means.'

'Yeah. Well, my mother's a special case.' The girl lapsed into another reverie. 'That's the thing. I've got just about the worst mother anybody could wish for, and even she would never *kill* anybody. It seems such a mad idea. I need to see this Anita person for myself – and find out why she might have wanted her daughter's husband dead. What did he do to her?'

'She can't possibly have killed him,' said Simmy. 'She's a solicitor.'

This time, Bonnie hooted with laughter and Simmy heard her own words with a wry acknowledgement of her own naivety. 'Well, they are supposed to be pillars of the community, above reproach and all that sort of thing.'

'The Hay Poisoner was a solicitor,' said Bonnie. 'Although Ben says there's a strong chance he didn't really do it.'

Simmy let that pass. References to famous crimes were a regular part of Ben and Bonnie's conversation, and she had almost never heard of the names they mentioned. She went back to Bonnie's question. 'I don't know what he did to her. Nobody's said anything about that to me. She seemed worried about him on Friday, when he was missing and they found that old man's body. You're right, I suppose, that it's rather peculiar to have two bodies at the same time.'

'It's a red herring,' said Bonnie. 'A distraction. Ben would want to know the name and the exact circumstances in both cases. The old man might have been deliberately placed for the police to find, to muddy the waters.'

'I doubt it. And even if that's right, it didn't work for long, did it? They found Declan sometime on Friday evening,

103

which must have been very soon after he died.' She frowned. 'I can't remember what Moxon said about that.'

'He should have told you more of the details. It's not fair to drag you into it without more explanation.'

'Yeah.' Simmy heaved a sigh. She wanted to go home and shut the door behind her. There had been altogether too many tears that day, as well as unanswered questions and a strong feeling of impending disaster. 'You know what?' she realised. 'We're useless without Ben. He'd slice through all this messy stuff and get to the main point. We don't even know what that is, do we?'

Bonnie pouted. 'I know what he would say, mostly.'

'Go on, then.'

'Well . . . he'd want the basics. Where and when did Declan die? What evidence is there that it wasn't an accident? Why is the Anita person everybody's main suspect? Background. Chief players.' She was groping her way, channelling her boyfriend's assumed ideas. 'Oh, this is silly. I'm going over to his and I'll make him listen. He must be able to take an hour off his revision. Nobody's that busy.'

'You'll be lucky. His mother won't let you in.'

'Yeah, she will. Now he's eighteen, she lets him do what he likes. Besides, they've got some bother with Natalie, and that's distracted them.'

'One of the twins, right?'

Bonnie nodded. 'She's gone all teenage and bolshy. There's a much older boyfriend hanging around and they can't decide what to do about it. He's got piercings all round his ears.'

'You've seen him, have you?'

104

'Once or twice. He seems harmless to me, but she's only fourteen. I never took any notice of boys at that age,' she said piously, as if fourteen was far in the remote past.

Simmy often tried in vain to imagine the daily lives of the Harkness family. Busy professional parents, five offspring, a big house and relaxed attitudes. Helen, the mother, was a sensible woman who Simmy much admired. Wilf, the oldest of the children, had left home and was away at university after considerable dithering as to his choice of career. Ben was followed by three sisters: Natalie, Tanya and Zoe, a trio of trouble, as he would sometimes characterise them.

'Good luck, then,' she said to Bonnie. 'But just remember: if he fails any of his exams, they're going to blame you.'

'He won't fail,' said Bonnie, with complete conviction.

Simmy found her car, drove home, phoned Christopher and fed herself, all without giving a single thought to Staveley and its suspicious inhabitants. Instead, she focused on the business. Ordering all the necessary stock for later in the month, buying in new cards, thinking up fresh wares for the summer such as hanging baskets and variations on that theme. She even jotted some ideas on a pad as she ate her supper. The mental barrier she'd erected against unwelcome thoughts was holding up nicely until the phone rang and all the defences collapsed when she heard her mother saying, 'He's been rushed into hospital. Your father's had a stroke, and they've taken him to Barrow.'

'Didn't you go with him?'

'I couldn't. There are guests. I can't leave them here on their own.'

'Yes, you can, Mum. You can't just *abandon* him.'

'That's why I'm ringing you,' said Angie Straw, with exaggerated calm. 'You get a choice. Either go and sit by his bedside, or come here and supervise a family of four and two dogs.'

Simmy didn't hesitate to take the less attractive of two very disagreeable options. 'I'll do the guests,' she said. 'Your place is at his side.'

Angie groaned. 'He'd far rather have you with him than me,' she said.

'Even if that's true, I have the shop to think about.'

'I'm not staying there all night. I'll come back and do the breakfasts tomorrow.'

'Is he conscious? What happened exactly?' Simmy was trying to accommodate the new crisis, concern for her father slowly overwhelming all other thoughts. 'How bad is it? They can do amazing things with strokes now, can't they?'

'He was dozing by the Rayburn, with the dog on his lap, and when he woke up he said his head hurt, and one of his eyes had gone funny. I knew what it was, right away.' Angie sounded inordinately proud of herself. 'I dialled 999 and they whisked him off in no time.'

'Poor Dad.'

'I'm sure he'll live to tell the tale.'

'Actually, I don't see why anybody has to be there this evening. The B&B people can manage, surely? If you're going to be back for the breakfasts, that's all that matters, isn't it?'

There was silence at Angie's end. 'Well . . .' she began, 'we never *do* leave them. They always want to ask something. They come down and sit in the games room, and we chat to them.'

'I know. But there's no rule that says you've got to be there.'

'I think there might be, actually. Why won't you come?'

'I will if you insist, but I can't see what use I'll be. You might be gone for half the night. Where would I sleep?'

'The back room's empty. Or you could use our bed, if we're not there.'

The conversation was imbued with a sense of urgency that did nothing to resolve the practical questions. Angie was famously calm in a crisis, to the point where it was hard to be sure that she was in fact feeling any of the usual emotions. Simmy was not deceived. 'Go, Mum,' she urged. 'I'll come down and check that everything's as it should be. Phone me on my mobile if there's any news. Give him my love. I'll go and see him tomorrow.'

'All right.'

The next ten minutes were spent in dealing with her own reaction. Some people, she reminded herself, lived in a perpetual state of drama and disaster. Their relatives were constantly in and out of hospital, or prison. They never had any money, their children went off the rails, their cars broke down, the rain came in through leaky roofs and their dogs attacked small children. And still they survived. Some even seemed to thrive on chaos. Simmy needed to man up and confront the immediate demands being made on her, without falling apart. The shop could be neglected for a few hours, for a start. Nothing else mattered at all. *Poor old Dad*, she kept repeating to herself. Such a patient, amusing, harmless man. Whatever could be done to soothe him must take priority over everything else. Firm resolution took hold of her, although only for a few minutes. Driving down to Windermere, she discovered tears running down her cheeks for the second time that day.

Chapter Ten

Wednesday started slowly, after the late night. Following a string of phone calls from her mother, Simmy ascertained that Russell probably had not suffered a full-blown stroke after all. 'They call it a TIA,' said Angie. 'He can come home sometime tomorrow.'

Which was now today. The release of tension was draining. She could feel the energy flowing out of her. 'So what happens next?' she asked her mother. 'Is it likely to happen again? What does TIA stand for?'

'Transient something episode. A mini-stroke in other words, I suppose. They want to put him on those pills – whatever they're called. He won't like that.'

'Neither will you,' said Simmy. She knew only too well that Angie deplored medication with a far greater passion than did her husband.

'There's sure to be side effects,' said Angie gloomily.

'I expect they know what they're doing,' said Simmy,

too weary to be diplomatic. Sometimes Angie was too much, never missing a chance to make her views clear. 'I'll come over after work and see how he's doing.' She ended the call before her mother could say anything else.

Bonnie was in the shop before her, looking flustered. 'It's all kicking off,' she said. 'Three orders for Mother's Day on the computer, and there's been a phone call already. And it's still ages away yet.' She coughed, and then frowned. 'My cold's turning into a cough,' she complained. 'Just when I thought it had gone.'

'They do that,' said Simmy. 'Will you be okay?'

'Probably. I'll have to be with all this work, won't I? Anyway, I don't feel poorly.'

'That's good. At least we can get all these orders done in good time, with them coming in nice and early. The next two weeks are going to have to be extremely well organised. We mustn't forget anybody.'

'But how does it work? I mean, how many can you actually deliver in one day? And do you do them on the day before, or the actual day? It's a Sunday.'

'Last year most people came and collected them on the Saturday. Melanie was amazing. She had everything lined up and ready to go. We did deliver about five on the actual day, at an extra cost.'

'Sounds fun,' said Bonnie, without a trace of irony.

As Simmy told her assistant what had been happening overnight, she felt a sudden compulsion to learn more about the Staveley business. Whether from superstition or a surge of fellow feeling, she knew she had to do whatever she could to help. There were people suffering – not least the likeable Debbie and her daughters. However misguided her suspicion of her mother might be, Debbie should not be ignored. And if Simmy could somehow prove useful in convincing the daughter of her parent's innocence, that would surely be the best possible outcome. Simmy's own parents were becoming vulnerable and dependent, and through a somewhat odd association, she found herself wanting to do what she could for other people's as well.

'But Dad's going to be okay,' she ended up saying to Bonnie. 'So, what about you and Ben? Did he spare some time to go over the killing of Declan Kennedy with you?'

'Better than that,' smiled the girl. 'He's found answers to at least half those questions we came up with yesterday. It's all over Facebook if you know where to look. And he thinks we have an obligation to try and see that justice is done.' The words emerged as an obvious quote from Ben. 'For a start, we're going to see Debbie Kennedy this afternoon. He spoke to her last night.'

Simmy was speechless. *What about me?* she wanted to whine.

Bonnie was ahead of her. 'And he thinks you should go and talk to the Townsend woman again. Did she leave you an address? Did she say where she lives?'

'I told you. Anita's got a house in Staveley, and Gillian lives in Kendal somewhere. I don't know the address of her office or her house.'

'We can find out easily enough.'

Simmy looked helplessly at her calm little friend. Quite at what point she had capitulated so completely was unclear. The whole previous day had been one of changed minds and irrational emotions. 'But I have no idea what I'm supposed to say, or why I even think any of this is sensible.'

'Ben wants us to find out about *evidence*.' Bonnie's face was full of importance. 'The serious stuff. He says he can't give it any more time before Friday, but then he's factored in a whole evening clear of revision. We've got until then to come up with something.'

It was so patently a game that Simmy lost patience. 'How does he think we can do that? Just barge in on people and interrogate them? Even the police don't do that – at least not without really good reason.'

The girl sighed. 'We're not barging anywhere. We've been *asked* to help. They *want* to talk to us. Both sides, in fact, which is amazing when you think about it. Between us we can get the whole picture. Look – today's Wednesday. When can you go to Kendal, do you think?'

'Oh, Bonnie! My father's been rushed to hospital. They're going to need me at Beck View this evening, and probably tomorrow. We've got a flood of orders to deal with here. I'm every bit as busy as Ben is, in my own way. And you can't go off to some unknown house by yourself. You'll get yourself murdered as well.'

'I can. Of course I can. That Debbie person isn't going to kill me, is she? Even if she wanted to, she wouldn't do it with two little girls in the house.'

'What about her brother? Matthew Olsen, he must be. Maybe he killed Declan, and is throwing the blame on his mother as a smokescreen.' Hearing her own words, Simmy paused. She sounded just like a character from a nineteen-thirties detective novel, or worse, someone out of the Famous Five. Even Ben and Bonnie were more mature and rational than that. 'Listen to me,' she moaned. 'I'm turning

112

into a Keystone Kop or something. It's all your fault.'

'I know,' smiled Bonnie. 'But you know you like it, really. I can tell you're hooked. I even spotted the moment it happened, about twenty minutes ago. When you were telling me about your dad, which is funny.' She turned her head aside for another cough.

'You couldn't have spotted anything. I didn't say a word.'

'I'm right, though. So, what you do is close up a bit early at the end of today, go round to your mum's and check on everything there. Maybe peel a few potatoes or something. Then down to Staveley – no, Kendal. No, hang on. You'll have to get the Townsend woman's home address, because she won't be in her office then, will she? You can phone her and tell her you're coming. After all, she *wants* you to go and see her. She'll be thrilled. And maybe you can see Anita Olsen as well if she's there. The cherry on the cake, she is. Ben's going to be jealous. Remember to ask open questions, let them talk about anything they like, and try to get some proper evidence.'

The conflicting emotions were ripping at each other inside her head – or wherever else emotions might dwell. Somewhere near the ascendant was gratitude for being included. The old childhood fear of being in permanent isolation due to the lack of siblings never quite went away. Then came panic at the prospect of a whole new slew of unpleasantness. People behaving badly, telling lies, hating each other – and telling her all about it. Persimmon Brown did not relish that sort of thing in the least. Why else had she chosen flowers as the core of her working life? Another strand of panic arose from the crowding demands being made on her. Where would Christopher fit in? How long

113

was all this going to take? Would she be despatched by Ben and Bonnie on a long succession of quests, once she agreed to the first one? And Moxon? Wouldn't he be furious to have her and the others trampling all over his investigation yet again? Well, no, probably not. Hadn't he come along in person to talk to her about it? Hadn't he known then that he was starting something, despite his apologies and assurances?

Bonnie was manipulating her phone, tapping and swiping, until within about forty seconds she had the address of the solicitors' office in Kendal. And its phone number. 'Call her now on this number,' she instructed Simmy, who meekly obliged. 'Better than using her mobile, if she's at work. You might interrupt something important.'

'I'm afraid she's with a client. Can I take a message?' said the young man who answered the phone.

'Yes, please. Say Simmy Brown called. The florist in Windermere. She can phone me back when she's free, can she?' Bonnie rolled her eyes at the wimpish tone. Simmy gave the shop's number and finished the call. 'There. Satisfied?' she snapped at Bonnie. What was she doing, she asked herself. She could still tell Gillian Townsend she'd only called out of politeness and didn't really want anything. She'd been given a second chance to bow out, but she knew she was already in too deep. If nothing else, she had to ensure that Ben and Bonnie didn't do anything too reckless.

'For now,' said Bonnie, with a knowing look. 'Why's everything so quiet today? We haven't had a single customer, and it's nearly ten o'clock.'

'It's cold out there. And dark. Hardly anybody's out

114

yet, look.' She waved at the empty pavements, and the heavy grey sky. 'I think they said it would brighten up a bit later on.'

Weather predictions inevitably brought her father to mind again. Like virtually every other Englishman of his generation, he could not begin a day without knowing the forecast, whether it was pertinent to his plans or not. In Russell's case, he could always claim relevance for his B&B guests, if not for himself. 'You'll need to take waterproofs,' he would tell them. 'It might look nice now, but there'll be rain by midday.' Or the converse. 'You'll be fine. It'll all have cleared up by eleven, and you'll be much too warm if you wear those jumpers.'

It did brighten up, imperceptibly, so that by three o'clock the sun was forcing its way through the thinning cloud. It was an abiding regret to Simmy that the lake wasn't visible from anywhere in central Windermere. It seemed an ironic quirk of geography that the town named for the mere should be so detached from it, while Bowness and Ambleside got the full impact. They had the swans and the sailing boats, the ice cream and the vivid colours. Windermere sometimes seemed drab by comparison, and very much too quiet.

Angie had phoned at eleven to say her husband had been restored to her, rather diminished and traumatised. 'He hasn't said more than three words to me,' she complained. 'I'm not sure he realises what's been going on.'

'I'll be there soon after five,' Simmy promised. 'But I won't be able to stay all evening. I've got to go and see somebody in Kendal.' She was relying on her mother being too distracted to take any interest in her daughter's doings. As far as she was aware, there had still been no proper news reports of the dead Declan from Staveley, and even if there had, nothing would link him to Simmy. She was determined to keep the whole thing well beyond her parents' ken, having seen how distressing previous episodes had been for her father.

'Kendal? About flowers?'

'Sort of. If you work out which jobs I can do, I'll knuckle down to them as soon as I arrive, and be off again about seven. I can come again tomorrow.'

'Well, all right, then. Thanks. See you later.' Angie sounded tired and beyond caring whether her guests got their full English breakfasts, or even clean duvet covers.

Then Gillian Townsend returned her call, giving her home address, and effusively grateful for being so co-operative. 'I can't thank you enough,' she gushed. 'You're being wonderfully kind.' It was almost enough to make Simmy change her mind yet again. It didn't strike her that she was being in the least bit kind. Just too spinelessly compliant for her own good, as usual.

'Looks as if your plan's going to work,' Simmy told Bonnie, bringing the girl up to date. 'My dad's home again and not causing too much trouble, from the sound of it. They'll both just want to go to bed by about eight, I expect. I can get things straight for them, and then I can scoot down to Kendal, heaven help me.'

It worked out even better than expected. At seven o'clock, she was driving down the A591, passing the cluster of houses that was Staveley, just off the main road, and heading down to Kendal, the nearest town of any size. In another ten minutes, she was encouraging

116

her satnav to find the small street on the eastern side of town which Gillian had given as her home address.

At precisely the same moment, Ben and Bonnie were cycling along the same road, enough heavy traffic thundering past to terrify a parent or friend who might have seen them. But they survived unscathed, turning left into the quiet oasis that was Staveley. 'We turn right over the little bridge by the bus stop,' said Ben, 'and then I think it gets a bit complicated.'

In fact, they found their destination largely by accident, wheeling the bikes down an odd little alleyway strewn with grey slate chippings that emerged into a road full of older houses, most of them painted white. 'Unpretentious,' remarked Ben approvingly. 'This is the one, I believe.'

The door was answered by a man with dark-brown hair left quite long on his neck, in a denim jacket. 'Hi, I'm Matthew,' he said. 'I'm here helping Deb and the girls.'

'That's kind of you,' said Bonnie. 'It must be so awful for her.' She was then seized by fifteen seconds of racking cough, exacerbated by the effort of cycling.

The man waited, saying nothing until she'd stopped. 'Tell me about it,' he nodded, then, 'Say what you like about Declan, he was always good to his family. Best dad I know, bar none.'

Matthew seemed to be about thirty, with a slight local accent. 'Are you married?' Bonnie asked, with an air of childlike innocence.

'Oh, no. Not even close.' He laughed. 'Too fond of my own company – and spending my own money as I like. No danger of me getting tied down any time soon.'

Despite his efforts at bonhomie, the two youngsters were wary. 'Debbie wanted to talk to us,' said Ben. 'Is this a good time?'

'It's the time you said you'd be here, isn't it? She's all ready and waiting for you, anyway.' He took them into the front room, which was much the same as thousands of other front rooms across the land. A three-seater sofa, with a small tear on one of the arms; a Chinese carpet with attractive sculpted shapes depicting flowers; large television and associated technology; a shelved alcove containing ornaments, clock, candlesticks and two books. On the wall above the fireplace was a picture of a clown done in bright primary colours.

'I like the picture,' said Ben, to nobody in particular.

'I like the carpet,' said Bonnie. Together they had identified the two things that indicated the individuality of the family in residence.

Debbie was on the sofa, a pen in hand and large notepad on her lap. She was wearing a baggy jumper and leggings, her hair unbrushed. 'Oh, hello,' she said. 'Here you are already.' She waved vaguely at an armchair to her left. 'Sit down.'

Ben took the chair and Bonnie settled comfortably into a corner of the sofa, bringing up her knees and turning to look at Debbie. 'You look like a little cat,' said the woman. 'All curled up like that.'

'Let's hope she's as clever as a cat, then,' said Matthew, who was lounging against the window sill, out of everybody's line of sight.

'Don't stand there,' his sister told him. 'If you're staying, sit where we can see you. Come here next to

118

me.' She patted the sofa and he meekly did as instructed, Ben watching him closely.

Debbie dived straight into the main matter. 'You know what I need from you, don't you?' Barely pausing for their nods, she went on, 'I need to find hard evidence that my mother was responsible for my husband's death last Friday. We all know she did it, but not exactly *how*. I know you two have been helpful to the police over this sort of thing before.'

'Well . . .' Bonnie began. 'Not exactly with anything like this.'

'We'll do our best,' Ben interrupted her. 'You've been making notes, I see.'

'Yes, I have. My head's not working too well at the moment, so I try to write everything down.' She held up the pad, which already had a page full of writing, at least. 'This is the third page. Some of it won't be relevant.' She sighed. 'I went back to when I first met Declan, you see. And then I thought I should take it even further – to when my mother first met him. It all got a bit long.'

'Very helpful, I'm sure,' said Ben encouragingly.

'So let me give you the essentials, to start with, then you can ask me for more detail. Declan did law for his degree and applied for a job with Olsen and Townsend in Kendal. That's my mother and Gillian Townsend.'

'Except they weren't called that then,' said Matthew. 'It was Hudson and Olsen when he first applied.'

'Right.' Debbie sighed, before going on, 'Anyway, they rejected him out of hand. They obviously took against him for no reason at all. There were hardly any other applicants, and Dec was *completely* suitable.'

'Which was the senior partner at the time?' Ben asked.

'My mother. Gillian was only a junior. She was promoted far too soon, purely as a way of keeping Declan out.'

'But you hadn't met him then?' Ben said. 'You didn't see any of this going on at first hand?'

'No. It was about three years later that he and I got together. But he was always talking about it. My mother said he wheedled his way into my affections to make sure she'd have to give him a job eventually. Which was extremely stupid of her.' Her face hardened at these words. 'She twisted it all round to make him look bad. He'd got a job he liked by the time I met him, anyway. It was really his father who kept banging on about a proper profession and wasting his degree.'

Ben smiled patiently, which Debbie rightly interpreted as a nudge to bring the story up to the present. 'So that went on for years and years. The whole time we were married, really. My mother was always criticising him and trying to undermine us as a couple. He couldn't do anything right in her eyes. My father was almost as bad, although we never saw very much of him. He's been in the army for twenty-five years, and only left a little while ago, when they forced him to retire. He's always been very fit and hadn't any other interests. He's younger than my mother.'

'Where is he now?' asked Ben.

Debbie became suddenly tearful. 'We don't know. I've been texting and emailing him, about Declan, but there's been no answer. He's got a flat in St Albans, and we thought he was there, but he doesn't seem to be.'

'So they're not together? Your parents?' said Bonnie.

'Well, they're not divorced, but they do live very separate

lives. It was never much of a marriage, was it Matt?'

Her brother waggled his head from side to side, in a non-committal gesture. 'Get to the point, okay.'

Debbie sniffed, reminding everyone that she had just been violently widowed and was resistant to broaching the subject of her husband's untimely death. 'Well, then my mother announced she was retiring, and Gillian insisted on giving her a big send-off here in Staveley, and Declan's father woke up and said now was his chance to get the job, at last. There was a ghastly argument a few weeks ago, with my mother saying horrible things about Dec, and accusing him of ruining my life because we couldn't afford a proper holiday – as if I cared about that. Matt was there as well, trying to stick up for us.' She gave her brother a feeble smile. 'And then, not much later he was dead. All smashed up on the road like a fox or a pheasant. No more nuisance for the solicitor sisters. That's what we call them. And I *know* they did it, and they think they can get away with it.'

'You think Gillian Townsend was involved as well?' Ben asked, eyebrows raised.

'I can't see how it could have been managed otherwise. Somebody must be lying about the timing, and it can't be that florist woman, can it?'

'She's our friend,' said Bonnie.

'Yes, yes. I'm not dissing her. It's lucky, that's all, that she can vouch for their whereabouts on Friday.'

'So let's look at the timing,' said Ben. 'There has to be some way of working out when it happened, surely?'

'Okay. I know now that Declan stayed Wednesday and Thursday night with a man called Roger, who lives near Crook. Roger called me on Saturday, desperately sorry that he'd let Dec persuade him not to say anything. He thinks Dec would still be alive if he'd let me know where he was. He might be right, I suppose. He's horribly upset about it, mostly because when I phoned him he lied and said Dec wasn't there. He told me all he knew – which wasn't very much. Declan went there right after the row, apparently. He just rushed off that evening, and never told me where he was going. That was on Wednesday, and when I couldn't find him on Thursday, I panicked and reported him missing. Then they found a body between here and Kentmere and I was terrified it was him. That was Friday morning. So when they told me it was an old man, I had about two hours of relief before they came and told me they really had found Declan dead, after all. It felt like some terrible joke.'

'Where did you think he was if he wasn't with this Roger bloke?' Ben asked.

'I had no idea. I just thought he was laying low somewhere, thinking about what I'd said to him. I wasn't very nice.' She turned her face away in misery.

'*Lying*,' said Ben and Bonnie in a single breath, interrupting her final words.

'What?'

'It's lying low, not laying low,' said Ben. 'Sorry. It's rude, I know, but we're on a campaign to get people to understand the difference. Otherwise, there's a whole generation getting it wrong.'

'Bit late, aren't you?' said Matthew. 'Everybody says laying low now.'

'Well, they shouldn't,' snapped Bonnie righteously.

Debbie was looking from face to face in disbelief. 'It doesn't *matter*, does it?' Ignoring the disagreement plain on both young faces, she looked down at her notes, and then went on, 'He did that sometimes. Went off for a long drive after a row, or turned up at a friend's house without warning. I tried to make him text me, and usually he did, but not always. And it was worse this time. He was really upset.'

'What was the row about?' asked Ben. 'Was it between you and Declan?'

'I don't want to go into that,' she muttered, wiping her eyes with a tissue. 'It's not relevant.'

'How can you be sure of that? Didn't the police ask you?'

'You're not the police. You don't have to know every single thing about us.'

'That's true,' said Bonnie, with a glance at her boyfriend. 'Obviously.'

'Why was he on a bike?' said Ben suddenly after looking at the clock in the alcove.

'Well, he couldn't take the car, could he? We've only got one, and I need it for work and the girls.'

'Did he cycle a lot?'

'Not really. It was an old bike he'd had since he was about sixteen. Only about three gears and the chain kept coming off. But he only went as far as Crook.' Tears choked her. 'I thought he was *miles* away, after I spoke to Roger. I thought he must be down in Barrow or somewhere, not just up the road. He could have *walked* there.'

'That would have been just as dangerous,' said Bonnie. 'I mean – he'd still be vulnerable to fast traffic.'

Ben threw her a grateful look. 'So now we need to know what makes you think it was done deliberately. Why doesn't anybody think it was an accident?'

Matthew cleared his throat. 'They can tell from his . . . injuries,' he said.

Debbie's face seemed to close up, as if braced for a blow. 'They didn't want to tell me,' she said. 'But I made them. The car hit him twice.' She said the words flatly, without inflexion.

'Twice?' Ben leant forward, eager for detail. 'How?'

The young widow gave him a long look full of pain. 'It hit him and the bike, then it hit him again. Drove over him, actually. And the person quite likely rolled him out of sight after that, with his legs and back and face all broken.'

'You mean they stopped and got out of the car? Wouldn't that be risky? Another car could have come along and seen what was happening.'

'It's not a very busy road,' said Matthew. 'And if it was planned, it wouldn't take long. The noise would be the main worry, if anybody was out in a field or garden. But nobody's come forward as a witness. Nobody useful, anyway. One man heard something, that's all.'

'So – you think the driver waited for the road to be deserted, then dashed up behind the bike, smashed into it, then what – turned round? Reversed? And went back to make sure he was killed? And *then*, got out and pushed him into a ditch? How long would all that actually take?' Ben looked to Bonnie for assistance.

'They wouldn't turn round,' she said. 'Just reverse quickly, then jump out to make sure the job was done, jump in again. Less than a minute, probably.' She was pale, her voice low, her expression apologetic. 'How absolutely horrible.'

'I didn't believe it when they told me. But it fits with the awful damage to his body.' Debbie couldn't go on for a moment. Then she swallowed and spoke again. 'The initial impact would have sent him up in the air, over the car even, landing on his head. His legs wouldn't have been hurt.'

'Not wearing a helmet,' Matthew added. 'Didn't even possess one.'

'Someone was waiting for him, and that means they knew where he was staying, when he was likely to go out, which way he'd go. That's if it really was planned,' said Ben. 'Did the police check his phone?'

'They couldn't find it. He didn't take it everywhere with him. But I think he did have it, and I think the killer took it, because I think she sent him a text that made sure he'd be where she wanted him. Probably pretending to be me, asking him to come and talk to me at The Watermill in Ings – something like that. I think that's what my mother did and then she took his phone and threw it away where nobody could find it. And if she gets away with it, I don't see how I can carry on.' The long-suppressed tears broke through the defences and she slumped back on the sofa, her hands over her face.

'That's a lot of "think"s,' said Bonnie, after a decent interval. 'It's all guesswork, isn't it?'

'I *know*,' wailed Debbie. 'That's why I need you. I want you to work out where my mother – Anita Olsen, the bitch – was, and how she managed to get another car, because the police have checked hers and it's not at all damaged, and then kill Declan with it, and turn up at Gillian's old mother's cool as you like, to talk about a party. A *party*, for God's sake.'

'Which is where Simmy comes in,' said Ben with a nod.

'Yes, but it's your *mother*,' said Bonnie, not for the first time. 'How will you carry on if she's convicted of premeditated murder? How can there be such terribly bad blood between you?'

Debbie shook her head obstinately. 'You said that before, at the shop. Not all mothers are loving and caring and unselfish, you know.'

Ben took over. 'Bonnie knows that very well,' he said. 'Her own mother was hopeless, inadequate, neglectful – which is why she's finding it so hard to understand.'

'I don't get that,' said Debbie. 'But it doesn't matter. You have to take my word for it.'

'And mine,' said Matthew, reaching over to pat his sister's arm. 'She was a monster.' He looked at Bonnie. 'I'm guessing you were rescued from yours. We weren't so lucky. We were stuck with her, living in what looked like a perfectly ordinary family to anyone outside. She even managed to divide us from each other until we saw what her game was.'

Ben looked at the clock again. 'We'll have to go,' he said. 'I just hope the lamp works on my bike. It's dark, look. Sorry to cut this short, but you've given us plenty to think about.' Bonnie got up to follow him, her expression showing her reluctance at being thwarted of hearing more of the family background. The movement activated another spell of coughing, giving rise to a look of concern on Ben's face.

They let themselves out, only to be confronted by a large man coming up the garden path. He stopped walking and stared hard at them. 'Who are you two?' he demanded.

'Oh, nobody much,' said Ben. 'Your daughter-in-law will explain, if you're interested.'

'Are those your bicycles?' The man waved towards the road. 'They shouldn't be leaning on the hedge like that.'

'Sorry,' said Ben. 'I don't think they'll do any harm, actually. Especially not at this time of year.'

'Don't answer back, laddie. And how did you know I was Debbie's father-in-law?'

'Gosh, Mr Kennedy, I think *everybody* knows you around here. You're our most important local politician, after all.'

The man snorted, trying to conceal his gratification. Bonnie made a similar sound, more quietly. 'Well, I hope you haven't been upsetting poor Debbie. That's all I can say.'

'I'm not sure she could be any more upset than she is already,' said Bonnie. 'Now, please excuse us. We're late.'

When the man had disappeared into the house, the two allowed themselves to laugh. 'You were wonderful,' Bonnie applauded. 'Pompous old pig he is.'

'He's been on the town council for about fifty years, and thinks he's king. The world revolves around Spencer Kennedy, and he makes sure everybody knows it.'

'Pity we don't think *he* killed Declan,' said Bonnie. 'He'd be a perfect suspect. Just think what fun we could have.'

'Don't speak too soon,' said Ben. 'If there's no evidence against Anita Olsen, the field might yet be wide open.'

Cycling back was much less enjoyable than the earlier ride. It was cold; Bonnie's nose and eyes streamed and she couldn't wipe them; when she coughed, the wind seemed to blow it right back down her throat; headlights dazzled them and they couldn't hear each other. They went first to Ben's house in Bowness, where Bonnie was given hot chocolate and a large cotton hanky. 'I'll walk home from here,' she said. 'My legs are too tired to pedal any further.'

'I'll drive you,' said Helen Harkness.

'No, you don't have to. It's barely half a mile.'

'I insist. And Ben – go and do some revision. You said you'd be back by half past seven.'

'Did I?' Ben was distracted by thoughts and theories concerning the Staveley people. 'What is it now, then?'

'You got back at ten past eight. It's nearly half past now.'

His shrug was too small to cause offence, but Helen wasn't pleased. 'Poor Bonnie. Look at you! You'll get pneumonia at this rate, as my granny used to say.'

'It was good, though,' Bonnie assured her. 'We were *amazing*.'

'Don't tell me. I seriously do not want to know anything about it. All I want is for the two of you to survive. That's not a lot to ask, is it?'

The youngsters knew better than to laugh. For Helen, given recent experience, the ambition was not at all amusing. 'We will, I promise,' said Bonnie, with a cough.

Chapter Eleven

By the end of the day, Simmy had forgotten that Anita Olsen was staying in Kendal, too upset to go home to Staveley where she presumably lived alone. Once again the two mismatched women stood side by side to greet her, just as they'd done the previous Friday. Not so much shoulder to shoulder as shoulder to elbow, Simmy thought to herself. She knew she was going to have to pay very close attention to the conversation she intended to conduct with them. She would also have to take care over her own side of it. No mention of Debbie Kennedy, for one thing. The main challenge was to explain her change of heart and account for her presence in this very bland little terrace house.

The first surprise was the discovery that there was a Mr Gillian Townsend. He was sitting in an armchair when Simmy was taken into the front room, reading a dry-looking magazine. 'This is Robin,' said Gillian. 'Robin, this is the flower lady I told you about. Mrs Brown. She's got that shop in Windermere.'

The man looked up, his face comically blank. 'Good evening, Mrs Brown,' he said, like a well-trained schoolboy. Then he looked to his wife. 'Do you want me to go somewhere else?'

'Actually, that might be helpful. Haven't you got some emails to send or something?'

'I expect I could think of some.' He got up with no hint of complaint, although the look he threw at Anita as he left the room did suggest a degree of resentment. Husbands famously resented visitations by friends of their wives, after all. The tall woman showed no sign of noticing the look.

'Sit down,' said Gillian. 'Can I get you a drink?'

Simmy had snatched some random bites of food at Beck View but had not stopped for tea or coffee, so was thirsty. 'Would coffee be an awful nuisance?' she said.

'No, of course not.' The slight hesitation before these words gave them the lie. 'Could you bear instant?'

'Absolutely. I prefer it, actually.'

'Neet?' Gillian asked her friend. 'I'll do some for all of us, shall I?'

'I'll do it,' said Anita, already halfway to the door. 'You need to rest. You've done far too much already today.' She left the room with a warm smile at her colleague, having made no enquiries about milk or sugar.

'She's still not entirely with it,' Gillian apologised, a moment later. 'All this business with Declan has upset her dreadfully. The family were already having trouble before this happened, and now . . . well, it's all too much for her, I think. There's likely to be a dreadful injustice if we can't do something about it. And now she's worrying that I'll make myself ill with it all.'

'Oh? You don't seem entirely well, if you don't mind my saying.'

'I'm all right. It's a chronic condition that flares up from time to time. I've lost quite a lot of weight, believe it or not.' She laughed, and plucked at the baggy garment she was wearing, showing that beneath its folds there was much less flesh than appearances would suggest. 'All my clothes are too big now.'

Simmy still wanted to ask the same question she'd voiced rather too many times – *But how does this concern ME?* But then she remembered that she had come quite willingly, because Ben and Bonnie wanted her to, and that if she could help avert an injustice, she had a moral duty to do so. She had involved herself and could hardly blame or complain. All she could do now was make the best possible job of it. 'Could you explain some of the background for me?' she asked. 'I really don't know anything at all. I'm still wondering how on earth I can be of any help.'

'But didn't that police detective explain it to you? He said he would. It was funny, you know, his face when I told him you could confirm what we told him about Friday. It went all soft for a second or two, and he was obviously glad to have an excuse to see you. He's fond of you, isn't he?'

'Not in the way you mean, no. It's just that we've got to know each other quite well over the past year or two. He knew I wouldn't want to be drawn into another violent crime. He was probably worried about how he'd approach me.'

131

Gillian said nothing at first, glancing from Simmy's face to the carpet and back. Then she began slowly, 'The trouble is, you have been helpful already, just by being willing to hear our side of the story. It was Anita, you know, who first suggested we ask you to do the flowers. She knew a bit about you, from things in the paper last year, and someone she knows in Ambleside had been speaking favourably about you. She got me to phone you last week. I'd taken a little while to get around to it, I must admit.' She sighed. 'It's such a shame about the party. We were all looking forward to it so much – especially my mother. She keeps saying we ought to go ahead with it, regardless, but you *can't* do that, can you, when there's been a death in the family?'

'What does Anita say? After all, it's her party, isn't it?'

'Oh, well, she knows there's no choice in the matter. To be honest, she's not entirely thrilled at the prospect of retirement, either.'

'So why not keep working for a bit longer?'

'There are several reasons. Most of them are my fault, I suppose. We couldn't avoid making changes any longer.' She sighed. 'Anyway, Anita's got much more pressing things to worry about now. She's a person of interest to the police. You know what that means, don't you?'

'More or less.'

'Well, it means they're actively looking for evidence against her. They've listened to those awful children of hers, and are intent on building a case for the prosecution. They've crawled all over her car and asked a lot of very intrusive questions. It's a disgrace, quite honestly. In all my years working in the law, I've never seen anything so blatantly unjust.'

The door was pushed open then, and Anita came in with a tray. On it were three porcelain mugs, with milk jug, sugar bowl and a plate of mixed biscuits. 'Hope I've done it right,' she said.

Gillian gave a little squeal. 'I haven't used those mugs for about ten years. Where did you find them?'

'On the top shelf in the cupboard over the toaster. I thought they looked so pretty I couldn't resist using them.'

'Robin's mother gave us a set of six when we got married. These are the only ones left now.' She turned to Simmy. 'He does break things rather a lot. Some men are so clumsy, aren't they?'

Robin Townsend had seemed a fairly well-balanced man to Simmy, with no discernible tremor. But she could imagine him losing focus and accidentally swiping delicate china off a surface.

The coffee was hot and strong and Simmy drank it with enthusiasm. 'You were saying "blatantly unjust" when I came in,' said Anita. 'Presumably in reference to my situation with regard to the police.'

'That's right. I wanted to explain to Mrs Brown what a scandal it is. I'm sure it isn't all the fault of her friend, Detective Inspector Moxon, but he has to have a hand in it.'

'Evidently he does. But I really don't think you need to get quite so agitated about it. They can't get anywhere without proper evidence, and since there isn't any, it will all come right. Probably before we know it.'

Simmy remained silent, wondering at the roles of these two women. The calm suspect trying to reassure her inflamed legal advisor struck Simmy as incongruous. Then she corrected herself – nobody had actually said whether or not Gillian had taken a formal part in the case. There probably wasn't even a case at all, until someone was arrested and charged. 'You're both solicitors, aren't you?' she asked. 'Working in the same practice.'

Gillian nodded energetically. 'Yes, yes. I told you that last week. We've been equal partners for fifteen years now. Anita was senior to me before that, but when her partner left, she replaced him with me.' She gave her colleague a big smile. 'We've always got along wonderfully. We'd worked together for ages before I was promoted, you see. I was over forty, and thinking that was my perpetual station in life – a junior solicitor.'

Anita responded with a tight smile of her own, indicative of painful gratitude and affection, overlaid with other more urgent matters. Simmy was still groping for any clues as to the essential personality of this woman. She had an air of martyrdom, which was only to be expected. She looked tired and stiff, as if she'd spent a night trying to sleep on a sofa that was too small. Her grey hair was wavy and slightly greasy, in need of a wash. A resemblance to her daughter Debbie could be discerned, not so much in the features as in the reaction to trouble. Carelessness over how one looked, and a whiff of despair, had characterised them both. But Debbie did have her mother's greeny-blue eyes and small chin, as well. *Don't mention Debbie*, Simmy reminded herself.

'So you're going to be Anita's legal representative, are you, if it comes to that?' she asked, boldly cutting to the chase.

'Well, no, not exactly. I'm not a criminal lawyer. I couldn't handle the defence in a full-blown trial. But I can gather the evidence and pass it to a barrister, and stay closely involved. But it won't come to that, will it?' Again she beamed at her friend.

'I hope not,' said Anita. 'Apart from anything else, it would waste months of our lives. These things go on forever.'

'I wouldn't know,' said Simmy.

'Really? Haven't you been part of a number of criminal investigations since coming to live here?' Gillian's voice was gentler than the words would suggest. Nothing accusatory in her tone. But it left Simmy in no doubt that she had been thoroughly researched, and that the findings were the reason why she was here now. A thought came to her that stopped her breath, and made her momentarily dizzy.

'Did you know all that about me when you phoned on Friday about flowers for the party?'

'Pardon?' Gillian frowned. 'What do you mean?'

Simmy waited, refusing to repeat the question, which had surely been clear enough. The little woman looked around the room for an answer, finishing up with a wide-eyed gaze at Anita. 'No, not at all. There's no florist in Staveley, so you were the next closest.'

'There are several in Kendal, though. Why not use one of them?'

'Because we were holding the party in Staveley. What are you suggesting, anyway? Some sort of ridiculous conspiracy?' Gillian laughed scornfully. 'Don't forget that on Friday we had no idea that Declan had been killed. We knew he'd gone missing, but we weren't especially worried. He hadn't been gone very long.'

'Oh, but wasn't there something on the news about a

body being found in Staveley, and weren't you worried that it might be him? That's how I remember it, anyway.'

Anita leant forward, still holding her mug of tea. 'You're right, up to a point. But I was really more worried about my daughter, who easily flies into a panic.'

Oops, thought Simmy at the mention of the forbidden Debbie. *Proceed with caution.* 'Yes, I remember. You said she was terribly concerned about her husband. You said he'd been gone for a day or two.'

'Oh, well, as it turns out, he was only up the road in Crook,' said Gillian. 'We're not sure what he was doing there, but we think he might have left messages for Debbie that she never saw. I mean, you can *walk* from Crook to Staveley in an hour at most. And Anita thinks they could have had an argument and he went off to cool down.'

'Crook? I was there myself on Friday,' said Simmy. 'I'd hardly ever been there before, which is a bit embarrassing after all this time.'

'Yes, you told us that when I phoned you on Friday afternoon. We thought it was all very nice and convenient, didn't we, Neet?'

Anita nodded.

Simmy was clutching at every word, Ben's example on her shoulder. Even if she chose not to share everything with him, she still wanted the picture to be as complete as it could be. 'Was he staying with somebody there, then?' she wondered.

Gillian made a sound like a snort. 'Nobody will tell us. There's been a news blackout, with the police keeping everything close to their chests. I suppose Debbie knows a lot more, but . . . well . . .'

136

'My daughter and I are not currently communicating,' said Anita, with the same formal delivery that Simmy remembered from their first encounter. 'I can't deny that there is bad feeling between us. It hasn't always been as extreme as it is now, let me assure you. But I imagine it must be blatantly obvious to you.'

Simmy nodded uneasily. 'Had he gone back to Staveley when he was run over?'

'No, no.' Gillian was impatient. 'He was killed in Crook. He was cycling along that fast bit of road, this side of the village, and some swine mowed him down and left him to die.'

Simmy's heart lurched. 'Do they know what time that was?'

Gillian shook her head. 'It's extremely difficult to pinpoint the precise time of death, you know. In any case they wouldn't tell us any details. All they said was that he died sometime that evening.'

Simmy shuddered. 'Horrible. What a dreadful thing to do. I mean – you couldn't be in any doubt as to what you'd done, hitting a person on a bike, could you? Even a rabbit makes quite a bang.' Simmy had been haunted for weeks by a rabbit she'd hit on the road to Troutbeck one morning. 'There must have been a loud noise. You'd think somebody would have heard it.'

'Exactly,' said Gillian. 'It has to have been some drunken pig, too worried about his licence or being somewhere he shouldn't, to own up to what he'd done. And probably hundreds of miles away by now, and the car in a scrapyard somewhere. But we've still got to do everything we can to find out whether it was somebody local, who knew Declan and had reason to kill him. That's the only realistic hope of exonerating Anita completely. Otherwise, there'll be a cloud of suspicion over her for ever, even if it can never be proved.'

Simmy nodded, thinking that the drunken pig theory was tempting, but probably not very likely. 'So you don't know why he was cycling along the road,' she summed up weakly.

'Of course we don't,' said Anita, with an expression bordering on contempt. 'That's the whole point, isn't it? Who could have known he'd be there? How could it possibly have been a deliberate killing?'

'Right!' crowed Gillian. 'Which is why it's so ridiculous to suspect Anita of having anything to do with it.'

'Yes.' Simmy could hardly disagree. 'And before there can be the slightest risk of Anita being charged, they'd have to have evidence from her car, and where she was, and motive – a whole lot of stuff. But mainly the car.' Wary of being sneered at again, she avoided eye contact with Anita. 'I don't really see why you need worry about it, given all that.'

'If only,' said Gillian. 'The awful thing is that Debbie and Matthew are both convinced that Anita – *their own mother* – was responsible. That's what we're up against, you see. That's why the police are so suspicious.'

'But they have to have evidence,' said Anita calmly. 'As Mrs Brown so rightly says.'

Mrs Brown was once again lost in contemplation of the horror of a relationship so bad between a mother and both her children that there could be accusations of murder arising from it. It was beyond her imagination's scope. What would Christmases be like? How would it affect the children? Who was going to acknowledge Mother's Day? What could Anita have done to earn such dislike?

'They must think there's something, though,' she said. 'Why else would they say what they did? Presumably you had some sort of problem with Declan?' *At the very least*, she added silently.

Gillian hurriedly spoke before Anita could react. 'It all goes back a long way. Declan did a degree in law, and graduated at about the same time as Jeremy retired. Jeremy was Anita's partner before me. So Declan assumed he could just walk into the business and become a partner in no time, before he was even twenty-five. I had to wait until I was practically twice that age.' Simmy heard something sharp in the final words, playing them again in her head, and filing them away for further consideration.

'Was he your son-in-law by then?' Simmy had thought Debbie Kennedy to be only in her early thirties, which made the idea untenable.

'No, no. That's the thing.' It was still Gillian giving the explanations. 'We told him there was no space for a third partner, not enough work, he was far too young and we thought he ought to go and get experience somewhere else first. Then we'd reconsider.'

'Sounds reasonable,' said Simmy, trying to avoid any more direct questions, much as she wanted to hear the full story. Far better to let it all dribble out in its own way, as Ben had told her.

'It was *perfectly* reasonable. But he didn't like it. We never quite understood his thinking, but he was absolutely intent on getting a position with us. Yes, we had a good reputation in the town, and we were making money quite nicely. But it was nothing special. He would have been the only man in the office – maybe that appealed to him.'

'He was fundamentally incompetent,' said Anita. 'That's the whole thing in a nutshell. He couldn't concentrate for five minutes, made the most terribly inappropriate jokes and was barely literate. Three extremely sound reasons for refusing to employ him.'

Gillian flushed. 'Yes . . . well . . . that's as may be. So, anyway, much to our horror, a few years after that, he started going round with Debbie, and ended up marrying her. That was about twelve years ago now.'

'Thirteen,' said Anita.

'Right. And they seemed quite happy. Two lovely little girls.'

Simmy wanted to say several things, but held her tongue. The picture was coming into focus quite nicely as it was. Anita gave her a direct look. 'And we still wouldn't take him on. He married my daughter in order to get a foothold, thinking we'd have to do as he wanted then. And Debbie thought so too. She's always been completely blind to his faults. The man wrecked my family. Even my son turned against me and took Declan's side. They sent him to argue with me, many a time.'

'But we really couldn't take him,' said Gillian, almost pleadingly. 'He was such a fool to keep on and on trying, when it was more and more obvious that it would never work. Although we often thought it was really his father pressuring him, rather that what Declan himself wanted. Left to himself, he'd probably have settled down quite happily.'

Simmy allowed herself a question. 'So what did he do instead?'

Both the older women drooped. 'Well, nothing to boast about,' said Gillian. 'He was self-employed, a sort of woodsman, I suppose you'd call it. The National Trust gave him quite a lot of work, and the Tourist Board as well. He had a big project at Grizedale, in the forest there. That lasted two or three years.'

'He earned good money, much of the time,' said Anita. 'Fresh air, good physical work. It suited him far better than huddling in a law office would have done.'

'Except there were unfortunate social implications,' said Gillian regretfully. 'You know how small-town solicitors have quite high status. He would have liked that for himself. His father's a prominent local politician, and a Freemason and in the Rotary and all that business, and never let Declan forget what a failure he was. In fact, *he* came to plead with us once, as well. It was all rather unpleasant, I have to say.'

'Very,' said Anita.

'What we need, of course, is to work out who *really* killed him. If we had someone else, with evidence to back us up, the whole thing would be resolved.' Gillian repeated urgently. 'Even though the chances are it was some stupid tourist going too fast in a big car, and we'll never find them, I'm not giving up yet. I've phoned about twenty local people, calling in every favour anyone in Cumbria owes me. If there's anyone out there who saw or heard what happened, I'm going to find them.' Anita gave a small cough. Simmy and Gillian both looked at her. 'Oh, I know what you're going to say. But I can't agree with you. The idea that it might have been someone else in the family is as awful as saying it was you. I don't know how you can think such a thing.'

'Like who?' Simmy blurted, eyes wide.

'Oh, I'm not naming any names, but just let's say a few people have made very unkind remarks, which Anita has taken to heart. I won't let her anywhere near Facebook, for one thing. I took one quick look and it made me sick.'

'Sicker than you were already,' said Anita, with an angry sort of fondness. 'And it's all my fault.'

'Don't be ridiculous,' said Gillian.

'I should go,' Simmy said, feeling suddenly surplus to requirements.

Chapter Twelve

Simmy texted Ben to say she was home and available for debriefing if he wanted. Within ninety seconds he had phoned her demanding a complete account of what had taken place in Kendal.

'First, tell me how you and Bonnie got on in Staveley,' she insisted.

'Not bad, considering. But I need to know what happened with you and the chief suspect.'

'We can't do it all over the phone, Ben,' Simmy objected. 'I thought we could, but we can't. There's too much.' She was beginning to feel rather silly, back to the Famous Five with the clues and observations and gut feelings all bursting to be shared.

'I've got a free period tomorrow, first thing. What if I come to the shop about eight-thirty, and we have an hour or so then?'

'I suppose that would be all right. It depends on whether

there are orders to fill, and people coming in. Thursdays can be busy sometimes.'

'We'll play it by ear,' he said, sounding much more grown-up than the Famous Five ever did. 'See you then, then.'

She should make notes, organise her thoughts and make herself worthy of the brilliant Ben Harkness. Instead, she phoned Christopher Henderson and talked about things other than murder and suspicion. He expressed concern for her father, having known Russell all his life. 'Bring him to another auction when he's better,' he offered. 'He enjoyed it last time, didn't he?'

'He loved it. I might do that, but it won't be for a while. I can't get away from the shop before Easter.'

'I was thinking about the holiday. I googled Lanzarote,' he told her. 'It looks idyllic.'

'It is. Did you find anything affordable?'

'If we go during term time, it's not too bad. I was thinking the first week of June. How does that sound?'

'A long way off. I want to go tomorrow.'

'So do I, but we'll have to wait. I'm coming over on Friday evening, okay? In fact, I'm coming whether it's okay or not. The following weekend is going to be hectic for me, and the one after that you'll be obsessing about all the Mother's Day stuff. It'll be June before we know it at this rate.'

'Friday will be lovely. I'll do some proper cooking. Unless you want to go for a Chinese in Kendal? It's ages since I had a Chinese meal, and I've got a craving.'

'Oh?'

Even before he spoke she'd realised the possible

interpretation of her words. *Stupid*, she snarled at herself. A stupid Freudian slip, she suspected. 'No, not that sort of craving.'

'Chinese is always good, but can we postpone it a bit? I won't want to go out anywhere.'

'What about a takeaway?'

'Mm,' he said with singular lack of enthusiasm. 'Why don't we cook something together? See how we work as a team now we're grown up. Don't you remember when we were twelve and took charge of that portable barbecue my dad had? We did the whole thing on our own, risking all sorts of injury and danger. It was probably illegal even then, to let minors handle glowing charcoal.'

'I remember the sausages were a bit raw on one side. Your sisters spat them out.'

They reminisced contentedly about their shared life, meeting every summer for seaside holidays before suddenly falling in love at the age of sixteen. For one glorious fortnight they'd been besotted, impervious to their families and everything else. Despite the jokes made from the day of their birth about their destiny being settled, their marriage inevitable, their parents took fright at the reality. Christopher was doing too well at school to embroil himself in a premature relationship. Nothing could be allowed to interrupt his university course and subsequent career path. Simmy had no particular ambitions, but could see that tying herself to the only boy she'd ever taken seriously might be unwise. So there were no more joint holidays after that. They wrote passionate letters, spent hours on the phone, and met infrequently. Things changed as they moved into their respective sixth forms, and they let each other go with surprisingly little complaint.

Now, they assured each other that it had really been for the best. That they had experienced other people, other places (especially in his case) and come back together older and much wiser. The only regret – which she knew was irrational – was that she was convinced that if she'd married Christopher at the age of twenty-three, they'd have a whole litter of little Hendersons by now.

'You know what I thought, as soon as my mother told me about his stroke – or whatever it was? I thought, *Now he'll never know the fun of being a grandfather*. I thought how cheated he'd feel, as he died. Even more cheated than he's been by my mother refusing to have more children. I know he wanted more than just me. He'd have been so good with them.'

'Stop torturing yourself, you daft thing. He wasn't so terribly special. You were an easy kid, he was proud of you, and you got along very nicely. Don't romanticise it, Sim. Things are as they are, as a friend of mine in South America used to say.' Christopher had spent some years travelling, dropping out of his planned career path more drastically than early marriage to Simmy could possibly have caused. Not so much a gap year as a gap decade, as his mother once said.

Both his parents were recently dead, amidst considerable horror and confusion. Simmy assumed he was still recovering from the resulting damage, which was another reason not to hurtle too precipitately into anything permanent with him. 'I expect you're right,' she said mildly. 'And it's academic now, because he's not going to die. They think he'll be back to normal in a week or so – whatever normal is.'

'There's a chance that some sort of blockage has cleared itself and he'll be better than he was before.'

'Really? Do you know of that ever happening? Or are you just being insanely optimistic?'

'I knew someone who used to have terrible migraines, and then had a small stroke, and after that never had another migraine. Same sort of thing.'

'We'll have to see.' It didn't really sound like the same thing at all, but she wasn't going to argue with him. They carried on for a few more minutes, chatting inconsequentially, enjoying the sound of each other's voice and the sense that things between them were warm and easy, despite enforced distance and extraneous complications.

It was mildly exciting to set out early the next morning with the intention of meeting Ben and Bonnie and comparing impressions of the Staveley people. All three coincided at the front door of the shop, laughing at the impeccable timing. 'It's no good,' said Simmy. 'We really are the Famous Five, even if there are only three of us.'

'What a thing to say,' chided Ben. 'This is real life and death, not a silly story for kids.' He took out a notebook and looked for a place to lean on. Yet again Simmy regretted the shortage of chairs, or space to put them.

'We'd be better in the back room,' she decided. 'Then people can't see us from the street. They might try to come in early and buy something if they think there's someone here. It wouldn't be the first time.'

They gathered around the workbench, all focusing on

Ben's notes. 'Okay,' he said. 'We need to pool everything we know, from both sides. Simmy, I think it's best if you give us the facts as you heard them last night.'

She felt as if he was challenging her to do a good job and in consequence made every effort to impress him. 'Declan was hit by a vehicle on the road from Crook to Staveley, sometime fairly early on Friday evening. That's when he was found. He and his wife and her brother have all been hostile towards Anita, mother of Debbie and Matthew, because she and Gillian Townsend refused repeatedly to employ him in their law firm. Gillian is prepared to gather evidence in Anita's defence, and pass it to a barrister, if it comes to the point of her being charged with murder or manslaughter. Gillian's much more outraged by the idea than Anita seems to be. Their only real strategy is that they should try to find who did do it, even though it's likely to have been a tourist who's long gone by now.'

She relaxed at the end of this little speech, feeling rather pleased with herself.

'Well, we knew most of that already,' said Bonnie, deflatingly. 'And it wasn't a random tourist, that's for sure.'

'Did you?' To Simmy it had felt like a whole string of revelations, neatly and efficiently summarised.

'You think the Townsend woman genuinely believes Anita's innocent?' asked Ben. 'She's not just trying to protect her?'

'That's how it looked,' Simmy nodded. 'She seems totally convinced, in fact.'

'Right. Well, we got some more background, but it doesn't contradict anything you've just said. Debbie's accusing both her parents of all sorts of character defects, but mother's a lot worse than father.'

'Oh! I thought of something else. Declan's father is a bigwig in Kendal, who always thought his son would go into a proper profession and make him proud. He's mortified that Olsen and Townsend thwarted his ambition.'

'Probably not enough to commit murder, though,' said Bonnie. 'We met him, actually. He was coming up the path as we were leaving. A right stinker he is, too. I wouldn't be totally surprised if it turned out to be him who did it, on second thoughts. Except what father could kill his own son? That would be worse than the mother-in-law doing it.'

Ben smiled. 'Bon's not at all happy with the notion of parents killing their children – are you? It is fairly grim, I agree. But they really do seem to believe Anita Olsen is capable of it.'

Simmy sighed. 'Anita thinks he married Debbie in order to pressure her to take him on in her office. Anita's known him since he was a student – or just after. He did law, but was never any good at it. It would have been professional suicide to employ him.'

'Did she say that? In those words?'

'Not quite,' Simmy admitted. 'But that's what she meant. It was one of the few times she said more than a couple of words. Gillian did nearly all the talking.'

'Debbie thinks it was because they wanted to keep the place all-female. She thinks that's actually illegal. Discriminatory,' said Bonnie, enunciating the final word with care.

'She's wrong, of course,' said Ben. 'At least, it would

be impossible to prove. They didn't take anyone else on instead of Declan, did they? They probably just kept saying there was no vacancy.'

'But it's all the wrong way round,' Simmy realised. 'All this stuff would be more likely to provoke Declan into killing Anita.'

'We thought that at first,' said Bonnie.

Ben took over. 'But then we asked – why now? Is there something about the timing? And we remembered that Anita Olsen is retiring. And that means there definitely *would* be a vacancy.'

Simmy gave this some thought. 'Surely he doesn't – didn't – think he could apply again after all this time? He must be really stupid if so. But, of course, Gillian isn't very well. She might be forced to give up work, which would leave the whole business up for grabs.'

Bonnie chimed in, 'I bet Debbie would have wanted him to give it a go. She seems to think Gillian is soft enough to be persuaded. It sounded as if they don't have such a strong animosity towards Gillian.'

'But why does that make Declan the victim?' Simmy's mind was struggling to keep up. She was becoming painfully aware that her initial masterly summary had been woefully incomplete. More details kept occurring to her.

Ben took over. 'It makes a sort of sense. Anita had simply had enough of him. He was a very persistent pest, after all, and there was no way she could risk Gillian capitulating. It probably wasn't planned, but when she saw him biking along the road, she grabbed her chance.'

'That's what Debbie thinks, I suppose.' Simmy was growing rather tired of hearing what Debbie thought, but there was no escaping the fact that the new widow had a remarkably clear set of ideas as to what had happened.

'More or less. Well, a bit more, actually. She's got an answer for everything,' said Bonnie. 'In fact, Anita might have known where Declan was,' she added.

'Oh?' Ben and Simmy both looked at her.

'Yes, because Debbie said she'd had a call from a man called Roger. He said Declan had been staying with him, and asked him not to say anything, so he lied about it. Remember?' Ben nodded patiently. 'So,' the girl went on, 'someone could have seen him while he was there and told Anita about it.'

Ben pushed out his lips, in an exaggerated show of taking this seriously. 'A bit of a stretch, kiddo,' he said. 'It's possible, of course, but how could we ever prove it?'

'Hang on.' Simmy's next thought sharpened her voice. 'Wait a minute. You're both talking as if Anita's guilty. When did that happen?'

Ben and Bonnie each took a long breath. Then Ben said, 'Yes, of course. Of course she's guilty. Anita Olsen killed her son-in-law. There's no doubt about that. It all fits. It's a horrible thing, I know. Bonnie's very upset about it. But that doesn't change the fact.'

'What fact? Or *facts*, surely? I'm just as sure as you that she didn't.' Simmy's tone was firm. 'You haven't *seen* her. She's being so dignified and restrained, so grateful to Gillian – and me, in a small way. She seems stunned by it all, but still hanging on to her self-respect. She's desperately upset by the way her children are behaving. And it sounds as if everyone except Debbie thought Declan was a bit of a waste of space.'

'Name those people,' said Ben. 'It's no good talking about "everyone". The same as it won't work to blame some faceless tourist. That's too easy. It's much more constructive to follow the sort of line Bonnie just suggested – try to find a thread of evidence to show Anita knew where he was and where she might best have a go at him.'

'And we need to know what that row was about,' added Bonnie. 'That's what started the whole thing off. We're not even sure who was there when it happened. Was he fighting with Debbie, or Anita, or who?'

'You're right,' said Ben, admiringly. 'The whole business probably hinges on that.'

'So why wouldn't Debbie tell us about it?'

'I guess because it reflects badly on her.'

'If her last words to Declan were something nasty, she's sure to be feeling terribly guilty,' said Bonnie.

'We're on different sides.' Simmy repeated her discovery flatly, but the truth of it was deeply upsetting. 'How can that be?'

'No, Simmy, no we're not. Not in a way that matters to *us* as people. It's just an intellectual puzzle. It'll help us work it all out together, don't you see?' Bonnie was urgent in her efforts to reassure. 'If you take Anita's part, speaking for her, and we do the same for Debbie, there'll be a proper balance. Like in a real trial. That's the best way to get the right answer. That's how we reach justice.'

Simmy could hear Ben's thoughts coming through the girl's lips. Ancient Rome came to mind, and Greek democracy and even the Icelandic Thingvellir, which Ben had delivered a lecture on, a week or two ago. 'You won't have time,' she told him. 'It'll interrupt your revision.'

'The timing's awful,' he agreed, with a small frown. 'If there was a remotely rational education system in this country, it would be an ideal addition to the work I'm doing. As it is, you disturb the curriculum at your peril. In the long run, though, the experience will be very useful. It's a bonus that the Staveley women are both solicitors. They know the law. That gives them power. You're probably on the winning side, if that's the way you want to look at it.'

'Where does Anita live?' Bonnie asked. 'We couldn't find that out.'

'Oh . . .' Simmy thought hard. 'Somewhere in Staveley. She pointed it out, vaguely. There's a row of big old houses overlooking a field, or village green. I think it's one of them. But she's staying with the Townsends in Kendal, now—'

'Did you say Townsends, plural?' Ben interrupted.

'Yes, there's a husband. He's called Robin and he looks fairly fed up at having a guest. I suspect there's no date for her to go home.'

'You never mentioned him,' Ben reproached.

'Sorry. I don't think he's very relevant.'

'Is he a solicitor as well?'

'I don't know, but I assume not. He'd be taking more of an interest if he was.'

'Are there any children?'

'I don't know. All the talk was about Anita, not Gillian and her family.'

'It all sounds very *cosy*, the way those two women are together. Partners at work, bosom buddies now, like babes in the wood, facing the big bad world side by side.' He sounded alarmingly grown-up to Simmy, speaking as an adult in judgement on other adults. Insightful and in control. She knew that Bonnie regarded her beloved as a sort of hero, a figure from ancient Gaelic myths, groomed for glory from an infant. And now Simmy found herself harbouring the same sort of feeling towards him. There was something golden about him, something rare and precious. There had been a terrifying episode the previous year where they thought they'd lost him, which had served to cement the general belief that he was far too important to be allowed to vanish. Ben himself had learnt lessons about vulnerability and fear, but the essential message had been that you can think yourself out of almost any tight corner, if you stay in control of yourself.

But his words made her giggle, despite all that. 'Lucky you didn't say "shoulder to shoulder",' she said. 'Have either of you actually seen Anita and Gillian together?'

'We haven't seen Anita at all,' said Ben.

'Well, she's tall. About three inches taller than me, in fact. And Gillian must be at least ten inches shorter. They look like a comedy act.'

'Wasn't there a famous pair of comedians, about a hundred years ago? My gran had them on a video that she used to play when I was about four. Hilda something, and a very tall woman called Cynthia.' Ben shook his head. 'Not important.'

'We could find them on YouTube or somewhere,' Bonnie suggested.

'Not important,' Ben repeated. 'Although . . .'

'What?'

'I don't know. Something about appearances being deceiving. People assuming the tall one's in charge, when it's completely the other way around. Like that Hitchcock story, *The Glass Eye*.'

154

'Is that important?' Bonnie asked. 'Because it's time to open the shop.'

'Who would you say is in charge between Anita and Gillian?' Ben asked Simmy.

'Probably Anita, but they seem fairly equal. Anita's older; she took Gillian on as her partner, so she was senior in the business. They're both quite clever, I suppose, but Gillian's so animated and talkative, she might seem a bit of a fool at times. She's low on energy because of her illness, but it'd take an awful lot to stop her.'

'Hm,' said Ben. 'So, are we done for now?'

'You tell me,' said Simmy, who was feeling as if she'd done a hard day's work already. 'I can't imagine where you think we should go from here. If anywhere,' she added.

'We wait, for now. Something's going to happen, police-wise. That'll dictate our next move.'

Now he sounded like someone playing a computer game, and Simmy's patience grew thin. 'Oh, Ben,' she sighed.

'What?'

'Why don't we just leave the whole thing to the police and get on with our normal lives?'

His look of forbearance was insulting. Here was another example of deceptive appearances. Simmy, old enough to be his mother, was firmly in the role of sidekick to Ben Harkness. 'What happens in *The Glass Eye*?' she couldn't resist asking.

'It's classic,' he enthused, suddenly boyish again. 'There's a ventriloquist who a woman falls in love with. Big and handsome, with a dummy on his knee. And then, in the final scene, it turns out that the big man's the dummy and the little one's the real person. It's fantastically frightening.

The dummy's glass eye falls out and rolls across the room.'

'Yuk!' said Simmy, and Bonnie giggled again. 'Did your gran show you that as well?' Ben's gran had died when he was fourteen, and only got mentioned infrequently. From what Simmy could glean, she had been quite a character.

'No, actually. That was my Uncle Robert. The one married to Mum's sister. He collects old horror movies. He's got some amazing stuff, but I haven't been allowed to see much of it until now. He says I can go and stay there after the exams, if I want.'

'First I've heard of it,' said Bonnie, all giggles forgotten. 'When did this happen?'

'You can come as well,' said Ben easily. 'He lives on the coast of Northumberland, near Lindisfarne. I'm sure I've told you about him.'

'So when did he show you this glass eye thing?'

Ben sighed, and cocked his head at her. Such unworthy emotions as jealousy were strictly beyond his scope, and Bonnie knew it. She forced a grin. 'Sorry,' she said. 'Too many questions.'

'Right. And it sounds as if you've got a customer,' he said to Simmy, as they all heard a knock on the locked street door. 'It's ten past nine already.'

'I'd better let him in,' said Simmy. 'Stay there a minute.'

She recognised the man right away. 'Hello, Mr Daniels,' she said. 'How are you now?' The man's wife had been in hospital for a month and he had made a point of taking frequent bunches of flowers for her, despite the virtual ban on taking them into the ward. 'They will let me put them on the window sill,' he'd said. 'Which is a lot better than nothing.'

'We're doing well,' he replied to her question. 'Thank you for asking. But now my sister's broken her leg, so these are going to be for her.'

It was undeniably a rich tapestry of critical human moments that passed through the doors of a florist shop. Simmy had at first been slow to grasp just how rich it could be, with a broad spectrum from a new baby, through broken legs and surprise parties to funerals. Not to mention retirement celebrations and dinner parties. Just when she thought she had experienced the entire range of flower-related events, another one popped up to add to the list.

Mr Daniels went away with a smile and a return wave to Bonnie's overdone farewell. 'There you are – a happy customer,' said the girl.

'Are we finished?' Simmy asked them. 'Can I get on with my work now?'

'Knock yourself out,' said Ben, hitching up his schoolbag. 'See you, Bon.'

And he was gone.

Chapter Thirteen

The start of a normal working day came as a relief to Simmy. The demands of the business kept her contentedly occupied all morning, with a last-minute order for birthday flowers scheduled for the afternoon, and another batch of early requests for a Mother's Day tribute. The necessity of keeping meticulous records of all these orders forced her to concentrate. Bonnie attempted, once or twice, to open a conversation about Staveley and the dead Declan, but was swiftly silenced. 'Not now,' said Simmy. 'I've got to think about getting all these flowers organised. You don't seem to be coughing much now. Does that mean I can rely on you to be fit when the work gets heavy?'

'Definitely. But I still don't know how you'll manage. There'll be dozens of deliveries that weekend, at this rate.'

'I know. Although we can encourage people to come and collect them, like we did last year. At least half of them will be happy with that, I think. Even so, the orders are up on last year by about forty per cent, so far. I can't ask Melanie to come back and help – her hotel's going to be just as busy as we are.'

'Corinne might lend a hand,' Bonnie suggested. 'I could ask her if she could do a few deliveries for you.'

Corinne's car was notoriously battered and unreliable, and Simmy hesitated before agreeing. The only acceptable way for flowers to be delivered was in the van. There had been times when she had insisted that Melanie should walk some distance through Windermere and parts of Bowness, rather than let her own shameful vehicle be identified as the delivery transport for Persimmon Petals. It might not be so easy to make Corinne do likewise. But someone in the shop wrapping and organising the bouquets and sprays would be useful. 'Thanks,' she said. 'She might be able to help you here, while I drive round all day.'

In fact, the more she thought about it, the more appealing the prospect became. Corinne knew short cuts and side streets better than either Simmy or Bonnie did. She could make an itinerary for deliveries, area by area, saving Simmy precious time. The prospect of a relentlessly hectic day began to mutate into a much less challenging exercise. 'Yes, ask her,' she decided. 'That's a great idea. I'll pay her the proper wages.'

After their meagre lunch, Bonnie suddenly asked, 'Have you heard any more about your ex? A date for the trial or something?'

'Not a word. I'd forgotten about it.'

'Did you tell Christopher? Was it awkward?'

'I did, yes. He didn't say much, really. Moxon hadn't heard anything, either. When he came in on Monday, that's what I thought it was about.'

159

'It's hard to feel sorry for him,' said Bonnie. 'Stalking's such a horrible thing. And he can't be a complete mental case, if he was married to you, can he?'

'You think I wouldn't have married him if he'd been deranged?'

'I'm sure you wouldn't. I can imagine you going with somebody boring, or incompetent, or unambitious, but not a nutter. Your mother would never have allowed it, for one thing.'

'Are we allowed to say "nutter"?'

Bonnie shrugged. 'Don't see why not.'

'My mother did think he was a bit boring, but she made no objections. She's not like that, actually. She would never directly have tried to stop me marrying him. And I have to tell you that I wouldn't have listened to her. She's so critical of practically everybody that it would have been futile to try and find somebody she approved of. Luckily, my dad thought he was quite a good son-in-law, on the whole.'

'Really? What did they talk about?'

'Oh, I don't know. Tony's quite outdoorsy, so there were trees and country sayings, weather and bits of history. He wasn't that different from us, you know. He fitted into the family quite nicely. And his mother really liked me. Still does, apparently.'

'Mm,' said Bonnie, appearing to be somewhat out of her depth. Relationships between adults could still leave her confused and nervous. Ben had wisely opted to postpone that whole area of experience for a future time, concentrating on training his little protégée in more cerebral matters. In a rare moment of disclosure, he had told Simmy how much he loved and valued Bonnie. 'But

160

she's delicate,' he'd worried. 'Fragile, in a lot of ways. I'm scared of hurting her, emotionally. It has to go slowly, if we're to survive long-term.'

Simmy had drawn unsettling comparisons between the young couple and herself and Christopher at the same age. Ben was so much more intent on his life plan, so clear-sighted and confident. He knew where and how Bonnie fitted into this plan, and what measures had to be taken to ensure a successful outcome.

She shook herself out of disagreeable reminiscences and dragged her thoughts back to the present. 'How did you get to Staveley last night?' she asked Bonnie.

'Oh – on the bikes. It was scary on the big road, especially coming back in the dark, but good fun. My legs are so strong now, it's amazing.'

The bikes had been bought shortly after Christmas, Ben subsidising his girlfriend's purchase with money received from various relatives. 'My mum used to give me money, but that's stopped now,' said Bonnie. 'The rich boyfriend's gone, I suppose.'

When Simmy first met the girl, she'd noticed the good clothes that sat rather oddly on the small shoulders. It had taken her some months to conclude that they were paid for with money from an ashamed parent. Bonnie's mother was a mysterious, even sinister, background figure; feckless, incompetent, gullible. Her enchanting little daughter had been treated more as a rival than a responsibility, left to her own devices and seldom protected from the untrustworthy whims of a succession of boyfriends.

'I'm quite glad I didn't know that,' Simmy confessed. 'I'd have worried about you.'

'How did you *think* we were getting there?'

'I didn't think about it at all. It's only just occurred to me to wonder.'

Bonnie's expression betrayed exasperation. If Simmy couldn't think things through better than that, she wasn't going to be much use as part of their team of amateur detectives, was the implication. It highlighted the unavoidable differences between adulthood and adolescence. 'I had other things to think about,' she defended. 'Like my father, and Tony and Christopher and the shop, and money, and the crack in the wall of my sitting room.' The last was very much scraping the barrel, she knew. The crack wasn't serious; the house wasn't falling down. But every time she saw it, she worried.

'Okay,' muttered Bonnie. 'I get it. And I'm glad, sort of, that you're not trying to make me tell you everything the Staveley people said.'

Simmy heaved a sigh. 'I really hate this secrecy, as much as you must do. I don't understand how we've got ourselves into it. All the people seem so *nice*. Anita and Debbie are both quite normal pleasant people, after all. There's no sense in all this animosity, as far as I can see.'

'It's unreal,' Bonnie agreed. 'But then, as Philip Marlowe says, all murderers are unreal, once you know they're murderers.'

'You'll have to tell me who Philip Marlowe is. I'm sure I should know, but I really don't.'

'Raymond Chandler. *The Long Goodbye*, and quite a few others. He's a private eye.'

'Oh. Right. You've read those books, have you?'

'I've read *everything*,' the girl boasted. 'It takes me three days to finish a book. Ben says you really get to know the world through detective fiction.'

'And Ben would know,' said Simmy, with an uncharacteristic flash of sarcasm. Then, in swift atonement, she went on. 'I had a text from Tanya Harkness just now. She's offered to come and help when the Mother's Day stuff needs doing. I suppose that's thanks to you? I told her to come in and see me on Monday after school.'

'She won't be as good as Corinne, but she knows her way around. She can get things organised for delivery, and take any telephone orders. She's definitely the best of the three sisters.'

'I'm looking forward to meeting her.'

'She looks just like her mother. The twins aren't identical at all. Ben's quite sorry about that. He keeps imagining the tricks they could play on people, if they were.'

'Sounds like a narrow escape for Helen, then.'

'Helen's embarrassed to have such a lot of kids, according to Ben. He thinks the twins were an accident, and should never have existed.'

Simmy winced. 'He should know better,' she said.

Moxon materialised five minutes after Bonnie had gone home, ten minutes before Simmy intended to close up for the day. She was much more pleased to see him than might have been expected, since he couldn't possibly be bringing good news. Her pleasure arose from a handful of negatives. He wasn't young enough to be her child; he wasn't ordering flowers; he wasn't going to get complicated about emotions; he wasn't either of her parents. Compared to those, his probable reason for being there was almost a relief.

She had forgotten about Tony yet again. Since Moxon had expressed complete ignorance of the events in Worcestershire or Gloucestershire or wherever it was, she had dropped the connection in her mind between the two men. The detective represented Staveley and the death of a man on the road. He might have come to say the case was resolved, nothing more to be done. Good news was, after all, conceivable.

'We heard from the people in Worcester,' he said. 'About your ex-husband.'

'Oh drat.'

'It's nothing too troublesome, actually. They want to confirm your contact details, that you are who his team say you are, and the basic facts of the matter at the time when he first met the woman. They could have done it all online, through normal databases, but they went the extra mile for some reason.'

'So now what?'

'From what you told me, I really can't see any benefit to their case in summoning you in person. You can't add any material testimony, can you? What do they think you'll say? That the midwife clearly fell instantly in love with your husband and gave him every encouragement, so that his subsequent behaviour was entirely rational? That's the only defence I can think of. Unless they want you to say he'd had mental health issues for years, which you and he covered up, which would explain the total absence of any medical notes to that effect.'

'Stalking is quite mad, though, isn't it? By definition.'

'The jury's out on that, as they say.' He smiled. 'I imagine your friend Mr Harkness is enjoying the legal complexities of the matter quite a lot.'

'He would be, if he wasn't so busy. His exams start just after Easter, and he's drowning in revision. I don't know how he does it.'

His direct look suggested that he did not quite believe her. 'You're telling me he's taking no interest in this Staveley business?'

'Ah. No, not quite. He seems to be able to snatch an hour or two of free time for that.'

'So I gather.'

Her thoughts whirled to hidden cameras, surveillance of the Kennedys' house, spies in the quiet streets of Staveley. 'How do you know that?'

'It's a small world,' he said. 'Word gets around.'

'Maybe so, but *how* exactly?'

'You must surely be aware that most people record every detail of their lives on Facebook and all those other platforms that live inside mobile telephones. It often feels as if there are no secrets left in the world. Debbie Kennedy is no exception. Her grief is loudly proclaimed, along with her anger at her mother, the police, and the world in general. She has embraced your young friends as her best chance of achieving justice, extraordinary as that might seem. She believes the police to be corrupt and incompetent, wary of prosecuting a well-known local solicitor because of the professional networks they share. Quite hurtful stuff, I have to say.'

'Gosh!' said Simmy. 'Am I the only person missing out on all this?'

'Assuredly not – although most of those still avoiding it are somewhat older than you. Demographically speaking, you should be right in the midst of it. But it's dangerous to generalise. We see people in their nineties merrily tweeting, and sixteen-year-olds who've abandoned the whole thing. One of our PCs said the other day she thinks there might be a backlash under way. That it's all unravelling and in a few more years it'll be back to privacy and real live personal relationships. Won't that be nice.' He sighed.

'So Debbie's wrong in assuming you wouldn't arrest her mother if you thought she was guilty.' She stated it as a fact, not a question. Simmy Brown, daughter of Angie Straw, might have been raised in an atmosphere of cynicism towards the police, but her own experience had taught her to trust them.

'Of course. But it's not about thinking she's guilty, is it? It's about finding evidence against her.'

'And that's not going well?'

'I can't say much, as you know. But her car's in the clear. If it was her, she didn't use her own vehicle.'

'It wasn't her,' Simmy said.

'You can't be sure. Does Ben Harkness agree with you?'

She had wanted to avoid that question. It still bothered her that she and Ben were both so certain, when one of them had to be wrong. She shook her head. 'Apparently, Debbie Kennedy has convinced him.'

'And that counts for something. Doesn't it?'

'Does it? I don't know. It has to be some very nasty family stuff at the heart of it. I know some of it – how Declan wanted Anita to employ him, and how unpleasant she was to him. I wouldn't want to be the object of her contempt, I must say. But that doesn't explain why she would kill him. Much more likely to be the other way around.'

'Yes,' he said, portentously. 'And doesn't that make you

think perhaps she knew that, and took pre-emptive action?'

'Killed him before he could kill her, you mean? That's awfully melodramatic. She's retiring from the business. Declan wasn't going to be her problem any more. It would make more sense for *Gillian* to kill him, than Anita.' She put her hand to her mouth, hearing her own words. 'No! I didn't mean that. Gillian's really nice. Full of good feeling. She'd never do anything like that. She really seems to like people, and wants everyone to be friends. But she is quite ill, as you said last time I saw you. I can't see her working for much longer. And that must have a few implications.' She stopped herself again, hearing all the wrong sort of accusations about to emerge.

'You seem to know her rather well. How many times have you seen her?'

The flash of triumph was warm inside her. So not everybody tweeted their every movement, after all. Not Anita Olsen or Gillian Townsend, for a start. 'I was there last night. At Gillian's house in Kendal. They seem keen to get me on their side, for some reason.'

He was disappointingly unimpressed. 'I'm sure they do,' he nodded. 'Because they know full well that you have a special direct line to me, which they must be eager to exploit.'

'Oh.' Deflation made her shoulders sag and her jaw relax. 'I never thought of that.'

'I could be wrong, but it's unlikely. Our names have been linked a few too many times in local news stories for anyone to miss the connection.'

'I suppose they have.' She treated him to a frank and friendly smile. A year earlier, she'd have been too wary to behave in such a way, worried that he would take it as an invitation. Now she knew better. He was fond of her, certainly, and concerned for her at times, but nothing more than that. She presumed he had got wind of her new relationship with Christopher and could be relied on to be glad for her.

'So you should be careful,' he told her. 'Don't be too trusting. Don't commit yourself to anything. I know Gillian Townsend slightly, and agree she comes over as all sweet and girlish, bouncing with energy. But she's had some knocks in her life, and she's no fool. She knows the law inside out, and won't be afraid to make good use of it.'

'Oh dear,' sighed Simmy. 'You make it sound horrible. I'm not such a hopeless judge of character, am I? My impression of her is of somebody entirely sincere. She never shows a shadow of a doubt about Anita's innocence.'

'You've made a few mistakes that I can think of,' he said. 'Like the time you got yourself into such a pickle in Bowness, remember? That was almost culpably naive of you. And you were still being worryingly reckless just a few months ago, if I remember rightly.'

'With hindsight, yes, I see I can be a bit foolhardy, I suppose. But I expect I'd do the same again. I mean – you have to trust people, don't you? The alternative is just too awful.'

'In general, yes. But on that occasion, when you knew there was somebody out there with malicious intent towards you, you were altogether too trusting. You might have died. Instead you appear to regard yourself as indestructible.'

'I know. I think it has to do with losing the baby. It feels as if the worst that can happen has happened already, so

I'm sort of immunised against any major disaster now.'

'Not logical,' he said gently.

'Not a bit logical. Ben said I was too dumb to live, that time last winter. Apparently, that's what Americans say when someone in a crime thing on the telly goes willingly into danger. I never dreamt it would apply to me. I do think I've been a bit more sensible since then, on the whole. And surely you don't think Gillian Townsend is going to kill me?'

'I hope not,' he said, without a smile.

Chapter Fourteen

She had heard nothing from her mother all day, leading her to hope this meant there was no bad news from that quarter. Despite – or perhaps because of – the growing concern over her father, there had developed a distance between Simmy and her parents. She withheld much of her own daily life from them, and had told them nothing of the past few days' events. No mention of Tony's trouble, and certainly not a word about the death of a man in Staveley. The growing pressure of Mother's Day was another taboo subject. She could provide practical help at the B&B in a limited way, but was on her own when it came to wanting anything in return. It was a point everyone reached eventually, of course. Parents lost the capacity to support, advise or even listen, as they faded out of the world. Even Angie, still vigorous and entirely competent, was losing her grip on the rapidly changing reality around her. Her temper, never altogether sunny, was worsening as the truth of this dawned on her. More and more aspects of daily life made her furious. Frustrating regulations, obstructive bureaucracy, small-minded people on every side – it all ran counter to her lifelong philosophy conceived in the nineteen sixties. More and more she looked like an isolated throwback, refusing to adapt as almost all of her contemporaries had done.

Simmy presented herself on the doorstep just before six o'clock, pleasantly surprised to find the door unlocked. One of Russell's disconcerting symptoms of mental decline was a paranoia that meant everything had to be kept firmly locked and barred. The reversion to normality was, though, not necessarily a good sign. It probably meant that Angie had taken control, because her husband was too unwell to resist. Russell might be suffering agonies of anxiety at being overruled.

'Hello!' she called, having walked into the hallway. 'Anybody home?'

'In here,' came a low voice from the dining room. 'Thank goodness you've come. I expected you forty minutes ago.'

Simmy went in to find her father sitting on the floor surrounded by broken china and her mother standing over him. 'What on earth—?' she began. 'Is he all right? Has he had another thing?'

'No. He's just being very stupid,' snapped Angie. 'Decided to dust all the ornaments on the high shelf, and managed to sweep everything off in the process.'

'Oh, Lord.' Simmy surveyed the wreckage, with the rueful old man at the centre of it. 'What were you thinking, Dad? You never clean the china. And I did it a few days ago anyway.'

'It needed it.' He spoke as if his position was easily defended, his wife not entirely in the right.

'He was standing on a chair,' said Angie, slapping an out-of-place dining chair. 'Lucky he didn't break that as well. They're not meant for that sort of thing.'

'I was all right until you startled me. You made me lose my balance.'

'How long have you been sitting there like that? Have you hurt yourself? For heaven's sake, Dad, you've only just got home from hospital,' Simmy burst out.

'He's been sitting there like that for close to a quarter of an hour,' Angie replied for him. 'I can't make him stand up.'

Simmy recalled recalcitrant toddlers going limp as their mothers tried to make them stand. It was a strategy that Russell might well choose to adopt in his alarming reversion to childish ways. Not that Angie was rash enough to attempt to physically manhandle him. While not a big man, he was far too much for one person to manage. Simmy doubted that the two of them together could move him very far.

'Have you had supper?' she asked, hoping to approach the problem sideways.

'Not yet,' Angie sighed. 'I was just serving it. It'll have gone cold by now.'

'What is it?'

'I made a chicken casserole, actually. It's sitting on the kitchen table.'

'Well, it'll soon warm up again, won't it? Come on, Dad. It sounds great, and if there's enough I want to stay and have some with you.' The temptation to lapse into hospital-style baby talk was hard to resist. She was already speaking in a fashion quite foreign to the usual banter between father and daughter. He evidently noticed this and gave her a hard look.

'Can you stand up, or do you want us to call another ambulance for you?' Angie was far less inclined to skirt around the issue. 'It's one or the other. Make your choice.'

It worked, albeit slowly. Russell turned onto all fours, then pulled himself upright with the help of the misplaced dining chair, taking most of his own weight on his right arm. Both legs looked too wobbly to support him. The women hovered, arms out like fielders, but not actually touching him. 'Does it hurt anywhere?' asked Simmy.

He shook his head. 'I fell quite gracefully. Shame about the pots.'

Angie was picking through the wreckage, extracting three unbroken items and placing them carefully on a table. 'Serves me right for hanging onto them all this time,' she murmured. 'I knew they'd get broken one day.'

'They should have been safe enough up there,' said Simmy, thinking of all the visiting children who'd rampaged around the room without a single breakage. 'And so many of them gone.' She spotted a piece of a handsome blue jug she knew she had been fond of as a small girl. 'I used this jug every morning,' she said mournfully.

'I'm sorry,' said Russell crossly. 'But your mother startled me. I was perfectly all right until then.'

'You'd have broken them trying to dust them, in all probability,' said Angie. 'What were you going to use, anyway? I can't see a duster anywhere.'

'I forget,' he said. 'It doesn't matter any more, does it?'

'It does matter,' Angie hissed at him. 'You know how I hate it when anything gets broken.'

The words took Simmy back to childhood days, where Angie would become a raging fury if her careless child broke something. She had seen her mother weep over a glass ornament or china mug lying in pieces on the floor. By some unspoken bond, Simmy understood that it made life itself feel fragile and vulnerable to destruction. She felt a similar hollow sense of loss, and the futility of trying to keep things safe. She would watch her mother erect another section of defensive wall against such feelings, trying not to care or invest too much in possessions. By extension, Angie sometimes seemed to reduce her investment in people as well. Simmy had assumed that it was the same for everyone, and that a broken cup was a universal tragedy. It had been Tony, her husband, who taught her otherwise. When one of their wedding present plates slipped out of his hand and ended up in three pieces on the floor, he showed no sign of distress. 'We can get another one,' he said.

'Not easily. They discontinued the line soon after my cousin bought them for us,' she'd told him.

'Oh, well – we're never going to need more than five, are we? It's only a plate, after all.'

She had left the room in confusion, questioning the strength of her own sense of loss at the wreckage not just of a plate, but the whole set, which was now forever incomplete. The damage seemed to lodge somewhere inside her, just as it did with her mother.

Christopher, of course, would understand. He would be as horrified as Angie was at the destruction wreaked by Russell. He worked with precious pieces of china and glass, after all. But then, Simmy wondered whether he might see them only as manifestations of monetary value. With every breakage, the scarcity value of the survivors increased. When Simmy told him what Russell had done, he was quite likely to suggest she come to his saleroom and buy replacements.

They escorted her father unsteadily back to the kitchen, where Angie put the casserole back in the Aga to warm up. Russell became impatient for his meal, and Simmy herself was hungry. There was an uneasy silence, hurt feelings and dawning suspicions swirling around. All because Russell had given a disturbing little smirk at his wife's words. 'You know how I hate it when anything gets broken,' she had said, and he had lifted his chin in a kind of triumph. Was it possible that he had done it on purpose, in a furtive piece of sabotage, or even aggression? Her sweet soft-hearted father was surely not capable of such a deliberate act? But perhaps his damaged brain had released age-old resentments that he now felt free to act on? Perhaps, like Tony, he was much less predictable and dependable than everybody thought.

The meal was a disappointment, with the potatoes crumbly with overcooking, carrots gone cold and the casserole not adequately reheated. It was another small sadness in a day that had contained a number of threats to Simmy's equilibrium.

It was half past eight when she got back to Troutbeck. She'd swept up the broken china, putting all the pieces in the dustbin as if disposing of a dead pet. Angie had still said little, which Simmy found worrying. The demands of the bed and breakfast guests were predominant, and perhaps provided a useful outlet. It was, after all, familiar and constructive work. It earned money and provided distraction. But without reliable help from her husband, Angie would struggle to maintain the same level of efficiency. The quality of her attention would drop, and the numbers of guests she could process would likewise fall. But it was less than two days since Russell's 'episode' or 'accident', or whatever they chose to call it. The shock itself would go a long way towards explaining his changed personality. He ought not to be out of bed, let alone climbing on chairs. It was far too early to predict how he would be in the coming months. All his basic functions had been unimpaired, and with modern medication, he might easily make a full recovery. 'Look at Peggy, in *The Archers*,' Simmy muttered to herself. The woman was in her mid nineties, and was returned to complete normality after a full-blown stroke. If that was anything resembling real life, there was considerable hope for Russell Straw.

The cottage, as always, was in darkness, but less chilly than usual, because she had adjusted the timer on the thermostat to get the heating going at four-thirty instead of six. It felt wasteful, but the east winds of March were behaving in their traditional fashion with the result that it felt colder than it had in January. For a florist, Simmy's failure to properly appreciate the month of March seemed perverse. 'Yes, the flowers are lovely,' she admitted to Melanie, who first observed this anomaly. 'But it's always so disappointing, somehow. The handful of nice days only seems more tantalising, so it's all the more depressing when it's cold and wet for weeks on end.'

There were no messages on her landline, no interesting letters on the doormat, and no lurking visitors leaping out from the garden shadows. 'Just me, then,' she murmured. Nearly two years of living alone had not made it any more palatable. Another anomaly, she supposed. An only child should be accustomed to her own company, even preferring it to society. But Simmy liked people. She liked being part of a lively group, all talking at once. She liked watching faces and listening to different accents. These repetitive evenings, from Monday to Friday, week after week, were weighing her down. The hours from seven to ten dragged tediously, imbued with a sense of waste. Time was passing, everyone was getting older, and nothing was changing. She couldn't allow it to go on.

At least it was only an hour or so till bedtime, having devoted half the evening to her parents. And this could be the pattern for quite a while. Tiring and unsettling as it might be to watch the decline of Beck View, it would at least resolve the issue of what to do at the end of the day. She could take charge of the evening meal, giving her mother the chance of a rest, and ensuring that all three of them ate properly. She could assess her father's condition more closely, and even perhaps have a word with his doctor. She could behave like a fully responsible grown-up daughter – even if the day when that was necessary had come twenty years sooner than anticipated. Russell was not yet seventy, Angie a few years younger. It wasn't right that they should be tipped over into old age so soon.

The day ended on a note of resignation. Simmy Brown had never been one to make things happen, being of the view that they happened anyway, and the best thing was simply to react as required. Not everybody operated on the same basis, of course. In fact, almost none of her immediate circle took the line that she did. Perhaps, she thought, as she snuggled down beneath her warm winter duvet, that was why they were her friends in the first place.

Chapter Fifteen

'Friday. It's Friday,' she told herself when she woke up. It was generally her first thought every morning – keeping track of the days, orienting herself in the real world, and shaking off the all-too-powerful dreams that she was prone to.

There was a delivery to be made sometime during the morning, to a house in Helm Road, which was where the Harkness family lived. That would take no time at all. There was no reason to rush, as she had for the meeting with Ben and Bonnie. But her early night meant an early awakening, and it was barely seven. Birds were singing outside, rehearsing for spring. The predominant species was evidently crows or rooks, however, which were very far from tuneful. They always seemed to be having violent arguments amongst themselves, with special grievances aired first thing in the morning. They favoured a large ash tree not far from her window, and she knew they'd wake her most mornings at an unsocial hour for some weeks to come.

When she turned her phone on, having left it charging overnight, a text message pinged through.

Can we meet today, please? Perhaps lunch somewhere? Gillian.

Simmy's main reaction was exasperation. Just as she was hoping to let the whole Staveley/Kennedy business drift into the far distance, here it was again. And once again, she had no realistic choice in the matter. Ben and Bonnie would never forgive her if she tried to back out of her part in it, and however much she might insist that it was ridiculous, and a waste of time, and risked annoying the police, they would still make her do it.

She replied quickly, before she could think too much about it.

Okay. I can be at the Elleray at 12.30.

She didn't sign it, unsure as to how to style herself. 'Simmy' seemed too friendly, while 'Persimmon' felt the opposite. For the nine hundredth time she cursed her mother for foisting the name on her. If only there could be a sudden surge of popularity for it – a soap opera character given the name, or a pop singer adopting it would fit the bill nicely. People wouldn't be so hesitant about using it then. Even DI Moxon found himself unable to utter it, mostly using 'Mrs Brown' but opting for 'Simmy' in times of crisis.

The Elleray was her default establishment for eating and drinking. It was close by, easy to park and the service was quick. Bonnie would have to cope in the shop for an hour or so. It wouldn't be the first time, by a long way.

Gillian did not acknowledge the suggested time and place, which Simmy thought slightly rude, but not indicative of any change of plan. Indeed, when she arrived at twelve twenty-five, there was Mrs Townsend standing against the wall of the pub, watching the passing traffic. 'I haven't got long,' said Simmy. 'I don't close the shop at lunchtime, so Bonnie has to manage on her own.'

'Suits me.'

They made rapidly careless choices of food and drink, and settled on a table that Simmy had used before. The bar was very long, full of light and poorly patronised. 'It might get busy any minute now,' said Simmy. 'Better go down the far end.'

'I've never been in here before. I don't come to Windermere much.'

Why would you? Simmy silently wondered. Kendal provided everything that Windermere could, and a lot more besides. 'I bet you go to Bowness, though,' she said aloud.

'Well, yes. Clients, and so forth,' she said vaguely. 'They've got those hotels . . .' Which neatly summed up the geographical variations of the area. Bowness did indeed have smart, versatile and welcoming hotels. And the hotels had views of the lake, meeting rooms, discreetly professional staff. Windermere had boarding houses, bed and breakfasts and not a glimpse of the lake.

Their sandwiches came quickly, and they ate as they talked. Simmy noticed the way Gillian took small bites, chewing thoroughly. It put her in mind of Bonnie and her discomfort where food was concerned.

Eventually, the main point was broached by Gillian. 'The thing is, I might have to call on you at short notice, and ask you to act as a witness. There's nothing concrete yet, but I've been putting feelers out. I *know* somebody in Crook must be able to help, but there's nothing definite yet.'

'Witness?'

'You did seem to want to help us,' Gillian reminded her.

'I know, and I do. I just don't understand what you're asking me.'

'Nothing yet. Just be available, if you can. I know you've got the shop, and it's busy. I wouldn't ask you, but there is literally nobody else who would carry such weight as you. You're known to the police as someone of integrity. You've got no axe to grind. And – well, I can't rely on myself as I used to be able to. It's Crohn's disease, you know. Did I tell you?'

'DI Moxon said that's what it was. I don't know very much about it.'

'It's quite debilitating. It can completely immobilise me sometimes. If I had somebody with me, I'd be so much happier.'

'But you won't tell me where we'll be going?'

'I would if I knew. I think by tomorrow I'll have a much better idea. Don't worry about it. It sounds much more mysterious than it really is. It involves a little group of old gents meeting every Friday evening at their local pub. It's likely something will emerge tonight.'

'Has it got something to do with the Roger person who Declan was staying with?'

'Who? Oh – *him*. No, no. Of course not. *He* wouldn't help us to save his own life. Debbie's already got to him, well and truly.'

'Oh.'

'I know it sounds horrible. Debbie's such a sweet girl, and she hasn't done anything to deserve all this trouble. I hate to say it, but I think she's rather lucky to have the ghastly Spencer Kennedy to watch out for her. He'll make sure she's all right financially, at least. Everyone wants to make things as good as they can for the poor girl – even my mother worries about her.'

'I still can't begin to understand what went wrong between Anita and her children. Wasn't there some sort of terrible argument last week, that made Declan go off without a word?'

Gillian absently pressed a hand into her belly, as she did habitually. 'That was something between Debbie and Declan. Anita wasn't involved in it at all.'

'But she did know he'd gone off without saying where. You were talking about it on Friday.'

'My mother again, I'm afraid. She never stops trying to bring everybody back together. She told Anita about it, thinking she might force her to make some effort to help her daughter. She came into our office on Friday morning and stayed for ages, mostly talking to Anita. I managed to raise the subject of the party – which is where you came in. I suppose my mother and I are alike in that way – we're always trying to find something positive to focus on.'

'That's nice. I think I'm a bit the same, actually.'

'Of course, it can backfire sometimes,' said Gillian regretfully.

Simmy looked at her watch. 'I'll have to go soon,' she warned.

'All right. I'm very grateful to you for coming. I couldn't have said what I have over the phone.'

'Well, I'm still confused. All I've gleaned is that somebody might come up with some evidence and you want me to be with you when you follow it up.'

'Exactly. That's it exactly.'

'And it'll be in Crook, because that's where Declan was knocked off his bike. And a car hitting a bike would make quite a lot of noise. There might have been shouting, screaming, all sorts of things.'

'Quite possibly,' nodded Gillian. 'Now, one last point I need to make, which is that *you* were driving along that road at just about that time, weren't you?'

'Yes, but I didn't hit him,' said Simmy stupidly.

'Don't be idiotic. Of course you didn't. But I want you to think hard about that stretch of road. About half a mile past the main village, such as it is. The road runs straight, but undulates. It would be easy to miss a pedestrian or cyclist until it was too late, if you were speeding – and that adds weight to the theory that it was an accident all along. It's desperately important that we establish what time it happened, you see.'

'I don't think I can help with that. I didn't see anything. Aren't there ditches along the road? And the light was going. And you don't expect to see crumpled bicycles and dead men on the side of the road, do you?'

'I'm just saying you might want to have a think about it, now you know he was very likely there as you passed. Something you saw from the corner of your eye and then completely forgot. Maybe you could drive along that way again, this evening, at the same time, and see if that jogs your memory. That could prove really helpful.'

'But why?'

'Why do you think?' Gillian smiled to soften the words. Her eyes were wide and warm on Simmy's, and she put down her glass to press Simmy's hand. 'I know you'd help us if you could. You've met Anita, you can see how distressed she is by all this suspicion. We *like* you, and the way you've been so friendly and nice. And of course, when we do get around to the retirement party, it'll be lovely having you do all the flowers for it.'

It was all so easy and amicable that Simmy had almost no qualms in agreeing to drive over to Crook again in the hope of jogging her memory. 'But I don't think I can do it this evening,' she demurred. 'The thing is, my dad's not well, and they need my help with the bed and breakfast business. It's all a bit of a crisis, really.'

Gillian smiled again, adding a little laugh. 'What a very British way of putting it,' she observed. 'Your whole life in meltdown, and all you can say is, "It's a bit of a crisis". Funny old lot, aren't we?'

'My life isn't in meltdown,' said Simmy. 'Dad's doing very well, actually, considering the scare he gave us. And everything else is going along quite nicely. It's just my parents who need some help.'

'Oh, sorry. Silly me. But *I* need your help, Simmy. Can I call you that? I suppose it's *my* life that's in meltdown, and I was putting it onto you, stupidly. I honestly am very worried about poor Anita. And given that I'm her legal representative, I owe it to her to try and get her out of this ridiculous trouble she's in. If only we could somehow get a lead on who actually killed Declan, it would all come right. You do see that, don't you? It's clutching at straws, obviously, but seeing that you drove that very stretch of road at roughly the same time that it happened, it would be neglectful of me not to check that out. I mean, how brilliant it would be if you *could* remember some little detail that pointed us in the right direction.'

The coincidence finally hit Simmy. That she should have been on that road at all was remarkable. With the timing, and the links to Anita and Gillian, it was almost beyond belief. And yet, such things did happen. It was a small area, with few roads, and sooner or later flowers would be delivered to every tiny hamlet within seven or eight miles of Windermere. 'Wasn't it an amazing coincidence,' she said. 'That I should pass that spot on the way to you, just at the time Declan was hit?'

'Amazing,' Gillian nodded. 'Although it was the rush hour, if that means anything around here. I suppose it does – the bypass does get very busy in the late afternoon.'

'Bypass?'

'The dual carriageway, between Ings and Kendal. The Staveley people still call it the bypass. It used to go right through the village, you see. Now Staveley's as quiet as anything. All they get is visitors going up to Kentmere.'

'You've known the area a long time, then?'

'All my life, apart from when I was a student, and a few years after that. Robin and I are both local – we went to the same school, although he was four years ahead of me. We both went to a reunion, five years after I left, and got together then. It was rather romantic, actually.'

Gillian smiled again, her face pink with remembering.

'A bit like me and Christopher,' said Simmy. 'Although not very, I suppose.'

'Oh?'

But the clock was against them, and the food was all finished. 'I've really got to get back to the shop.' She stood up. 'I don't see that I can be of any use to you, you know. I understand how desperate you must be to track down that car, but surely the police are in a better position to do it? They'll have got tyre marks and located the exact spot . . . all that sort of thing. And they'll be watching out for a car with scratches or blood or whatever on it.'

Gillian sighed and nodded. 'I know. But we can't just sit around doing nothing, can we? And you seemed like a gift from heaven, if that doesn't sound daft. You really are a very dear girl, you know. Even my mother took to you, and she takes quite some pleasing, I can tell you.'

Flattered, Simmy merely smiled and made her departure. Nobody had called her a dear girl since her grandmother had died.

Bonnie appeared calm and contented, back in the shop. Simmy had not mentioned her assignation with Gillian, merely that she might take longer than usual because she had an errand to run. Bonnie naturally assumed it was something for Angie, and asked no questions. Now Simmy was not sure whether or not to come clean, and if so, how much to disclose. Ben and Bonnie were, after all, not favourably disposed towards Anita, and by extension, Gillian. It felt as if a trial had already begun, with each side keeping its powder dry, its weapons under wraps.

The implication that trust might be misplaced, and tricks played, was disturbing.

'Two more orders for Mother's Day, and I sold a dozen tulips,' the girl reported. 'Nothing else happened.'

'Oh well, that just about covers the rent for a couple of days, I suppose,' said Simmy. 'I wonder whether the Hawkshead Hotel will want me to do flowers for them again this summer?'

'Call them and ask. Or even better, make it sound definite that they do want you. There'll be new people there, who'll just assume it was agreed at some point. Say you're phoning to check that Easter's the starting date.'

'You're very businesslike,' Simmy smiled.

'I am, aren't I?' Bonnie smirked. 'It's fun as well.'

'Good.'

'But not as much fun as working with Ben on this Staveley case. That's really brilliant, even with him hardly having any time for it.'

'Is it?'

'Well, it's not so good if you think we're on opposite sides. We're not, you know. It's just the best way of getting to the truth. Based on the legal system that's lasted for a thousand years, or whatever it is. Dialectic, that's what Ben calls it.' Bonnie frowned. 'I'm still not entirely sure what that means.'

'Well don't ask me.' Simmy laughed. 'I think even my dad might struggle with that one.'

'It's all to do with opposites, answering one argument with another on the other side, and testing them for credibility. Like they do in a trial. Except it's got dreadfully corrupted, especially in America.'

A customer interrupted what threatened to be a lengthy diatribe, for which Simmy was thankful. The indecisive woman could take all the time she needed, as far as Simmy was concerned. When she finally left, it was half past two. 'Is Ben coming in today?' Simmy asked.

'Don't know. That experiment's gone wrong, so he had to start again. But it'll be quicker this time and he's got Dave Rowland to help him. That's another sixth-former doing biochemistry.'

Sometimes Simmy worried that Bonnie lived too much through her boyfriend, with hardly anything in her own life apart from him. How would the poor girl manage when Ben disappeared to Newcastle in the autumn? There had been hints of an intention to go with him, which would leave the florist in need of yet another new assistant. That prospect made her feel weak.

Gillian's request nagged at her, with her attempted refusal seeming more and more churlish as the afternoon went on. It wasn't much to ask, after all, and she could make a loop through Crook and Staveley and back up to Beck View in about twenty minutes, even if she crawled slowly along the stretch of road where she believed Declan Kennedy had met his end. It wouldn't matter if she didn't get to her parents' house before six. They probably wouldn't even notice. She wouldn't be doing anything to annoy Moxon or concern Ben, but merely refreshing her murky recollection of Friday's drive. To leave it any longer would probably only dim the memories even more.

She wouldn't say anything to Bonnie. The matter had not arisen so far, and even if it did, Simmy had questions of her own. The youngsters had told her almost nothing about their visit to Debbie Kennedy, which made it easier to withhold her own findings from them. Although 'findings' was putting it a bit strong. What had she 'found' anyway? Nothing that wasn't common knowledge, as far as she could think. Anita disliked her son-in-law, but the animosity was much stronger in the other direction. Anita was a perfectly pleasant, if somewhat remote, person. She had a loyal and affectionate friend in Gillian, but Gillian's husband was not so enamoured. There was a son, Matthew Olsen, who Simmy had not yet met. Oh – and where was Mr Olsen senior? Ben Harkness, of course, would not have left without ascertaining name, address and possible motive. Even now, given the fact of his existence, Ben would easily find him. And whose side might he be on, if located? Only then did the possibility strike her that Debbie and Matthew might well have already supplied these details and a lot more, when the youngsters went to Staveley. If so, and they had withheld it from Simmy, that would be upsetting. In fact, the increasing sense of being in opposition to them was already getting her down. Talking to Bonnie had become awkward, with unaccustomed silences where they would previously have shared everything.

Another Mother's Day order came in, and Simmy began to give serious consideration to the logistics of so many deliveries. 'Did you ask Corinne if she'd help out, the weekend after next?' she remembered to say.

'Oh – yeah. She's not sure, to be honest. There's going to be some gig in Penrith she might want to go to.' Corinne had developed a passion for music festivals in the past few years, to the point of offering her own performances on occasion. Simmy had heard her singing once or twice, and not been unduly impressed. The songs and the guitar reminded her of singers favoured by her parents – Joni Mitchell, Joan Baez, Maddy Prior. Corinne might look like a woman of the twenty-tens, but she sounded like someone from the 1970s.

'Oh. Well, I do need to know for sure. It would make a huge difference.'

'We've got Tanya, don't forget.'

'Assuming she's old enough to be of any use.'

'She's fourteen and fairly sensible. I've been getting to know her better, and she's definitely the best of the three. Natalie's a total pain, and Zoe's never around.'

'I can't ask somebody of fourteen to do too much. It's bad enough with you looking so young. And Corinne would be so useful working out the quickest routes.'

'I'll tell her you really want her. Let's hope it's awful weather. That might change her mind.'

'We can't rely on that. I was *depending* on her.'

'I'll tell her, but don't hold your breath,' said Bonnie again, showing far too little concern for what felt to Simmy like a major disappointment. 'Doesn't look as if Ben's coming.'

It was only five minutes after the boy's normal time to turn up. 'His timetable's all different now, though, isn't it?' said Simmy.

'Not so much different as non-existent. They don't have proper lessons any more, just loads of revision, and practicals and special small-group stuff for some of the subjects. I don't know how the teachers cope with it. They've got all the other years to deal with as well, and their timetables haven't changed. I guess I won't see him until tomorrow, now.'

Simmy found herself unable to recall much detail from her sixth-form years. The first term had been spent mooning over Christopher, followed by endless dithering over what she wanted to do by way of further education. It all felt like a very long time ago. 'I expect they let him get on with most of it in his own way,' she said.

'Yeah,' Bonnie nodded. 'He knows more than most of them by now.'

'Oh, well, Saturday tomorrow.' It was fatuous, no doubt, but she found herself very much anticipating the end of the week. In the summer she might keep the shop open until well into the afternoon, but at this time of year it was quite reasonable to close soon after one. She and Christopher would have the next day together, not doing anything very much. The very laziness of it was appealing, with no firm plans and the prospect of a cosy Sunday adding to a sense of luxurious possibility.

'You'll be seeing Anita Olsen again, will you?' Bonnie's question was strikingly casual. Simmy was instantly alerted.

'No, I don't think so. What makes you say that?'

'Nothing special. But you've been acting as if the whole thing wasn't happening, and I can't stand it any longer. I can't actually think about anything else. That Declan was a real character, you know. His wife and kids adored him, but plenty of people didn't.'

'How do you know that?'

'Facebook,' said Bonnie tiredly. 'What else?'

'Show me.'

The girl brandished her phone, tapped it a time or two and started flicking the screen with a delicate finger. 'There, look.'

Simmy focused on a succession of comments. *Old Dec finally got what was coming . . . Shame to die so young, but you can't say he wasn't warned . . . He lived in a world of his own most of the time . . . The original Walter Mitty – no idea of his own limitations . . . What? Declan dead, and never repaid what he owed me? . . . Come on, mates, have a thought for his family . . .*

'I see what you mean,' said Simmy faintly. 'They don't care what they say, do they?'

'This is mild,' Bonnie told her. 'People say terrible things to each other, most of the time.'

'So I gather. Do you think one of these people might have killed him?' She paused to think a moment. 'Do you think his mother's seen all this? Or his wife?'

Bonnie shrugged. 'Daughters, probably. Wife possibly. Mother – not so sure. If Anita's really the killer, she'll be glad, of course.'

'Oh?'

'Glad there were so many others who might want him dead. Muddies the water. The police are going to be all over this, trying to track them all. It'll keep them well busy.'

'I still can't get much of an idea of him. Everybody seems to have a different impression. To hear Gillian talk, he was a real loser, wheedling and whining about something he was never going to have. And these Facebook people obviously didn't like him much. And yet poor Debbie was so fond of him.'

'Yeah. But it's the same with everybody, isn't it? What the family sees of them is nothing like the person they are outside – in the pub and all that.' Bonnie paused. 'That's a bit muddled, isn't it, but you know what I mean.'

'I do, but isn't it mostly the other way round? I mean, people are usually nastier at home than they are in social situations. Declan sounds as if he was more popular with his family than anyone else.'

'Not with his mother-in-law,' Bonnie reminded her. 'She's family as well.'

'Yes.' Simmy wanted to add, *And she might well see him more objectively than anyone*. But she didn't, because yet again, her thoughts tipped the balance the wrong way. So many of them supported the notion that Anita Olsen had indeed killed her daughter's husband, and yet that notion remained unacceptable, not least because it would destroy poor Gillian Townsend if it was true.

Simmy resolved in that moment to make time to do as Gillian had asked, and drive down through Bowness and along the road through Crook. It seemed just as untenable to not do it as to do it. It was ridiculous, intrusive, a waste of time and against her basic nature. But she could not adequately justify rejecting the request. And that was because Gillian was such a nice person, sincere and well-intentioned – and she had called Simmy a 'dear girl'.

Chapter Sixteen

The sun was close to setting as she drove down to Bowness, and when she turned east towards Crook, the dazzling reflection in her mirrors made her realise how blinded drivers might be as they came towards her. Had it been like that last Friday? Had Declan been heading west on his bike, the sun in his eyes? Was that a probable piece of evidence that the whole thing had been an accident? He might have ridden straight into an oncoming car, or at least failed to avoid it, to the driver's horror. She resolved to mention this to Ben, and maybe even Moxon.

Much to her surprise, flashes of unconscious observations from the previous week came back to her. The solitary church tower a field or two away to the right had attracted fleeting notice then, and did again now. She would have to ask somebody what it was. The road leading to Staveley went off to the left – another detail she'd forgotten, having automatically followed the sign the first time she'd driven that way. The pub and the small cluster of houses that marked the centre of the village preceded the turning by a short distance. And much of that distance, on the right-hand side, was now decorated with a strand of blue police tape and a modest accumulation of floral tributes, blessedly minus their usual cellophane. 'Hmm,' Simmy muttered. 'Nobody came to me for any of those.' She had slowed to a crawl, scanning the length of stone wall and grass verge, wondering how it could have been possible to miss seeing a mangled bike and its rider lying there. The ground was bumpy, and there was a shallow ditch, but in early March there was hardly any long grass. There was, however, a small tree of some sort, with branches low down. Blackthorn, Simmy decided. And all the trampling that had taken place all week might well have reduced tussocks and ridges to the relative bareness that was there now.

At the junction, where she had to turn left, she stopped just after making the turn, pulling the car as far off the road as she could, but still leaving scant room for anyone to pass. The putative rush hour was not at all evident yet. She had not met a single vehicle since leaving Bowness. Quickly she jumped out and walked back. Without knowing what she was doing, she examined the site of Declan Kennedy's death, and tried to think.

Nobody had told her which way the cyclist had been facing, but she had assumed he was going towards Bowness. That fitted with him being on the southern side of the road. And now she was close enough for a proper look, she could see that there was in fact more of a ditch than she thought. And more dead, straggly grass with plenty of long stalks to provide a screen. Had he been somersaulted over the car, to land brokenly up against the stone wall? Had he been wearing a helmet? From what she had gathered of his character, she supposed not. Although nothing she'd heard fitted with him riding a bike at all. He hadn't sounded sporty or environmentally conscientious. Perhaps it was a borrowed bicycle, and he was unused to riding it, wobbling and dazzled and doomed. So many unknown factors made her quest thoroughly frustrating.

Gillian had asked her to try and remember whether she saw anything. Well, she remembered the isolated tower, and the way the fields rose gently on both sides of the road. The stone walls and the pub standing proudly at the centre of the small village. She did not remember anything at all about the sides of the road, or any hint of a collision. No stray shards of metal, no blood, no residual ghostly shimmerings on the air. She could see no other conclusion than that she had passed before the incident took place. In fact, that now seemed almost certain, the more she thought about it.

She went back to the car, just in time to move it for a large Land Rover to squeeze past. The driver gave her a friendly wave, in response to her grimace of apology. Fifteen seconds later, she met two more cars, and then a blue van. 'And so the rush hour begins,' she murmured to herself. A glance at her car's clock told her it was five thirty-five. People hurrying home from Kendal, of course. Soon there would be more, from points further south. Although a moment's thought provided a geographical correction. The road to Kendal ran eastwards, while she was now heading due north to Staveley. They wouldn't use this road. These commuters had probably come from Staveley, then – there was some industrial activity there, after all. But which way had Declan's killer been heading? To or from Bowness? Was it even possible to work that out?

The road crossed the main A591 and took her into the heart of Staveley, emerging alongside the bus stop where she had first met Gillian and Anita. How had such an innocent rendezvous turned into such a confused and frustrating business? She remembered the two women, one so much taller than the other, smiling at her as she arrived. Even Anita had smiled – something she had scarcely done during subsequent encounters.

The fish and chip shop was open, a small group of people standing outside. On a whim, she considered buying three dinners, to take to Beck View. She couldn't remember the last time she'd had the real thing, relishing the thought of crisp batter and succulent cod. The road home meant turning left, but the best parking for the chip shop was the other way. Impressed by her own decisiveness, she turned right, and stopped just around the bend from the bus stop. It was a wide space, most likely the village square at some point, its shape ordained by the little river that ran right through the settlement.

She joined the queue, rooting for money in her shoulder bag, and imagining her father's delight at her unexpected contribution. Nobody liked cod and chips more than Russell Straw did. He used ketchup like a child, abjuring vinegar as a travesty and a crime against the taste buds. 'Most people think that about ketchup,' Angie would say.

'Nonsense,' argued her husband. 'By far the greater part

of the population regard it as an absolute necessity. You, my dear, are too much in your ivory tower to know.'

Then the woman at the front of the queue turned to leave, and Simmy saw a familiar face. Familiar, but not readily identifiable. Their eyes met, each with a sudden hesitation. 'Hello,' said the woman warily. 'Haven't I seen you somewhere recently?'

'I've got the flower shop in Windermere. I expect it was there.'

'Of course! You brought me that lovely bouquet last Friday. In Crook. Remember?'

'Oh, yes.' She *did* remember the whole episode very clearly, and yet it had been entirely overshadowed by her efforts to satisfy Gillian Townsend. Of course, she had driven up the little road towards the golf course, found the cottage, delivered the flowers, and left again without a backward glance. The road had been to the right, on the same side as the abandoned church tower, before the pub and the turning to Staveley.

'You know – I was worried, afterwards, that you might have got involved with that horrible accident, where the man was knocked off his bike. They closed the road for *ages*, right through the night and into Saturday morning.'

'Did they? I think I must have just missed all that, then.'

'I think you did. It was later in the evening, after it was dark.'

'That was when they found him,' Simmy realised. 'Not when he was hit. Nobody seems to know what time that happened.'

The woman, who was about sixty, full of goodwill and community spirit, widened her eyes. 'That's the thing, isn't it? That's what makes it such a mystery. I mean – you've got to think it was done by accident, but then how could anybody just drive off and leave him? You can't really blame that silly Kennedy girl and her brother for kicking up such a fuss and saying it was deliberate murder.'

'You know them, do you?'

'Oh, no, not really. Just by sight. My sister lives in the next road.' She waved a hand towards the main residential part of Staveley, three minutes' walk away. 'I shouldn't call her silly, I know. Poor thing, with those nice little girls. It's most likely the brother more than her, anyway, making so much unpleasantness. I mean – aren't things bad enough already, without that?'

Simmy thought of a question that she should have asked days ago. 'Where does her brother live?' She was aware that the people in the queue were only inches away, virtually part of the conversation. One young woman with her back to them had murmured something to herself, apparently in comment.

'Not sure, actually.'

The young woman turned round. 'Matthew Olsen lives in Troutbeck,' she said.

'Really? So do I,' said Simmy, wondering whether she knew him from the village shop or pub, or as a regular morning commuter past her house. She knew the faces of a dozen men of varying ages and schedules.

'You're the florist, then,' said the interloper. 'from Windermere.'

Simmy smiled in acknowledgement, fighting the flush of anxious shame that arose from being caught gossiping about a sudden violent death in this community where everybody knew each other. She and the woman from Crook had been indiscreet, she realised.

But then the queue moved forward, and Simmy had to assemble her thoughts. Angie preferred haddock to cod, more for reasons of conservation than taste. Russell teased her about it every time. The first woman became concerned for her cooling dinner, and with barely another word trotted away to her car. The young one was giving her order to the man behind the counter. There were two men behind Simmy, wearing work clothes with splashes of plaster or cement all over them. One spoke to the other in what Simmy thought was Polish.

The fish and chips were well received, all the more so for Angie's complete failure to prepare an evening meal. 'You did say I was to leave it to you, didn't you?' she asked her daughter, with unusual vagueness. 'But when you weren't here by six, I began to wonder.'

'It's only quarter past. How's Dad?'

'He's a bit droopy today. Slept in late, and then spent most of the day on the sofa with a book.'

Simmy resolved not to worry until compelled to. 'Well, that's not so surprising, is it, after everything that's happened.'

Angie shrugged. 'He was full of beans yesterday, as if it was all a lot of nonsense. I'll never forgive him for breaking all that china.'

'I expect you will eventually. When does he have to go for a check-up? They'll want to keep an eye on him, won't they?'

'You'd think so, wouldn't you? In the olden days, there'd have been a doctor or at least a district nurse calling in every day. Now you have to fight for an appointment, and when you get one, they act as if they're doing you an enormous favour.'

'He's got pills to take, hasn't he? Maybe they've made him sleepy.'

'Very likely. Lord knows what's in them.'

Russell came into the kitchen willingly enough when told there was cod and chips waiting for him. They sat round the pine table, the Lakeland terrier at his master's feet. 'The poor dog's been neglected,' said Angie. 'He hasn't had a walk for days.'

Simmy resisted the implication that she should add dog-walking to the list of tasks she was taking on. It was already dawning on her that the help she currently provided might become permanent. It might even escalate, until she was spending every evening at Beck View and probably much of every Sunday. Would Christopher go with her, if so, she wondered. He had always got on well with Russell and Angie, but Simmy was wary of encouraging any thoughts that she and Chris were getting serious as a couple. She needed just a few more weeks before she'd be ready for that.

Throughout the hours spent that evening with her parents, she was mentally rehearsing her findings in Crook and Staveley. Not that they amounted to very much, but amongst the various snippets there could perhaps be something that would help Gillian and Anita. There had been no plan to meet again, mainly because Simmy had given no clear undertaking to do as Gillian asked. That left her free to duck the whole business, she supposed, if that was what she wanted. First, she needed some quiet moments in which to note down everything she'd seen and heard. Ben Harkness had taught her the value of recording even the most obvious facts, building up a picture and spotting connections.

And then what? If she did leap to a conclusion, as she suspected she might, what should she do with it? Go straight to Moxon, trusting him to act in the interests of truth and justice, or confine herself to the Kendal solicitors who might distort or embellish to suit their own ends? There ought not to be any dilemma at all, put like that. And yet, Gillian's evident fears that Anita would be scapegoated, thanks to local politics and family animosities, weighed heavily on her. The sense that the young detectives were withholding substantial amounts of information from her was perversely provocative. Never particularly competitive, she suddenly found herself wanting to show them she could play the game as well as they could. There was a generational element, too, with them taking the part of the son and daughter, while Simmy favoured the mother. And if plain and simple justice was the issue, then it was starkly apparent that Anita could not have killed her son-in-law. She would have had to be in two places at once, in two different vehicles, and in two different frames of mind. Nobody could wantonly slaughter a cyclist, then rapidly materialise in Staveley looking perfectly calm and unruffled.

Unless, perhaps, she had been actively aided and abetted by her friend and colleague Gillian Townsend. And that, to Simmy's mind, made the whole theory even more ludicrous.

Nobody could be more wholesome and law-abiding than Gillian. Despite her regular lapses in judgement, Simmy was thoroughly persuaded that she was right this time. If Gillian Townsend was party to a cruel and premeditated murder, then she, Simmy, would eat every tulip and gerbera in the shop.

Chapter Seventeen

She stayed at Beck View until almost nine, chatting rather absently to her father, while washing down the kitchen surfaces and eyeing her mother with some concern. Angie was looking a decade older than she had at the start of the year. 'How many bookings have you got for the coming month?' Simmy asked.

'Oh, I don't know. Three or four lots of people a week, as usual, I suppose. There'll be some spur-of-the-moment ones as well. There's a couple the week after next bringing two dogs. That'll make extra cleaning.'

Simmy had been surprised to learn that people almost always let their dogs sleep on the beds. 'That's awful,' she said, when first hearing of it. 'Can't you stop them?'

Angie had laughed. 'Tell me how, and I might. We all pretend they'll be on a blanket on the floor, but that never happens, unless the animal's really huge. And actually it's just as easy to get mud and hair off a duvet cover as it is off the carpet, when you think about it.'

Simmy had never thought about it at all. 'Where do they eat?' she'd wondered.

'Mostly in the en suites, where they can wipe up any spilth.' *Spilth* was a word coined by Russell, or so they believed. How the language had managed without it, they couldn't imagine. Simmy's father used it as often as he could, in the hope of sending it out into the world for the benefit of mankind.

The Lake District was famous for its dog-friendliness, with shops and even some restaurants allowing them in. It had become a selling point, and Angie had no plans to limit access to canine holidaymakers. She rejected Simmy's suggestion that she should charge extra for them, too. 'They really don't involve any extra work,' she insisted.

'So the two dogs will sleep on the beds, will they?' she asked now.

'Probably,' shrugged Angie.

Back in Troutbeck she phoned Christopher, with a sense of having short-changed him all week. She had told him little or nothing about the death of Declan Kennedy, unsure of his reaction. Whilst auctioneering had a famously seamy image, floristry did not, and she was reluctant to spoil the illusion any further than she had already. There was a lurking shameful shadow associated with the way a simple delivery of flowers could pull her into murky human depths. Somewhere, she felt it must be her own fault; she was doing something wrong, or failing to watch her step.

But not telling him carried its own problems. With Ben sceptical about Anita Olsen's innocence, as well as being desperately busy, there was really nobody with whom to share her thoughts on the subject. Bonnie was in the other camp, Russell wasn't well enough and Moxon would very likely tell her she was overstepping a mark.

'I wish you could bring your dad to next weekend's sale,' Christopher said wistfully. 'It's going to be a bigger one than usual.'

'I wish I could, as well. But there's no way. I'm clearing the decks for Mother's Day, making lots of lists, and trying to get someone in to help. Besides, Dad's not really up to it yet.' She told him about the broken china, and how upset her mother was. 'She hides it, but I know she loved all those silly teapots and jugs.'

'She should come to the sale as well, and get some new ones. We've kept some really good pieces back, so we can call it a Spring Special. Focusing very much on china and glass. There's a few big collectors coming along, as well as a lot of online bidding.'

'I thought china was out of fashion.'

'It is and it isn't,' he said, rather to her irritation. 'I personally know of three different B&B ladies who go mad for bits of Beswick, and two more who'll snap up any Moorcroft they can find. Your mother might have some stiff competition, come to think of it.'

'Well, she can't go, either, so the matter doesn't arise. It's good to know she's a more typical B&B lady than she realises.'

'She is. The world's full of crazy collectors. She's just one more of them.'

Simmy laughed. 'She's not my idea of a collector at all. I imagined American men in panama hats, with pockets full of cash.'

'We almost never get anyone like that.' She could hear his mind spinning. 'Where did that image come from?'

'No idea. Maybe I'm thinking of butterfly collectors.'

'We do get them now and then, but they don't wear panama hats either.'

It was no good – the banter was far too inconsequential for her mood. Life was real and earnest, and instead of providing respite and solace, Christopher was simply diverting her from the serious stuff. 'I can't take another Saturday off for ages,' she said. 'It's the busiest day in the shop, during the summer. I don't know how we can work round that. The roads are going to be cluttered with tourists, as well.' Frustration blossomed as she spoke. 'It's going to be impossible,' she wailed.

'No it isn't. Where did this come from? For a start, I'm serious about a holiday, and we don't have to wait till June. I think we could get away for a long weekend at the end of April, both of us, if we really wanted to. It's unhealthy and foolish to go all year without a break. We need to stop being such workaholics – both of us. It's not healthy.'

The idea had barely penetrated Simmy's consciousness, despite his repeated references to it. Her parents hadn't been on a holiday for years, and now she was running her own business, she had simply assumed that it wasn't going to be an option. An occasional full weekend off was luxury enough.

'So we can have *two* holidays?'

'Well, one and a bit, anyway. I was thinking of something more modest next month. Maybe three days as a city-break somewhere. I gather Brussels is very underrated, and there's loads to see and do there. Plus a whole lot of chocolate.'

'Blimey!'

'Greedy, aren't I? But it would solve our logistical problems, and really test how things go between us. You don't know a person properly until you've travelled with them.'

'Mm,' she said, thinking of remarks she'd heard from women friends to the effect that it was often a mistake to try to travel with your man. 'It brings out the worst in them,' one friend had said. But Christopher had spent much of his adult life exploring the world, and was an expert traveller. 'I think you might find me a bit of a wimp. I'm not great with exotic food, and I can't speak any foreign languages.'

'We'll avoid Venezuela and Burkina Faso, then,' he said easily. 'I have to say I was underwhelmed by them both.'

'It would be lovely to have proper time together. I don't know why I'm being so lukewarm about it. Just that I feel a bit bogged down at the moment. It won't last.'

'No problem. But I am going to book it. Them. Both of them. Brussels at the end of April and Lanzarote at the beginning of June. Clear your diary, woman, and come away with me.'

'Yes, sir. And thank you. It's nice to have someone else make the decisions for a change.' At the back of her mind she could hear her mother expressing horror, not to mention her former assistant Melanie and Bonnie. Regardless of what they might think, it was true. She trusted Christopher to choose the right places to stay, the right mixture of sun and sea and food. 'I insist on paying my share, though,' she added.

'I wouldn't expect anything else,' he said, hitting the exact right note.

She sighed. 'I don't deserve you,' she told him.

* * *

It had been a busy day. Even in ordinary times, the approach of the weekend called for additional focus and preparation. While Saturday was the traditional changeover day for holidaymakers, implying that nobody would have time for shopping, it had become apparent that a large number of them felt the need for flowers to take home with them as gifts or souvenirs. The dog-sitter, abandoned old parent, or just the empty house waiting for them – all seemed to need a floral tribute.

Remembering the imperious text of the morning, she sat holding her phone after finishing the chat with Christopher. Everything in connection with Gillian was unfinished, the loose ends unavoidable. With a surge of energy, she decided to take the initiative, keying a message.

Went to Crook as requested. Have a few thoughts to share. When can we meet?

Stilted but good enough, she judged as she sent it. It was a week since her first meeting with Gillian and Anita; a week since Declan had died. The police must be growing agitated at the passage of time and the failure to resolve the investigation. Was Moxon sorry not to have greater involvement from young Ben Harkness, she wondered. Probably not, since there had certainly been times when Ben was more part of the problem than the solution.

No response had come to her text by the time she got to the shop next morning. Bonnie followed her in, two minutes later, and they both went to the computer to check for new orders. 'Four!' said Bonnie. 'That's good, isn't it.'

Before Simmy could answer, a customer came in, with an unmistakable air of belligerence. She carried a bunch of flowers. 'Uh-oh,' murmured Bonnie.

'These flowers were sold to me under false pretences,' the woman accused. 'Look at them. They're dead already.'

'When did you buy them?' Simmy asked.

'Only just over a week ago. I expected them to last *far* longer than that.' She brandished the blooms, which were unarguably at death's door.

Simmy glanced at Bonnie abstractedly, and went back to the irate woman standing six inches away from her. 'You're being unreasonable,' she said coldly. 'The flowers were quite fresh when you bought them, and you're telling me they were perfectly all right for nearly a week. What did you expect?'

'They were *not* perfectly all right. They were brown at the edges within five days. The buds fell off without opening. Everything drooped.'

Bonnie stepped forward. 'Did you keep the water topped up?' she asked.

The woman whirled round. She was short, dark and angry. 'Who are you?' she demanded.

'I work here. I remember when you bought the flowers. You had no idea what any of them were, and didn't listen when we tried to tell you how to look after them. I'm guessing you gave them an inch or two of water, in a hot room, and it was all gone in a couple of days. Isn't that right?'

The woman hesitated, avoiding the eyes of both Bonnie and Simmy. 'I gave them water,' she muttered.

'Well, I have no intention of refunding you,' said Simmy.

'There are limits to what I can be expected to do to ensure the flowers stay at their best. It's not my responsibility once you leave here with them.'

'Oh, yes it is. What about the Trade Descriptions Act?'

'What about it?'

'I bought them in good faith. You told me they would last two weeks.'

'Up to two weeks,' said Bonnie. 'That's what we always say. Some people can keep them nice for quite a lot longer than that, with a bit of common sense.' She tensed, waiting for a reproach from her employer, but none came. Instead, there seemed to be a beam of approval coming her way.

At last the woman went away, assuring them she would never cross their threshold again.

'Good riddance,' said Simmy. 'What a stupid person.'

'You were brilliant,' said Bonnie. 'You never said sorry even once.'

'I didn't see why I should.'

'Good.'

Simmy smiled ruefully. 'Not a great start to the day, all the same.'

'Come on, Sim – that wasn't the start. We've got all these new orders, look. That must be good – right? I mean – this is what we're here for. You'd starve if nobody wanted any flowers, wouldn't you?'

'Eventually, I suppose. Though I could always stack shelves at Sainsbury's.'

'No, no. You could work for Christopher. I bet that's a brilliant job.'

'Make up your mind.' She sounded tetchy even in her

own ears. 'To hear you talk, you want me to close down and move to Keswick.'

'I don't.' The voice was that of a child of five, guaranteed to elicit shame.

'Sorry. I'm in a mood today. I went to Crook last night, to look at the place where the Kennedy man was killed.'

Bonnie instantly reflated. 'Did you? Wow! I thought you weren't going to have any more to do with it. Did you find anything?'

'Not really. Are you and Ben seeing Debbie again? Should I be careful what I tell you? I still don't exactly understand what's going on in that department.'

'It's all got horribly stuck,' Bonnie admitted. 'Without any evidence, Debbie's got no hope of getting her mother convicted. The police were really good to start with, listening to her accusations and taking them seriously, but now I think they're changing their minds about it. They keep coming back to the car that hit him. They need to find it before they can get anywhere.'

'It's probably been crushed by now, don't you think?'

'Quite likely. Ben says this might be the one that got away.'

'What does that mean?'

'Escaped justice. Got away with murder.' Bonnie spoke slowly, as if to an aged and demented relative. Simmy could hear the silent *What do you think it means?* that Bonnie was too polite to utter.

'That wouldn't please DI Moxon.' The thought of the detective's frustration was upsetting. 'They must hate it when that happens.'

'It'll stay as an open case for ages. More or less for ever, actually. Cold cases, they call them.'

'Yes, I know,' said Simmy, meekly accepting the role of dim-witted old person. 'But people in Crook might yet come up with something. They seem to be pretty taken up with it all. They probably can't understand how nobody saw or heard anything that would precisely pinpoint the time it happened, and the sort of car it was. I mean, obviously other cars must have passed it at some point – why didn't they notice blood or dents on it? They must be feeling they've failed.'

Bonnie cocked her head. 'You've been talking to people, haven't you?'

'One or two. Nothing came of it that could be useful.' Reviewing recent conversations, she found herself unconvinced that this was true. Somewhere there must surely be some helpful detail, some snippet of evidence that could prove Anita's innocence. 'Except, it seems definite that it couldn't possibly have been Anita,' she finished. 'She'd have had to have been in two places at once.'

Bonnie grinned. 'That's what Ben loves about it. It's a great puzzle. But he needs a few more pieces – just like Poirot would say. And he'd be sure to think you'd got them, if he could hear you now.'

'You think it's down to me to provide evidence that would convict Anita Olsen? That's not going to happen, when I'm absolutely sure she didn't do it.'

'It's wonderfully complicated, isn't it?' said the girl happily.

'You could say that,' sighed Simmy.

Customers, orders, deliveries to Bowness and Troutbeck, new stock arriving – all kept them occupied for the morning. Simmy forgot all about her text to Gillian, and Bonnie was comprehensively diverted by the appearance of one of her former foster siblings with their new mother. 'Hey, Crystal!' she enthused. 'Remember me?'

The child, aged about six, looked at her doubtfully. 'Yes, you do. Of course you do,' Bonnie persisted. 'At Corinne's. I used to put you to bed, and sing to you.' She burst into a rendition of 'Unchained Melody' that was startlingly tuneful. 'Remember that?' she said when she'd finished. Everyone in the shop was staring at her.

The child looked dazed, and Simmy suddenly wondered how sensible it was to remind her of earlier times. She tried to catch the eye of the woman with her, but she was fixated on Bonnie. 'That was fantastic,' she said.

'Have you adopted her?' Bonnie asked.

'In the process. Her foster mother did a good job. It's really going to work out, isn't it, sweetheart?' She addressed the little girl, who nodded compliantly.

Simmy was impressed by the courage that must surely be required to take on a child with years of confusion and damage behind her. Only good people would do it, she concluded. Good, brave people – who were perhaps also desperate to experience parenthood. 'Have you got any others?' she asked.

'Two boys, in their teens. We adopted them as well.'

Simmy could think of nothing to say, other than to express her own feelings of inadequacy, which would not be fair or appropriate. Her own timid world of tiny families and high levels of apprehension was far removed from this blithe woman's – which was also the one inhabited by Bonnie Lawson.

The woman was buying flowers for a social worker who had performed various miracles, apparently. Bonnie knew her, and approved the tribute. Nobody was quite sure whether Crystal actually remembered her much older foster sister, but the song had been lovely.

'You're a very good singer,' Simmy said. 'That song's a funny choice, though.'

'Corinne loves it. She's got a CD with about twelve different people singing it. She used to play it all the time. She does it at her gigs.'

Bonnie was one of two remaining foster children at Corinne's. The hitherto inexhaustible mother figure had gradually retired over the past year or two, but Bonnie as the eldest and little Sebastian as an emergency case were still part of the household. The looseness of the arrangement reminded Simmy strongly of the way her own mother forced the world and its institutions to conform to her own value system. Angie demonstrated an assertiveness that Simmy herself found impossible to apply to her own life.

'It's over a week since I got that call from Gillian,' Simmy mused, after lunch. 'Seems ages ago. Not much has happened, really.'

'More than we think. Moxon's not giving anything away with this one. We don't know what he really thinks about the Olsen woman.'

'Or the Kennedy one,' Simmy flashed back. 'It boils down to a really sordid vendetta between mother and daughter. I imagine he finds it all pretty unpleasant. Especially when the likelihood is that Declan was killed by a speeding tourist and it was nothing to do with Anita.'

Bonnie shook her head. 'You know it wasn't that, don't

you? Nobody thinks that any more. It was deliberate and cruel and clever. All planned in advance. In the olden days, the killer would definitely have been hanged.'

Simmy shuddered. 'At least we don't have to worry about that.' An image of the tall dignified figure of Anita Olsen dangling from a rope made her feel sick.

'It certainly made the stakes very high. So many innocent people wrongly convicted and executed. Ben says it might have been as many as ten per cent of all those who were hanged, over a period of a hundred years. Can you *imagine* it?'

'I'm trying not to.'

Bonnie was showing signs of an unwholesome relish. 'Knowing you hadn't done anything, as they put that black bag over your head, thinking it couldn't possibly be really happening. The state killing you for no reason, in cold blood, nobody taking any responsibility for it. It has to be the worst thing that can happen to a person.'

'Weren't most of them at least guilty of *something*, though? They would never have been arrested if they were totally innocent.'

'Oh, Simmy,' Bonnie reproached her. 'That won't do, and you know it. Thinking like that might make the authorities feel better, but it's no excuse. The law has a penalty for a particular crime, and if you didn't commit the crime, you shouldn't suffer the penalty. Simple.'

Simmy could – as so often – hear the voice of Ben behind the girl's words. Ben always managed to make complicated moral issues sound simple. 'I suppose that's right,' she said doubtfully. 'But you can understand the police and lawyers and people needing something to console them, if they discovered they'd hanged the wrong person.'

'They don't deserve to be consoled,' said Bonnie fiercely.

'I don't expect they did it deliberately. It would have been a forgivable mistake.'

'Not the way I see it.'

'All of which brings us back to being thankful it's not like that any more. And I really can't see them convicting a retired professional woman with a spotless record, just because her daughter doesn't like her.'

'It wouldn't be because of that, though, would it? It would be because she drove over a man on his bike – *twice*, and then told a whole lot of lies about it.'

Simmy felt herself go pale. 'Is that really what happened? Somebody drove over him twice? Moxon said there was evidence that the whole thing was deliberate, but he didn't give me any details. How do you know? Who else knows?'

'I know because Debbie told me and Ben. Just about everybody knows – Matthew, and Debbie's children, and the whole of Cumbria by now.'

'How come?' Simmy was bemused.

'Because it's on Facebook and all the rest of it,' said Bonnie with a scornful sort of patience. 'How do you think?'

It became clear that the main source of the Facebook disclosures was Matthew Olsen. Bonnie showed it to Simmy, who was shocked by the detail and the incontinent language. Stark accusations of murder were made against his mother. 'I can't believe it's legal to do that,' said Simmy faintly. 'It's got to be libel. Or slander. Whichever it is.'

'Libel, because it's in writing,' said Bonnie. 'And Ben

thinks it might well be actionable. But Anita would have to take the action, and that doesn't look very likely to happen.'

'She's waiting until they find who really killed Declan. Then Matthew's going to be in serious trouble. Has Gillian seen this, I wonder?'

'Somebody's bound to have shown it to her.'

'Then she ought to tell Matthew he's in for a lot of legal stuff before very long. She's sure to press charges sooner or later, on Anita's behalf. Poor woman,' she groaned. 'I can just imagine her face.'

'Which woman?'

'Gillian. She's such a softie, and she's taking all this to heart. I think she must have lived quite a sheltered life, dealing with minor matters of law, and never quite letting herself see the worst in people.'

Bonnie blew out her cheeks. 'Come off it. Neighbours' disputes about leylandii. Making threats against other people's kids and dogs. Petty theft. Acrimonious divorces. Fights over inheritance. I mean – those are the softer end of the job, and they're all pretty horrible. She's got to have realised how awful people can be, by this time.'

'I don't know.' Simmy was wracking her brains for pleasant aspects of legal work. Conveyancing, perhaps? But no, people behaved abominably when selling and buying a house. She had to admit that there was nothing philanthropic or warm about the law and its implementation. 'I suppose you're right,' she conceded.

'So she might be soft on Anita, upset on her behalf, like you said. But we shouldn't assume she's always like that.'

'I like to think that knowing the law and making sure it's properly applied can involve at least some decency,' said

Simmy, hearing herself sounding pompous. 'Her clients probably trust her and like her, and make friends with her some of the time.'

'Yeah. So what if they do? What does that have to do with anything?'

Simmy couldn't explain, but she clung to the notion of Gillian's essential integrity as central to the whole business. 'Anyway, I'm seeing her again,' she said. Then three things happened at once.

Chapter Eighteen

Simmy's phone announced the arrival of a text message, at the same instant as DI Moxon came into the shop. Ten seconds later, a customer followed him. Simmy didn't know which way to turn, flapping at Bonnie to deal with the customer, clutching the phone in her pocket and smiling vaguely at the detective.

'Are you busy?' he said.

'Not really.'

'I won't take a moment. I just wanted to confirm that the Worcester people are quite happy with what we sent them, and they see no reason why you should be involved any further. They seem to think it might all be settled out of court, anyway.'

'Really? How could that be?'

'If the woman pleads guilty, and drops her counter-accusation against your . . . against Mr Brown, then it can be quickly dealt with. She'll be sentenced at a hearing, and that'll be the end of it.'

'Poor woman,' sighed Simmy, for the second time that morning. 'I hope they'll be lenient with her.'

'I imagine they will, especially if she has a competent legal representative. It's a sad story for all concerned.'

She was still fingering her phone, wondering about the unread text. It had to be from Gillian, and should therefore be concealed from Moxon. That made her feel ashamed of herself. But how could she tell him – what would she say? There was nothing concrete to disclose, and it seemed unfair to burden him with half-baked impressions. She forced herself to focus on the Worcester story instead. 'It seems wrong, in a way, though. I mean – there really *should* be a proper trial, with everything aired openly. Don't you think?'

He smiled. 'Perhaps in an ideal world. But trials are expensive, and very time-consuming. I'm not sure it would be in anybody's interest in the long run. Whatever lessons there are to be learnt have probably gone home by now. I seriously doubt whether he'll do any more stalking, and she's not going to stab anybody ever again. You have to weigh it all up in a balance, and look at the greatest good.'

Simmy looked at him, eye to eye. This was a good man, with a good brain and a good heart. Like Gillian Townsend, in fact. They both saw dreadful things done by malicious and stupid people, and somehow remained decent in themselves. 'That's reassuring,' she said with a smile.

Another customer added pressure, which Moxon was quick to understand. Bonnie was standing by the till with a worried frown. Her customer was tapping an impatient finger on the table.

'I should go,' said the detective. 'Bad timing, I can see.

But I need to have another word with you at some point. About the other thing.'

'Oh dear. I was hoping you weren't going to say that. Are you sure it's necessary?'

'Necessary, but not terribly urgent. A side issue. A loose end.'

To Simmy's ears that sounded like an announcement to the effect that the case was just about resolved, the killer identified, justice achieved. 'Loose end?' she repeated.

'Well, no, not quite. But there has been progress. By the end of today we're hoping we might be able to go public.'

'A bit late for that, when it's already all over Facebook, and presumably other places like that.'

His eyes widened and his cheeks flushed. 'You've seen that, have you?'

She nodded.

'It's outrageous.' He came close to spluttering. 'There'll be severe repercussions, I can promise you that.'

'Good,' said Simmy. 'I should hope so too.'

And then she had to rescue Bonnie, attend to the second customer, and generally get back to business. Moxon left without a farewell smile.

The text was from Gillian, but did not read as expected.

Thanks for message. Terribly busy. Will get back to you very soon.

Once again, Simmy felt that her efforts had been misplaced. Having swallowed her reservations, and gone out of her way to fulfil the woman's wishes, she was being pushed aside before things became really interesting. She had allowed herself to take the part of Anita against her daughter and son, keeping things back from Bonnie and Ben – and all for what? All because she believed in Gillian and her passionate defence of her friend. And that, she admitted to herself, was not nothing. Nobody else appeared to be supporting the accused woman, so Simmy had stepped into the breach. She took a steadying breath, quelling her unworthy feelings. Gillian would almost certainly be busy with the case in hand, tracking down evidence that would exonerate Anita. That was good, and if there was no need for Simmy's input then she ought to be glad.

A third customer put in an appearance, and Bonnie was wilting. 'Is everything okay?' Simmy asked her.

'Not really. I can't see a price for this.' She brandished a tired-looking succulent that had been on display for weeks in a corner of the shop. The woman trying to buy it was clearly losing her last scrap of patience.

'Oh dear. That's all my fault,' gushed Simmy. 'You can have it for three pounds. Is that all right?'

'Why? What's wrong with it?' the woman demanded suspiciously.

'Nothing. But it's going to need repotting, and it's the last of the line. I'm sure it'll serve you well for ages.'

The money was handed over, and Bonnie rolled her eyes.

The next in line wanted a spray of lilies, highly scented, still in bud, with three pink roses and plenty of foliage, to be constructed immediately. Simmy hurried into the back room to comply, hoping Bonnie could handle the latest arrival, who was elderly and shabby and sweet-faced.

When the bell above the shop door rang yet again, Simmy had just finished the spray and taken a generous payment for it. When she looked up, she met the gaze of a short woman she had not expected to see. 'Oh!' she yelped. 'Hello. I thought you were too busy to talk to me.'

Bonnie was still debating with the nice old lady who was dithering between a geranium in a pot and a bunch of deep-red tulips. She looked up at Simmy's tone of surprise, but obviously didn't immediately recognise Gillian Townsend. It was turning into a very complicated morning, and Simmy was once again torn between conflicting demands. Gillian would probably want to go somewhere private, which was really not feasible without Bonnie's agreement, and she would be feeling an intense curiosity guaranteed to keep her within earshot.

'It's happening just as I said it might yesterday. I need you to come with me,' said Gillian urgently. 'I've just this minute been told something that's going to get this whole business settled once and for all. But I can't do it by myself.'

'But—' Simmy stuttered. 'You mean *now*? I can't just drop everything in the middle of a busy Saturday.'

'Yes you can,' said Bonnie. 'I can hold the fort for a bit. Hello, Mrs Townsend. It took me a minute to recognise you.'

Gillian smiled briefly, but kept her focus on Simmy. 'Please,' she said. 'I did warn you. I'm depending on you. I've got to have a neutral observer, if this is to stand any chance of working. And really you're the ideal person for that. I promise we won't be more than an hour. Probably quite a bit less than that. We won't be going very far.'

'Go on, Sim,' said Bonnie, making shooing motions. 'You can't refuse. You know you can't. Ben would never forgive you.'

She couldn't pretend to be surprised after the conversation at The Elleray, and yet the reality of the request was a shock. Had she assumed everything would just settle down without any intervention from her? Even after her observations of the previous evening she still experienced the whole case as largely theoretical. But now her own moral character pushed her into agreeing to Gillian's urging. At some point on the road through Crook she had become committed to the investigation into how Declan Kennedy had died. She did not understand her reasons, nor how she could possibly provide any constructive assistance – but she still accepted that she was involved. 'All right,' she said. 'Give me a minute to make sure Bonnie knows what she's got to do.'

Gillian drove them down to Bowness, taking the left turn towards Crook, as Simmy had assumed they would. Her brain might be working a lot more slowly than Ben's or Bonnie's would have done, but she was getting there in her own time. 'I came along here last night,' she said. 'Trying to remember exactly what I saw last week. It upsets me to think I might have driven right past Declan and his bike without seeing them. It doesn't seem possible. I think it's more likely it happened after I was here. That's what the woman in the chip shop seemed to think.'

'Who?'

'She lives up there,' Simmy pointed to the right. 'She's the one I delivered flowers to before meeting you and Anita.'

'We still can't be sure what time it happened. If not you, then other people must have driven blindly past him. He could have been there for as much as two hours before anybody noticed. Of course, it was getting dark and everybody's always in a hurry.'

'Are we going to see the Roger man? The one he was staying with?'

'What? Oh – no. He lives a lot further on, where this road comes out onto the 591, shortly before Kendal. There's no reason at all to talk to Roger.'

'So where are we going?'

'Not far now. There's a track on the left, leading up to a farm. I know the people there. I helped them a while ago when their father died. Some family unpleasantness, which we soon sorted out.'

Simmy refrained from enquiring just how these people fitted into the picture, trusting that all would eventually become clear.

'Listen,' said Gillian, speaking rather more loudly than necessary. 'What I want from you is to watch very closely everything that's going to happen from here on. Don't ask questions or make comments. You're here purely as a confirmatory witness. I did wonder whether we should get it all on camera as well, but I don't think that's essential. And funnily enough, you tend to miss a lot if you're concentrating on filming. I want you to be able to give a full and totally truthful account of what's going to happen.'

'Including what you're saying to me now?'

'If asked, yes.'

It felt alarmingly staged, as well as uncomfortably exploitative. People didn't drag other people into their unilateral semi-legal investigations without raising anxiety. 'What if it gets violent?' she said.

'It won't. No chance whatsoever of that. We're just

going to look at something. Nothing more scary than that.'

The track to the farm was stony, rutted and steep. Gillian's car was robust and sufficiently high off the ground to survive the protruding rocks that occurred at random. 'My little car would hate this,' Simmy said with a nervous laugh.

'I imagine they get plenty of aggravation from the post man and other delivery people. Not that they're likely to get a lot of post. I can't see Jonah or Dorcas buying anything on Amazon.'

'Jonah and Dorcas? Are they Methodists?'

'They are, as it happens. Their other siblings are called Aaron, Martha and Luke.'

'I like Dorcas,' mused Simmy.

'She's like a person from another age,' said Gillian, before realising her misunderstanding. 'Oh – you mean the name, not the person. I don't suppose you've ever met her. She doesn't go out very much.'

The farmyard was dirty and very untidy. A ewe with two bedraggled lambs stood miserably against a barn wall. Two black and white dogs came hurtling towards them barking wildly. Even from a distance, Simmy could see their coats were matted and lumpy. Various farm implements had been left in the open on a scrubby patch of grass. Beyond them was a stone wall with a broken wooden gate leading into a scrubby field devoid of animals. There was a lot of mud.

'Did we go through some sort of portal?' she wondered aloud. 'Have we gone back two hundred years in time?'

Gillian laughed. 'Maybe we have, at that. Come on, then. There's Jonah, look.'

Jonah fitted the picture only too well. Bearded, wearing

a colourless coat tied around the middle with orange string, he could have been any age. Fascinated, Simmy watched his face as he approached the car. There was an almost glowing affability in it. His wide smile revealed a set of healthy teeth. His eyes were framed with crinkled skin; his hair was dark and wavy. 'Mrs Townsend,' he said, with a comical little salutation that involved bending his knees as if about to curtsey.

'Jonah,' she cried, throwing the car door open. 'This is *so* good of you. I can't tell you how much I appreciate it. I don't know what we'd have done without you.'

'Think nothing of it,' he shrugged. 'No skin off my nose.'

'I hope not. You realise what'll happen, don't you? It's a big thing you're doing, and don't you pretend otherwise. There's going to be uniforms crawling all over this place, if you and I have got this right.' She swept the yard with a sharp eye. 'You'll need to give those dogs a brush, for one thing.'

'Why – you think they'll call the RSPCA onto us?' For the first time, he fixed Simmy with an enquiring look, as if suspecting that she might be an inspector of some sort.

'Not if I can stop them,' said Gillian. 'This is Mrs Brown. She's just come along for the ride. Don't worry about her. Where's Dorcas?'

'Indoors. The pig's farrowed and there's one not doing too well. She's bottling it. She's always one for the pigs.'

Simmy had a wild image of a baby pig being forced into a pickling jar, until she realised he meant bottle *feeding*. She smiled at her own foolishness.

'Come on, then,' said the man. 'Can't hang about like this all day.'

His accent was local, but far less thick than his appearance might suggest. Simmy wished Ben could be there, to share his impressions with her. He might well already know that Jonah was a graduate in Medieval History or have a PhD in Spanish revolutionary film. Although such information would also be known by Gillian Townsend, of course. Farmers came in a host of different guises these days – city dropouts, as well as individuals who would have been on familiar terms with William Wordsworth. This man was surely at the latter end of that spectrum.

'Come on,' Gillian repeated his words to Simmy. 'Let's see what's what.'

Jonah led them back along the track a short way, and through a gap in a wall to a rickety shed. There were ruts, showing signs of tyre treads. 'Gets used a fair bit,' Jonah said. 'Not too boggy, considering.'

Boggy enough to cause problems for her shoes, Simmy noted ruefully. Gillian might have warned her about that. She had a pair of boots in the back room of the shop, which she could easily have changed into.

'There!' he said, with a dramatic wave. 'Is that what you were looking for?'

A white van was tucked inside the shed, nose first. Gillian almost ran to it, circling it eagerly. She had to squeeze past the passenger side, and then stopped a few inches from the front. 'Bumper's bent,' she said, addressing Simmy. 'Come and see.'

Simmy took a different route, arriving at Gillian's side having already observed a deep scratch on the driver's door and a broken wing mirror. 'It's been in an accident,' she said carefully.

Gillian nodded, pointing out the various cuts and bruises the vehicle had sustained. Jonah stood back, taking much less notice than seemed normal to Simmy.

'He uses it a lot, does he?' Gillian asked. 'And keeps it here between times?'

The man nodded. 'Said he'd not got space for it at home. Neighbours didn't like it, or some such rubbish. Been a year or so now, on and off. Pays me a quid or two when he thinks of it.'

'Where does he leave his car?'

Jonah looked blank. 'Pardon?'

'Doesn't he bring it here and swop it for the van? How else would he get here?'

On a bike, thought Simmy, without having any idea who they might be referring to.

'Oh, ah, that's right,' said Jonah. 'Bit far to walk. Must be seven miles or so. But he leaves it down at the pub. Doesn't like to risk the suspension on my track, see. Even the van gets a few knocks to the exhaust if he steers it a bit crooked.'

Gillian returned her focus to the van. 'Did you see this damage before now? Any idea when it happened?'

He gave her a reproachful look. 'You oughtn't to ask me that. All I'm saying is that Jack Taylor was in the bar of The Watermill a few days ago, asking around, on your behalf, whether anyone knew of a vehicle kept round Crook way, that might have reason to stay out of sight. Old Bob Corden was there, and he comes up here of a Thursday, most weeks, and passed the word along, on account of this van. No great mystery to it. Bob had his own ideas already, but didn't like to get onto you about

231

it. That's all I'm saying,' he finished, folding his arms.

'That's more than enough.' Gillian trotted back to the front of the shed. 'You won't touch it, will you? There'll be people up here before you know it. You did right, my friend. You've done a good deed.'

'You think it was him, then? Done it deliberately, you reckon?'

'We shouldn't get into that yet. You'll be asked a lot about when you last saw him, when the van was last used, where the keys are kept – all that. If you want to tell me anything that goes against what I'm thinking, then I'd appreciate it. Otherwise, we can let the arm of the law do our work for us.'

He rubbed his forehead with a stiff finger, and stared thoughtfully at the van for a long moment. 'Didn't see a thing, other than the headlights, might have been last Friday evening. Don't know what time it would have been. Now we're not milking any more, there's no strict routine. Lambing's just got started, and there's always some crisis going on. Spare key always hangs on that nail, look, so's I can move the van if need be.' He pointed it out. 'And might have been Friday when Dorcas cut her hand. But the days get mixed up, after a week or so.' He smiled. 'I'd best go and have a think. And Dorcas can see if she can clean the dogs up a bit.'

The two collies had followed proceedings from a safe distance, their gaze on their master. To Simmy's inexpert eye, they looked healthy and happy enough. She rather wished she could have been invited to view the baby pigs, instead of staring at a supposed murder weapon. Her role as observer was decidedly unfulfilling, at least thus far.

232

'We'll go, then,' said Gillian. 'Thanks again, and good luck.'

Jonah waved them off, with no sign of anxiety.

The drive back took just over ten minutes. 'As promised,' said Gillian, delivering her at the shop well within the hour. 'I am immensely grateful to you for coming. And for not bombarding me with questions. I don't know for sure what happens next, but you can expect the police to want to interview you. I'm sure you're bright enough to work out the implications for yourself, and wise enough to know you shouldn't speak of what just happened until you've been debriefed. You'll understand that this is the culmination of a lot of work on my part. I called in all sorts of favours. I must say, there's a huge sense of satisfaction in the way it all worked out, thanks to a lot of networking.'

'It helps to have been here a long time, I suppose.'

'It does indeed. And if that stupid man thought he could get away with it, he deserves everything that's coming to him.'

Simmy said nothing, fully aware that she still had very little idea of who the stupid man, owner of the white van, actually was.

Chapter Nineteen

Bonnie was not the slightest bit reluctant to ask questions. 'Where did she take you? What happened? What's going on?' and more.

'I'm not telling you anything at the moment,' said Simmy firmly. 'Gillian has been very persistent and clever, and it looks as if she's accomplished her mission. That's as much as you need to know. It's good news for everybody,' she added optimistically.

'Huh! I don't know how you can say that. Think of poor Debbie. What possible good news can there be for her?'

'I'm not talking about it,' Simmy repeated. 'We're all behind now. Aren't there some orders for this afternoon?'

'Only one. There's a couple at Troutbeck Bridge having an anniversary, remember? Her mother wants us to deliver flowers no earlier than half past two, because they'll be out until then.'

'That's the one that came in last week? She's very organised, isn't she?'

'Scarily so. She must be a terrible mother-in-law.'

'Oh, Bonnie – you can't know that. She might be absolutely lovely.'

'She's got control freak written all over her,' Bonnie insisted. '"Not before two-thirty. Shades of yellow, gold and crimson. Buds not too tight, but not fully open. Foliage feathery and not too dominant." Come on!'

'Okay. You win. I guess I should get cracking on following her instructions, then.'

She spent fifteen minutes in the back room, then emerged to find Bonnie intently tapping and swiping her phone. There were no customers, visitors or inquisitors, for which Simmy was grateful. Bonnie looked up, finally. 'Ben says we have to go and see Debbie again. What time are you closing up? He's free all afternoon, so if you can do without me, we can go right away.'

'How? Where are your bikes?'

'He's calling Debbie, to see if she'll meet us somewhere.' The phone pinged. 'Yes, it's all fixed,' Bonnie reported.

'But . . . what are you going to say to her? You can't tell her about me and Gillian and what we did today. Don't you *dare*.'

Bonnie was defiant. 'I don't *know* what you did, do I?'

'Just don't say *anything*, okay? It's all terribly delicate. Gillian has to do everything by the rules, one step at a time. She's only interested in the *truth*, don't you see? She's being very professional about it. If you go charging in with half-baked bits of theory, you might cause all kinds of trouble.'

Bonnie shook her head. 'That's not the way we see it, so I'm not going to make any promises. Ben says Gillian has an unfair advantage, and besides that, she's determined to save her friend, regardless of what the woman's done. He says we owe it to justice to add some weight to the other side.'

'But that's what the courts are for. You're acting out the whole trial in advance, and that can't be right, can it?'

'What's wrong with it? I don't see that we can do any harm.'

The persistent haunting memory of Debbie Kennedy swayed Simmy's judgement. Bonnie was right – there was no possibility of a happy outcome for Debbie and her daughters. They could never have Declan back, whether or not Debbie's mother caused his death. If Anita was innocent, there was still the corrosive hatred and suspicion keeping them apart. Yet again, Simmy wondered what in the world Anita could have done to alienate her daughter so totally. 'Oh, go on, then,' she said. 'Make sure you eat something, though,' she could not resist adding. Bonnie's relation to food was far less dysfunctional than it had been, but she was still apt to skip meals at the slightest provocation.

'Yes, Mum,' said Bonnie, with a look that told Simmy the girl knew just how much impact those little words would carry.

Ben and Bonnie stood conspicuously on the pavement outside the Elleray public house, where so many people arranged meetings. It was easy to find, with available parking and relatively little traffic. Drawing up to collect or deposit a passenger was simple. Even Debbie Kennedy, still giddy and distracted with grief and rage, managed it effortlessly.

'Aren't we stopping here, then?' said Ben.

'Certainly not. Far too public. We're going to Troutbeck, if you must know.'

The youngsters exchanged reassuring looks, banishing any notion of coercion or abduction. Between them they could overcome Debbie if they had to. But neither one had any real concern that it would come to that. Debbie was slight, and sad, and she clearly needed them very badly.

'What's in Troutbeck?' asked Ben, in a relaxed tone.

'My brother Matthew. Didn't we tell you he lives there?'

'You did,' said Bonnie. 'We forgot.'

'He wants to be in on whatever it is you have to tell us. We both want to thank you for this. Without you two, we'd have no idea what was going on.'

'We don't know anything much. We just thought it only fair to keep in touch,' said Bonnie.

'Surely the police are updating you as well?' said Ben. 'Haven't you got a FLO?'

'Pardon?' Debbie looked at him and almost hit a car in front, waiting at the roundabout near Hodgehowe Wood. 'Oops!'

'Careful,' said Bonnie, belatedly.

'Family liaison officer,' Ben explained. 'They usually have someone staying with the family while the investigation's going on.'

'They said something about that, but I told them not to bother. It made me think they must have me down as a suspect, as well. They tried to insist, but my father-in-law had a little word and they backed off.'

'Useful man.'

'He's been wonderful. Ever so kind and thoughtful, when he's so absolutely devastated himself. I mean – losing his only son is so terrible. His wife died as well, you know, not so long ago. She was only fifty-nine.'

'I suppose Matthew must know Simmy if he lives in Troutbeck,' said Bonnie.

'By sight,' said Debbie vaguely.

They were driving up the steady incline to the fellside village that marked the first point beyond Windermere where the classic atmosphere of the Lakes could be felt. From there the views were all of bare slopes and rocky outcrops, rising to Kirkstone and Kentmere and the northerly sweep devoid of human settlement. 'Troutbeck – Gateway to the Wilderness,' Ben had once christened it.

Matthew Olsen turned out to live in a stone cottage right on the road at its narrowest point. A small space at the side was the only place where a car could sit and it was already occupied. 'We have to park further on and walk back,' said Debbie. 'Parking's always a pain in Troutbeck.'

'And Ambleside, Grasmere, Hawkshead, Rydal,' said Ben. 'I could go on.'

'Not Staveley,' said Debbie with a girlish touch of pride. 'It's never a problem in Staveley.'

'That's because the tourists never go there,' said Bonnie. 'There's nothing interesting in Staveley.'

'That's why we like it,' said Debbie, choking slightly on the last word, as she heard herself saying *we*.

They were rescued from the painful moment by Debbie's brother coming out of his front door and watching them walk back from the place where they had parked rather untidily. 'You're not meant to leave it there,' he called.

Debbie shrugged. 'We're not going to be long, are we? These two can't stay very long, apparently. Can you find them some food, do you think?'

'Probably. I've got some nice ham, and the bread's not quite stale. I'll make sandwiches, shall I?'

'Go on, then. Hurry up.'

As before, at Debbie's house, Matthew obeyed with an exaggerated meekness. He came back barely five minutes later with a tray holding a plate of sandwiches, a dish of tomatoes and a jug of something that looked like orange squash. 'I'll just get some tumblers,' he said, and was back again in seconds.

'Well, are we all right now?' he asked. 'We must say thanks for coming – again. We very much appreciate it. We really do need you, you know.'

'No problem,' said Bonnie.

Debbie interrupted any further remarks by handing out food and drink as they all sat around the kitchen table. Then, without any further preliminaries she asked Bonnie and Ben to please tell her and Matthew everything that had happened since they last met. Ben waved at his girlfriend to convey the news.

Bonnie grimaced and looked at Ben. 'I feel bad, after Simmy told me not to say anything.'

'Did you promise her anything?' Ben asked.

'No. I really don't know very much, anyway. But it still feels awkward.' She sat hunched, both hands braced on the seat beneath her.

'You're not betraying Simmy,' he assured her. 'Just tell us whatever you gleaned. It's going to help everybody if we can get at the truth.'

Bonnie still wasn't happy, but she did as asked. 'Okay. So – Gillian Townsend turned up today at the shop and took Simmy off with her for an hour, saying she wanted a neutral witness to something. I got the impression she thinks she's found evidence to prove that Mrs Olsen didn't kill your husband. I mean – what else could it be? But I don't know any more than that.'

'That's a bit thin,' said Matthew. 'What are we supposed to do with a something and nothing like that?'

'Let's think,' said Ben. He turned to Bonnie. 'There must be a few more clues. Did you see which direction they went in, for example?'

Bonnie shook her head. 'Oh – but her shoes were mucky when she got back.'

'Mucky or muddy?'

'Um . . . muddy, I think. But maybe there was a touch of sheep in it as well. I could smell it. She'd obviously forgotten, because she didn't wipe them or anything. A bit fell off inside the door when she got back.'

'So, she went to a farm. That's a huge clue, Bon.' The boy was suddenly excited. He looked at the brother and sister. 'Does that mean anything to you?'

'Not really,' said Debbie. 'There's loads of farms around here. And maybe they were just standing in the road, where someone had been moving sheep. The place is awash with muck at this time of year.'

Matthew rubbed the back of his neck. 'The only farm I ever go to is the one where I keep my van, in Crook. That can't be it. There's no reason why Gillian should go there.'

'Why do you keep your van in Crook? That's miles away,' said Ben.

'It's just the way things worked out. I help the people once in a while, when they need an extra pair of hands. I've known them forever. They've got an old shed they don't use, and Crook's quite handy, really. I can be there in ten minutes from here.'

'What sort of van?'

'Ford Transit. I'm a white van man. It's a good little earner, I must say, especially since I've got in with the auction house up in Keswick. I can deliver the big stuff to anyone this side of the region. There's always something.'

'You mean the auction house where Chris Henderson works?'

'That's the one. You know him?'

Bonnie laughed, but at a gentle nudge from Ben, she bit back the explanation she'd been about to give. 'Only a bit,' she said. 'I suppose it's not such a coincidence, really.'

Meeting Ben's eyes, she signalled a question and got a complicated response involving a wiggle of his eyebrows and a tiny shake of the head. He also waved the piece of ham sandwich in his hand. 'Eat,' he ordered her.

'Okay.' She picked up the smallest sandwich and nibbled at it.

'You must be wondering why I've gone to all this trouble to bring you here,' said Debbie. 'It was Matt's idea, really. He thinks we ought to show you something that might explain why we seem to be such unnatural children. Matt?' she prompted. 'I know we weren't very forthcoming when we saw you the other evening. What day was that?' She rubbed her temples as if trying to suppress a headache.

'Wednesday,' said Ben.

'God, it seems *ages* ago. Well, we were being much too secretive about everything then. It's gone too far for that now. You deserve to know the full story. Matt?'

Obediently, he produced a large book. 'A photo album?' said Ben.

'Partly, yes, but with letters as well as photos.' The man put the volume down flat on the table where they could all see it, and opened the front cover. 'It's a somewhat Victorian tale,' he said, before talking them through an account of a childhood spent moving from one reluctant relative to another, not always with his sister, while their mother not only concentrated on her studies of the law, but also travelled abroad on a regular basis. 'I think we did tell you that our father was in the army,' he added. 'We almost never saw him.'

'But . . .' Bonnie floundered. 'That's not so unusual. It's not very different from how it was for me – and I don't hate my mother.'

'*She* hated *us*,' said Debbie forcefully. 'We were nothing more than a nuisance to her. And we were just normal kids, always trying to please her, to be good so she'd like us. It was pathetic, looking back on it now.'

'But . . .' Bonnie tried again. 'What about day care, social services, childminders? Or something . . .' she trailed off.

'Oh no. Nothing like that for us. We were a proud middle-class family, not needing anything from the state. After all, it was only for the first seven years. Then we could go off to boarding school for army children, and everything worked out perfectly, as far as she was concerned.

It was horrible for us,' said Debbie. 'We went to different schools, and were both utterly miserable.'

'Look at these photos and letters,' Matthew invited. 'Never the same faces or places. We were worse than nomads or Gypsies. They have their families with them everywhere they go. We were two bits of driftwood, barely even having each other most of the time. But we wrote to each other. Twice a week for years, we put it all down on paper, and kept every single word. These are just the special ones. There's a filing cabinet drawer full of the others.'

'But . . .' Bonnie was not giving up. 'How does that fit with your mother killing Declan?'

'It just does,' said Debbie flatly. 'He must have gone too far with her somehow, said something that sent her over the edge.'

'Are you saying you don't really know exactly why you think she did it?' Ben's tone was challenging. 'I assumed that was pretty clear, the way you've been talking.'

'Declan must have made some kind of threat to her,' said Bonnie. 'Something that meant she wasn't going to be safe or happy with him around. How about access to her grandchildren? Was Declan stopping her from seeing them?'

'We both were,' said Debbie. 'Not that she seemed to care about that.'

'Money?' said Ben. 'Who inherits her money?'

'She's only sixty-five. Nobody's thinking about money.'

'*She* probably is, being a solicitor.'

'The first thing is that you have to find evidence against her,' Matthew interrupted. 'She'll get away with it otherwise. From what you say, Gillian's fighting back, big time, and she's no fool. You need to find out what she thinks she's unearthed. Your florist lady's the key to that. You have to make her tell you.'

'Okay,' Bonnie nodded uneasily. 'But we don't like this business of being on different sides from Simmy. We're *friends*. I'm not doing anything to spoil that. She'll be cross enough already if she finds out what I've told you.'

'That's sweet of you,' said Debbie, on the brink of tears. 'I wish it was all different. Honestly, I do. Without Declan, I can't function. I feel as if I'm floating in a great dark cave. The only way out is to follow the hope that at least we'll understand *why*. I don't expect her to apologise, or ever be the least bit of use to me. All my life, I've vowed not to let her crush me, or stop me living a normal happy life. Declan gave me that. How could she take him away from me? How *could* she? I never did anything to her.'

'Buck up, kid,' said her brother. 'You've got to drive these two home again, remember. Dry your eyes, and think positive. You've still got me, don't forget.'

'Um . . .' said Ben portentously. 'Don't you think you ought to tell us about that row you had with Declan? It's been niggling at me for days – I know it's crossing a line, but it really might be important.'

Debbie's eyes filled again. 'You're right, I know. It's just that it's the saddest part of the whole thing. The last words I said to him were "You're such a selfish pig, Declan Kennedy. You know that, don't you?" I hear them over and over in my head. I *shouted* them after him, when he went off on the bike.'

Nobody tried to console her. Bonnie gave a sympathetic grimace, but Ben leant forward, wanting more.

'Oh well, I might as well tell you. I wanted another baby, and he didn't. All perfectly simple and ordinary, in the usual way of things. I always wanted a boy, you see. But he said we didn't have the space or the money and the gap would be too big, and then I'd be nagging for a fourth if the next was another girl. He was *right*, of course. It was me being hormonal and stupid that sent him off. I can't ever forgive myself. How can I?' Her face was grey with tragedy. 'Even Barbara couldn't find any way to make me feel better about it – and she did try.'

'Mrs Percival? You told her about it, did you?' Ben asked, not hiding his surprise.

'I tell her most things. She's like a second mother to me sometimes. To both of us,' she added, looking at Matthew. 'She's a very warm and loving person. I think she's a bit lonely sometimes.'

'But isn't she in the enemy's camp? She's Gillian Townsend's mother, isn't she? Have I got that right?' The boy was still bewildered.

'Yes, but she can think for herself. She lives just around the corner from here, and she's lovely with my girls. I think she feels they need a proper granny figure, so she stands in for my useless mother.'

'She must be very old,' said Bonnie.

'Maybe, but she's still full of energy. She's really taken to your florist friend, you know.'

'People do,' said Ben vaguely.

'Time you were off,' Matthew said again. 'That's enough for now.'

Ben and Bonnie said very little in the car, and very soon they were in Bowness, outside Ben's house. 'Keep in touch,' Debbie told them. 'We're relying on you.'

Chapter Twenty

Simmy was still in the shop at half past two, tidying up and scanning the list of orders for flowers over the coming two weeks. It was a substantial workload by any standards, more than enough to keep her occupied without any additional efforts devoted to the Olsens and Kennedys. But she accepted that it was far too late for such thoughts. Gillian had seduced her, with the fatal combination of flattery, need and intrigue. Anita was in trouble, and Gillian would jeopardise her own health – and perhaps reputation – to rescue her. Simmy Brown did not have it in her to reject claims for help in such a situation.

So when the woman at the centre of the whole business walked into the shop, Simmy was only very mildly surprised. 'I'm so sorry to trouble you,' the woman said. 'I know you must be busy. But I really did want to come and thank you for your support. Could we talk, just for a few minutes?'

Anita looked tired, but not excessively strained. Her

light-coloured eyes had grown smaller, set more deeply in their sockets. She had clearly washed her hair and given it more bounce than before. But her movements were stiff, suggesting a tightness that was more mental than physical.

'No problem,' said Simmy. 'You were lucky to catch me. I've usually gone by this time. Sit down.'

Anita took the seat, and began to talk. 'It would appear that Gillian has succeeded in her quest for evidence of my innocence,' she began. 'Rather to my surprise, I have to say. But it isn't all good news. If appearances can be believed, the person who killed my son-in-law was my son. Matthew did it. You'll know, of course, that Gillian found the vehicle concerned, and it's one he often uses.'

'Oh,' said Simmy, her head humming. 'Matthew? The one who lives in Troutbeck? That's definite then, is it?'

'Apparently. She's gone to the police with her findings and they'll do all their forensic tests and so forth.'

Simmy was stuck on the man's name, only very gradually grasping the implications of this revelation. Ben and Bonnie had been with him only a few days ago – had they shared a sofa with a heartless killer? Had they been in real danger? They'd gone off with Debbie again, probably meeting Matthew a second time. Panic gripped her before reason asserted itself. 'So it was *Matthew* who kept the van at the farm. Gillian was very careful not to say his name this morning.' She stared at the woman, sitting there so calm and unemotional, as she cast her own son into the ghastly role of murderer. But then, he'd done the same to her. It was a family that had moved beyond any recognisable bounds of normality, perhaps a long time ago.

Anita then began to speak warmly of her friend and

saviour. 'Gillian's been absolutely amazing, digging out the whole story, and then tracking down the actual van. It was in a shed of some sort, down a farm track – I suppose you know that. I can't think how she did it. It's like a miracle.'

'Is that all she's told you?'

The woman nodded. 'Just the basics. She hinted that things were coming to a head this morning. She's been out most of the day – as well as on the phone most of yesterday. Her poor husband has had enough of the whole thing. He blames me, of course.' She sighed dramatically. 'Like practically everybody else does.'

'But she told you about the van and the farm?' Simmy was trying to channel Ben, following whatever flimsy logical thread might offer itself.

'She sent a text that just said, "Vehicle found. Matthew's van on a farm. Police contacted. Simmy B witness to it all." Those are the exact words. I've had to construct everything I just told you, based on that. Now I'm here to see if you'll tell me the rest.'

Simmy was thrown back on her customary resistance to being dragged into the matter, at the same time as knowing it was far too late for that. 'I don't think there's any more I can add. I don't understand why a man – your own son – who lives in Troutbeck would keep his van in Crook. I don't know what he does for a living. I have no idea whatsoever why he would want to kill his sister's husband. And I don't actually think I'm the right person to be talking to you about it.'

A veiled look crossed Anita's face. 'There isn't anyone else,' said with a hint of tragedy. 'I've never been one for friends, except for Gillian and an old schoolmate who lives in Aberdeen now. I've never felt much need for them before now. But all of a sudden, I feel horribly alone. Most people who know me are crossing the road to avoid me.'

'That'll be because of all that stuff Matthew put on Facebook,' said Simmy. 'You really ought to sue him for libel, you know.' She stopped, letting her thoughts catch up. 'Well, I suppose you won't need to if he's convicted of killing Declan. It'll be obvious that he was just trying to shift the guilt on to you.'

Anita's pale face grew even paler. 'He's my *son*,' she whispered. 'How could he be so full of hatred?'

You tell me, Simmy wanted to say. The woman must have done something pretty terrible to earn the vitriol emanating from the man. But instead of speaking, she merely patted Anita's arm.

'You're thinking it has to be down to me,' Anita accused her. 'It's always the mother's fault, isn't it? With Debbie feeling the same as Matthew does, the assumption gets all the stronger. They've depicted me to themselves and everybody they meet as the worst mother who ever lived, because I gave so much attention to my work when they were small. I've had so many years of it now, carrying it around like a malignant tumour inside me. Nobody understands what I've been through, except Gillian. I think she has literally saved my life.'

'Well, it sounds as if she's saved you from being charged with murder, anyway. That's a pretty good start.' The look Anita gave her made her realise how flippant she sounded. 'Sorry – that came out wrong. But let's hope it'll all be settled quickly. I know it's never going to be okay for you where Debbie and Matthew are concerned, but perhaps you can . . . I don't know . . . start again somewhere else? Make some new friends.' She remembered that Moxon had mentioned Anita selling her share of the business. Perhaps that would see her rich enough to set up in a handsome house in a different area – or go on lots of cruises. Her imagination stalled at the potential opportunities for the woman.

'Perhaps I can,' said Anita. 'We can always hope, can't we? Meanwhile, I did want to thank you for being so supportive and co-operative. It has been much appreciated.'

'I didn't do anything,' said Simmy, in all sincerity. 'I can't honestly say I felt much like co-operating. I just couldn't think of a decent reason to refuse when Gillian asked me to go along with her this morning.'

It was still barely three o'clock. She had plenty of time until Christopher was due to arrive for the evening. And she needed to talk to someone.

'It looks as if my side won,' she said to Ben, when he picked up his phone. 'Gillian Townsend has found the vehicle that killed Declan, and seems to think she can prove it was being driven by Matthew Olsen. Anita came just now to tell me. She's a very sad woman, as you can imagine. Her son killed her son-in-law. There's no consolation for her in that, is there? It sounds as if she'll move away from here, where nobody knows the story, and try to start again.'

'Wow! Look, can you come over for a bit, and tell us the whole thing? We've not long got back from Troutbeck. We ought to pool our findings.'

'I've got half an hour,' she agreed, and was in Helm Road ten minutes later. She already knew the line Ben would take: demanding hard evidence and exact timings, hypothesising over how the truth could be quite other than the obvious. Asking questions that she could not hope to answer. It might not be fair to accuse the youngsters of playing a game, but neither were they wasting any energy on considering the painful feelings of the people involved. And since they had no access to the details of the police investigation, everything they said would be theoretical. And Simmy was by nature impatient with theories.

The twosome absorbed the latest information quickly and thoroughly. Bonnie was incredulous. 'That van at the farm belongs to *Matthew*? That's where you went this morning, and got your shoes mucky? But . . . we told Debbie and Matthew about that and he immediately started talking about his van. He was perfectly relaxed about it, chatting on. He couldn't have done that if he'd used it to kill Declan. Nobody could act as well as that.' She fixed Simmy with a fierce glare. 'He didn't do it. No way was it him. Oh – and did you know he works for your Christopher?'

'What?'

'Yes, he uses the van to deliver big stuff that people buy at the auctions. You'd think Christopher would have made the connection with Troutbeck and said something.'

'He never did. Maybe he doesn't like him. I still haven't met him – or if I have, I don't know which man he is. I expect I've seen him.' She felt unfocused and unsettled. 'I don't like this sort of coincidence.'

'It's not so unusual. I keep telling you that everybody knows everybody around here.'

'Yes. Well, I don't like thinking there's a murderer living near me. And Christopher won't like it, either.'

Ben gave her a stern look. 'We're telling you, Simmy. Matthew didn't do it. The police will find someone else's fingerprints and DNA in the van, you see. Until they do, I don't think we can say anything for certain about who's won.'

'Gillian doesn't agree with you. She's planned every step meticulously, to maintain the integrity of the evidence, if that's the right phrase. And everyone in the whole area seems to be rooting for her. They all like her and want to please her. She's a good person. And Anita knows it.'

'Hang on,' said Bonnie, waving a finger, as she arranged her thoughts. 'Hasn't she just interfered with that integrity, by telling you who owns the van? Now, when the police question you as Gillian's witness, you'll be influenced by knowing that. Because you didn't know before, did you? You'd never have let me go off with Debbie if you had. You'd have been scared that Matthew might kill me and Ben as well.'

'As if I could have stopped you. I was very worried this afternoon, for a minute or two. If I'd known what I know now I might have insisted on coming as well.'

'Or called Moxon. Except . . . well, I wouldn't have been in any danger, would I? All he'd want would be information.'

'Well, as far as I can see, Gillian's got it all sewn up. Evidence, probably motive, timing. She'll be presenting the whole thing to the police as we speak, and Matthew will be questioned and probably charged.'

'Hm,' said Bonnie again, with heavy significance. 'Or it could be that it works out to be something altogether different.'

'It's great that we're all talking about this together now,' Ben declared. 'No more need to take sides. That was never right, anyway. I mean – it was a vital part of the process, but now we should pool all our findings, and not hold anything back. As far as it looks now, Gillian Townsend has accomplished her mission to prove her friend's innocence, but in the process incriminated the suspect's son. How will that go down, I wonder?'

'If you mean, how does Anita feel about that, she's absolutely miserable,' said Simmy, conscious that she was being selective in this report. Anita Olsen's emotions had been a lot more complex than simple misery. 'She says she's failed as a mother, and she's going to have to move right away and start a new life.'

'At her age!' scoffed Bonnie. 'Some chance.'

'She's only about sixty-five. She might have another thirty years. People do it all the time – move to a new town and join all the clubs and whatnot. She might even do a bit of part-time work, I would guess. She's perfectly competent.' Simmy's continuing defence of Anita Olsen was as powerful as ever. 'And she's really *nice*. She'll make a success of it.'

'If she's as nice as all that, why do both her children hate her?' asked Ben. 'And it doesn't strike me that she's particularly popular around here. Nobody's leapt to her defence online.'

'I don't think she's a bit nice, actually,' said Bonnie. 'Simmy's trouble is, she likes everybody.'

'I do my best to keep an open mind about people,' said Simmy stiffly. 'She's just one of those women who can't see much need for a lot of close friends.'.

'Right. In fact, as far as I can tell, the only one is the Townsend lady.'

'And Simmy,' Bonnie persisted stubbornly. 'Simmy wants to be her friend.'

'Not if she moves away. Besides, don't forget there was going to be a big party for her retirement. That implies that plenty of people like her and want to send her off with a flourish.' Even as she spoke she knew what Ben was going to say – and he did.

'They might just be glad to be getting rid of her.'

'Oh, shut up,' said Simmy.

'We're not doing this right,' complained Bonnie. 'We ought to be thinking about that van and who might have been driving it, pretending to be Matthew. What about the timing on Friday? Is it even *possible* that it was Matthew? How did he know where Declan would be?' She looked to Ben for agreement. 'And we just *saw* him. He was talking about the van so openly. He didn't blush or stammer or anything. Nobody's that good at acting.'

'We said that before about him *and* Gillian,' Simmy reminded her.

Ben nodded abstractedly. 'The police will be going over the van for marks and fingerprints and so forth. It could yet turn out that it's a red herring – not the murder vehicle, after all. And we have no idea where Matthew Olsen says he was last Friday. That didn't come up when we were there, did it? Why would it, anyway? We'd got no idea he was the latest suspect.'

Bonnie shook her head. 'They were laying it on so thick about his mother having done it.' She frowned. 'What's Debbie going to feel now? She can't have the slightest inkling that it might have been her brother.'

Finally, thought Simmy. The first time the feelings of the people involved had been mentioned and it turned out to be a conversation-stopper. Ben was silent as he tried to compute this question. Simmy took pity on him. 'She's not going to be happy,' she said lightly. 'But the whole business is obviously focused very tightly on the family. There must be much more horrible things behind the scenes than any of us know about.'

'You never told us Anita's side of the story,' Ben remembered. 'Why does she think there was so much bad feeling towards her?'

'She thinks Declan only married her daughter to put pressure on her and Gillian to take him on in the business. When they still refused to do it, he and his father both turned very nasty and it's stayed like that for years.'

Ben scratched his head. 'That doesn't seem enough to warrant calculated murder, does it?'

'You were happy to go along with it until now,' Simmy reminded him. 'I assume Debbie must have told you pretty much the same story.'

'Plus a whole lot more. She was a rubbish mother, making it clear she wasn't interested until they got old enough to fend for themselves. By then it was too late, of course. They've never forgiven her for the ghastly time they had.'

Simmy looked at Bonnie, as the acknowledged expert on rubbish mothers. 'Did all that seem credible to you?' she asked.

'Sort of,' said the girl, with an uneasy twitch of her shoulders. 'Well, not really. I mean, you don't *hate* people, do you? You feel angry with them, and blame

255

them for things, but if you're even halfway grown-up you just get on with it, and accept that things are the way they are.'

'And Debbie and Matthew are both pretty reasonable individuals,' said Ben. 'As far as I can see.'

'She bosses him about,' said Bonnie. 'And he doesn't seem to be making much of himself, just driving a van around. How does he afford that house? He must have some other money coming in.'

'Maybe an auntie died and left it to him,' said Simmy.

'Could be,' Ben agreed. 'It is quite an auntyish sort of place.'

'Anyway,' said Bonnie loudly, 'none of this is helping to explain why it was Declan who was killed. What did he do? Somebody must have seen him as a threat, or obstacle. Somebody who didn't too much mind the consequences for poor Debbie. You have to think of the *motive*.' She looked fiercely at Ben. 'Don't you?'

'You certainly do,' he said. 'Good for you, putting us back on track.'

Bonnie smiled proudly. 'I'm getting better at this, aren't I?'

'You're brilliant,' said her beloved. 'Now, we mustn't forget there are other people to consider, though. Old Man Kennedy, for one. And old Mr Olsen for another. The two fathers, who might have much more significance than we realise. The whole thing might even have started with them, thirty years ago. Did they know each other? How did Declan cope when his mother died? I bet there's a more personal motive than what we've been told. Oh,' he burst out, 'I'd know all the answers by now if I wasn't so tied up with all this school work. I haven't given it *nearly* enough time.'

'I can do most of it,' said Bonnie stoutly. 'And you can spare an hour or two some evenings.'

'Yeah,' sighed Ben, looking pale and weary.

'Exactly what is it you think you have to do?' demanded Simmy. 'If Anita has been shown to be innocent, it all has to start again, presumably, with the focus on Matthew. And we don't know who Declan might have threatened or offended or . . . whatever. We should—'

'Don't say "leave it all to the police",' begged Bonnie. 'That's what people always say, and you know it doesn't have any effect on me and Ben. Even the police wouldn't expect us to do that.'

'They might *hope*,' sighed Simmy. 'The same as me.'

'Gillian Townsend must be pretty clever,' Ben remarked after a pause.

'And persistent,' said Bonnie.

Simmy shook her head. 'I'm not going to think about this any more today,' she said loudly. 'I should have gone home ages ago. I'm having a nice evening with Christopher, and a lazy day tomorrow. Then after school on Monday your sister's coming in, Ben. She says she can help out when we've got all the Mother's Day stuff to do. Although I suppose I could have a quick word with her now, if she's here.'

He looked completely blank. 'Sister? Which one?'

'Tanya. Didn't you know?'

He shrugged. 'She's the only one of them who might be halfway useful. But no, she's out this afternoon. Now, I've got to get on. Things to do, books to read. I'm behind schedule.' He sighed. 'It'll be eleven or later by the time I've got it all done.'

257

'Will I see you tomorrow?' asked Bonnie, managing not to sound wistful.

'The afternoon should be okay for a bit.'

They looked at each other with fond frustration, and Simmy took her leave.

Chapter Twenty-One

It was just after five when she got home, having spent nearly an hour drifting around the big supermarket, pausing every few paces, trying to decide what she needed for the next week. She got two steaks for the coming day, and two bottles of red wine. Ice cream, peas, extra bread, cheese and a big bag of mince would all help to replenish the freezer. Tins of tomatoes, sweet corn, beans and soup would stock the cupboard, and a selection of cakes and biscuits went into the trolley, followed by instant coffee, teabags and a bottle of squash. It was the first time for many weeks that she had bought so much at a time – and still she eyed yoghurts, fruit, smoked fish and cold meat, wondering whether she could make herself some interesting meals for a change, even when Christopher wasn't there.

It was surprisingly therapeutic, she found, focusing so much attention on food. Her mouth was watering, and on impulse she snatched at half a cooked chicken for the following evening, with some salad stuff to go with it. 'Enough,' she muttered. 'I'll never find space in the fridge at this rate.'

Wheeling it all to the car, in a small procession of housewives and elderly couples, she felt like a boringly normal person, fuelling herself for the days to come, anticipating the flavours of decent food for a change. Not a hint of murder or malice entered her head for a whole wonderful hour.

She drove home maintaining focus firmly on mundane domestic matters like giving the back bedroom a thorough dusting and decobwebbing. The cottage only had two rooms upstairs, plus bathroom and large cupboard. Christopher had inspected the one at the back on one of his early visits and bemoaned its neglected state. 'You could make a very nice guest room here, and have friends to stay,' he reproached her. 'Look at that fantastic view!'

Simmy had defended herself. 'I had someone last year. There's a bed, look.' The bed was a narrow affair with a hard mattress. The rest of the room contained surplus chairs, boxes and a bookcase of shamefully dull books that should have been dumped before she moved house.

It took five or six minutes to distribute her shopping to freezer, fridge and cupboard. Then her landline started ringing, and her breathing stalled. Instantly she was back in the world of mangled bodies and distraught relatives. Her strong inclination was to let it ring, but that was cowardly, and would solve nothing.

'You didn't answer your mobile,' came her boyfriend's reproachful voice.

'Sorry. I never heard it. Why? What's the matter?'

'Nothing, really. Just that I won't get to you until about half seven. Is that okay? We've got some pest bringing in a massive great stone trough, and he's had transport trouble. I've got to hang around until he's been and gone, so I can lock up.'

'That's no problem. It'll give me time to clear up a bit. Don't worry. We've still got the whole of tomorrow.'

The conversation ended with muted expressions of affection on both sides; Simmy assuring herself that it was all quite normal. Two adults living full lives, and finding insufficient space for each other. Nothing at all to worry about – even if they really weren't behaving much like a proper couple at all. Proper couples spent every single night together, ate all their meals at the same table, watched rubbish on the telly and argued about who put the bins out. And had babies.

Seven thirty came and went, and she began to worry. After ten more minutes, she gave in and called him. 'You are coming this evening, aren't you?' she said. 'You didn't change your mind?'

'Of course I didn't. What are you thinking? Sorry I'm a bit late, but I'm stopped at the lights in Ambleside, and will be arrested any moment if I don't put this phone down. Give me nine minutes.'

His estimate was surpassed by a whole minute, and there he was in the doorway looking young and cheerful and deliciously *normal*. No hint of murder or family feuds or vague apprehensions. Just a warm hug and a carefree bounce. 'Come on, then,' he urged. 'Let's get cooking. Isn't that what we decided?'

Simmy had found four pork chops in her freezer the

previous evening, and left them to defrost all day. She had apple sauce, three vegetables and a bottle of red wine. 'It's not very special,' she worried. 'But at least it won't take very long to cook.'

'Two chops each is a feast. Tell you what – we can do them in a sauce, with onions and herbs and things, and leave them in the oven while we pop down to the pub for a quick gin and tonic. You haven't got any gin, have you?'

She shook her head. 'The budget doesn't run to spirits.'

Christopher took over, chopping onions, browning the meat, fishing in a drawer for rather elderly dried herbs. Simmy watched in awe. 'You're terribly good at this,' she observed.

'It's fun, when there's someone else to enjoy it. Now in it goes, and we've got fifty minutes before we need to get the potatoes on. You've done a lovely job of peeling them,' he added, with exaggerated patronage. 'But we won't be needing apple sauce. I've put an apple in the casserole. Lucky you had one.'

'It's a miracle.'

'We should do this again tomorrow. Establish a routine. We've been awfully disorganised up to now.'

She sighed, thinking how easy it could be to make a person happy. 'I went to the supermarket,' she told him. 'And got everything we'll need from now till Monday morning.'

They walked the short way to The Mortal Man and were mutually delighted to be together. But Simmy could not entirely divest herself of thoughts about Declan Kennedy, his wife, mother-in-law and above all, his brother-in-law Matthew Olsen. The day had been filled with the whole business, and the sense of impending climax was inexorable. 'I gather you know Matthew Olsen,' she said, as they drank their aperitifs. There were people in the bar who could overhear what was said, if they wanted to. Too late, it occurred to her that the man himself might even be there, since she didn't know what he looked like.

'Do I?' said Christopher. 'In what context?'

'He drives a van for you.'

'Um . . . ?'

'I mean, he delivers things that people buy at your sales and are too big to go in their cars. A white van.' There had been no obvious flickers of recognition from the surrounding tables, making her feel safer about discussing the man, albeit in a low voice.

'Oh. There are a few of them. They don't work for us, exactly. They just hang around waiting to be needed. It's all very informal. There is one called Matt, now I come to think of it. Nice helpful chap. Very good with old ladies.'

'Not with his mother, he isn't, He loathes her.'

'So what's the connection? Why are we talking about him? What did his mother do to him?'

'He lives here in Troutbeck. I expect he comes in here to drink. I might know him by sight, but I've never consciously met him.'

'So?' Christopher was plainly puzzled and a trifle impatient.

'I'll tell you when we get back to the house. I shouldn't have mentioned it, really. It's just – the whole day has been so taken up with it all, I can't get it out of my head.'

He changed the subject willingly enough. 'So what's happening about your ex? Any more developments?'

'Oh – no. I'd forgotten all about it. Did I tell you

they've decided they don't need any more from me than I've already provided? It was clutching at straws to think I could be of any use to him. Besides, I'm inclined to be on the woman's side, more than his. He must have driven her mad, poor thing.'

'I'm on his side,' said Christopher with a laugh. 'Which is probably very incorrect of me.'

'There's a lot of taking sides going on,' she noted. 'Everybody seems to be against everybody else at the moment.'

'In what way?'

She glanced around the cosy bar. 'Better not go into that here,' she said.

He gave her a surprised look. 'What's all this mystery? Is it something to do with the Matthew chap? Have I been missing something?'

'Quite a lot, actually. I was hoping not to drag you into it, but I can see that's not going to work. Let's think about holidays instead.'

Obediently, Christopher began to rhapsodise about beaches and foreign food and quirky shops. 'Someone told me about a wonderful place in Teguise,' he told her. 'That's in the middle of Lanzarote. It has a huge market, but the shops are great as well.'

'You've been doing some homework,' she said. 'I never do that. I like to find out everything when I'm there. I want it all to come as a surprise.'

'But you've been before. How does that work?'

'There's still loads I haven't seen. Are we going to hire a car?'

'Of course. And we're going to get a ferry to another island one day, for a change of scene.'

264

'Oh good,' said Simmy.

Back at the cottage, after a scramble to get the vegetables ready, and the wine broached, she was reluctant to spoil the mood by talking about murder, suspicion and downright lies, but Christopher would permit no evasions. 'It's obviously bothering you,' he said. 'And what bothers you should bother me as well. Don't forget, it was murder that brought us back together. I can take it, you know. Probably better than you can, actually.'

'I know,' she said, and did her best to summarise events of the past week, concluding by saying, 'The trouble is, Ben and Bonnie are convinced that Anita did it, and I'm convinced she didn't.'

'In a nutshell,' he smiled. 'It sounds to me as if the key person in all this is the Townsend woman. If she believes in her friend's innocence, that must surely count for a lot.'

'She does. And she knows Anita better than anyone does. But Ben would say she's got a lifelong friendship invested in the Anita she knows and loves, so she's not trustworthy. But I'm so sure she *is*,' Simmy wailed. 'I can't bear to think she's deliberately falsifying evidence to get Anita off.'

'Could she do that, even if she wanted to?'

'I don't know. I don't see how. Everybody *likes* her, you see. They're all going out of their way to please her.'

'But do they like Anita?'

'Maybe not so much. But she seems all right to me. She's so hurt, because of the way her children are towards her. They're being absolutely awful, accusing her of murder. I mean – isn't that the most terrible thing?'

'Pretty bad,' he agreed. 'But families can get into ghastly emotional vendettas, at times. Sisters who never speak to each other, and fathers who ruin their daughters' lives.'

'Yes. But it's not often *mothers*, is it? That's even more horrible to think about.'

'We were both lucky, I guess. We had nice, normal, decent parents.'

She looked at him, head to one side. 'Three out of the four, anyway,' she corrected, referring to recent events concerning Christopher's parents.

He flinched. 'Okay. But nobody did anything bad to me, which is what I'm saying.'

'But Matthew doesn't strike you as capable of killing anyone. Is that right?' she pressed him.

'I really have no idea what he's capable of. The question's meaningless. But I'll keep an eye on him next week, if I can.'

He finished the last morsel of pork, with relish. 'That was amazing,' he said. 'Though I say so myself.'

'I could eat it all over again,' she agreed. 'I don't think there's anything that would do for pudding.'

'Cheese would be nice. Didn't I see some in the fridge?'

They finished the modest lump of cheddar, which started Simmy thinking of her next shopping list. 'And I don't imagine there's anything we might have for a nightcap, either?' he asked with a rueful grin.

'Nightcap! It's only quarter past nine.'

'So?' he grinned, and finally she really did forget all about the Kennedys and the Olsens and dented white vans.

She continued to forget them throughout a blissfully enjoyable Sunday, in which she and Christopher did very little. They buried their phones under a cushion, walked up Wansfell, turned up the heating when they got back, and shared another indulgent meal. 'I've earned this,' Simmy assured herself, once or twice. Earned a break from her parents, the shop and above all, the repellent details of a recent murder. Monday would come soon enough, with Christopher scrambling out of bed at silly o'clock and leaving her to face the new week as best she could.

Chapter Twenty-Two

Tanya Harkness was quite a surprise. Much darker than Ben, almost as tall, and with a clear gaze that Simmy quickly decided would go over very well with customers. She presented herself at half past three on Monday afternoon, looking at least sixteen despite being in school uniform. Bonnie politely stayed at the back of the shop, pretending to be rearranging some of the stock.

'It seems daft that we've never met, after all this time,' Simmy said. 'I've even been to your house several times.'

'Ben wanted to keep you all to himself,' said the girl. 'We often tease him about it.'

'I can't imagine why.' *I'm old enough to be his mother*, she wanted to say – a thought that came to her almost every day.

'He says you're a very rare person.'

'Don't tell me what he says,' Simmy begged. 'It's bound to be embarrassing. Let's talk about what you might be able to do for me when the Mother's Day madness kicks off. It's going to be absolute bedlam.'

'Sounds great,' enthused Tanya, somewhat prematurely.

'You haven't heard anything yet. There'll be orders on the computer, phone calls, both right up to late on the Saturday before it. I'll be out delivering most of that day, as well as Sunday. I'm offering a discount for Saturday delivery, which is a bit of a cheat, but it's the only way to cope. Bonnie and you will be here without me, keeping track of everything, making sure nobody gets forgotten. I'm going to let Bonnie do some of the bouquets – the simpler ones. The place is going to be so full, we'll hardly be able to move.'

'You haven't put me off yet. How much will you pay me?'

'Thirty-five pounds,' said Simmy promptly. 'Cash in hand.'

'What if I come on the Friday and Sunday as well? Not just Saturday. Sounds to me as if it would be good to get ahead as much as you can on Friday.'

Simmy shook her head. 'No, thanks. Friday's my problem. But Sunday morning might be a help. Say another fifteen for three hours? I don't have to pay someone your age the minimum wage, you know,' she added defensively.

'No, I know. That would be great.' The sparkling eyes and shallow breathing betrayed how excited she was. *Such a sweet child*, thought Simmy. From Ben's disparaging remarks about all his sisters, she had expected a far more disaffected and inarticulate creature.

The deal apparently made, Tanya began a tour of inspection, gently fingering the foliage and sniffing some of the blooms. When the doorbell pinged, she looked up, her face alight with interest.

DI Moxon glanced at her without recognition. Simmy wanted to make immediate introductions, but thought better of it. 'Hello,' she said, knowing she sounded resigned and profoundly unwelcoming.

'Hello,' he said. 'Can I have a word?'

'It'll have to be in here, then. It's going to get busy any minute now.'

'No problem. You'll know that Mrs Townsend is naming you as an independent witness to events on Saturday morning. All we want is for you to come down to the station and sign a statement to that effect.'

'The statement's already been written, has it?' she said stupidly.

'No, no. Of course not. We'll want you to give your own first-hand account of what happened. As much detail as you can. It's looking bad for the person concerned, I don't mind telling you.' He cocked his head. 'I'm not sure whether you're aware of his identity?'

'I am, as it happens, despite Gillian's efforts not to tell me. Mrs Olsen came the same afternoon and told me.'

'Did she indeed. I wonder what she did that for?'

'Muddying the waters,' said Tanya boldly. 'That's what Ben would say.'

Moxon looked from Tanya to Bonnie to Simmy and back again. 'Who's this?' he asked.

'Can't you guess?' Simmy gave a little laugh, partly sympathetic towards his confusion, and partly scornful. 'She's Ben Harkness's sister. Tanya.'

He rolled his eyes, and swept a theatrical hand across his

brow. 'Heaven help me, they're proliferating,' he groaned. 'Are you an amateur detective as well, young lady?'

'Sort of,' she grinned. 'I've been keying in some of Ben's notes, to save him time – and a bit of googling as well. I know quite a lot about the Declan Kennedy case.'

Moxon groaned again. 'How old are you?' he asked.

'Fourteen.'

'Far too young to get involved in any of this business. Miss Lawson's too young, as well. You *all* are. It's a scandal, the way you think you can get involved in serious police investigations. Absolutely scandalous.'

'Don't worry,' Tanya soothed him, sounding uncannily like her brother. 'I'm not at all involved. I just know about it, that's all. I'm not as clever as Ben, of course.'

'Nobody is,' sighed Moxon. Then he straightened up. 'Now then. Let's try to keep this on track, if that's possible. I have matters to discuss with Mrs Brown, which are not for your young ears. Either of you.'

'I'll try to come when we've closed up,' Simmy told him. 'Is that soon enough?'

'It'll have to be, won't it?' His expression was much milder than the words might suggest. He seemed relaxed and subtly complacent. Simmy interpreted this as coming from a satisfied investigator, case solved, primary suspect exonerated and new perpetrator identified. Moxon, like everybody else, obviously liked and admired Gillian Townsend, and wanted her to be on the side of the angels. Matthew Olsen was a much better candidate for their attentions, despite a singular absence of motive, as far as Simmy was aware.

'I'm glad I can help,' she said. 'I never could see Anita as a killer.'

'No. Well . . .' he said. 'There's still a way to go before we can present a proper case. The evidence is thin at the moment.'

'That's why you need Simmy,' said Bonnie, with an accusing look. 'Without her, you'd never make a case against Matthew, would you?'

'Be quiet, Bonnie!' Simmy said sharply. 'That isn't true at all, and you shouldn't use people's names.' She glanced anxiously at Tanya, who gazed blandly back. 'Though I don't suppose it matters,' Simmy admitted. If the girl had been helping her brother with his flow charts, she'd know all relevant names already.

Moxon's eyes had widened, and he seemed to want to say quite a lot. But he controlled himself and turned to leave. 'When you're free, then,' he said to Simmy over his shoulder.

'He's prejudiced in favour of Anita Olsen,' said Bonnie indignantly, as soon as he'd gone. 'He's not supposed to be. It's not fair.'

'You think he'd let it influence him? Of course he wouldn't.' Simmy was equally outraged at the imputation. 'He's the straightest man in the police force, and you know it.'

'I don't, and neither do you. You're exaggerating. He's probably no better or worse than average, in fact.'

'My mum thinks he's brilliant,' said Tanya. She gave Simmy a supportive look. 'The way he's always been so nice to Ben, letting him interfere with police work. Mum says that's extremely rare. Moxon's one in a million, she says.'

272

'He can see how special Ben is,' said Simmy. 'But he's not always very patient with him.'

'Who is?' laughed Tanya. 'Ben's a real pain a lot of the time.'

'Me,' said Bonnie. 'I never get impatient with him.'

'Oh you,' said Tanya. 'You don't count.'

It occurred to Simmy that her newest employee had no intention of going home soon. The interview, such as it was, had been concluded within moments, but that apparently did not mean she should leave, and Simmy hadn't the heart to tell her to go. 'You can stay and watch what goes on, I suppose,' she said. 'Bonnie can show you the computer, and where we keep things.'

Both girls nodded as if this went without saying. Two customers came in, and all was business and efficiency for a few minutes. Then it went quiet, and Simmy took some time to get the back room organised. A running order for Mother's Day, and a rough estimate of the orders they could expect over the coming week.

When she came out again, Bonnie and Tanya were bent over a large jotter pad, Tanya with a pen in her hand. 'This is Ben's flow chart,' Bonnie explained to Simmy. 'Or a copy of it, anyway.'

'There are five different versions,' said Tanya. 'This is the latest one. I've just had a new thought.'

'She's good at this,' said Bonnie. 'Makes me feel really slow.' The look on her face was not unadulterated approval. Even the ever-faithful Bonnie could not restrain a hint of jealous resentment against the sudden intervention of a young sister.

Simmy glanced at the computer. 'Four new orders,' she discovered. 'I feel weak already.'

'It'll be fine,' said Bonnie absently, her focus still on the jotter pad. 'Hey, Tanya – what's this about the farm shed? Why's it got a red circle round it?'

'I explained that at the start. It's the crux of the whole thing. That's where Gillian found the van, isn't it?' The girl looked at Simmy, not Bonnie, for a response.

'That's right.' Simmy saw no reason to conceal further details. 'Some old chap in a pub told her about it. At least . . . I think it was less direct than that. The farmer got to hear that she was looking for a dodgy vehicle and phoned her to say there was a van in his shed that she might find interesting.'

'Wow! We didn't know about that,' said Bonnie. 'Does that mean this man thought all along that Matthew Olsen killed Declan, but was keeping quiet about it? Or what?'

'I don't think he realised it was relevant, for a while. He lives up there with his sister, and I imagine they take very little notice of local news. They seem quite busy.'

'Huh!' scoffed Bonnie. 'Don't you believe it. Farmers are the biggest gossips alive. He'll have had his own reasons for staying quiet about it.'

'I don't think so,' argued Simmy, feeling strangely loyal towards the more than co-operative Jonah. 'He wanted to be useful to Gillian, that's all. She helped him a while ago, and he likes her.'

'Anita should be very grateful to him, anyway. He's going to be a central part of the case against her son.'

'I'm sure she will be,' said Simmy. 'She looked very relieved when she told me about the van belonging to Matthew.' She was aware that this represented a different

274

bias from her earlier disclosure, as well as threatening to be yet another detail that looked less than good for Anita. Any normal mother would be appalled at the news. Yet again, the truth forced itself through her reservations.

'When did she say that?' Tanya asked, her pen poised to make a note.

'Saturday. She came to thank me for my part in getting things cleared up. She told me then that it was her son's van in the shed. I've told Ben and Bonnie all this already.'

'I see.' The girl drew a new line from the red circle, and wrote *Anita told Simmy abt van and shed.*

Not for the first time, Simmy felt uneasy at the way these young detectives treated murder as if it were a game. She remained haunted by the image of Debbie Kennedy in the awful hat, her face smudged and her eyes blurred. Nothing was going to make things better for her, whether or not her certainties about her mother's guilt were overturned. Declan remained dead, whatever happened. And if it turned out that her brother had killed her husband, that could only compound her misery.

A thin stream of customers occupied the remainder of the day. Tanya stayed for an hour, and then took her leave with a cheery wave. 'What a nice girl she is,' said Simmy.

'She's changed a lot just lately. She was nearly as bad as the others until around Christmas. I think there's a new teacher she's trying to impress. And Ben's finally let her in. He would barely even talk to any of them when I first started going with him.'

'I'm not sure that's a good thing, actually. She's terribly young.'

'Don't keep saying that. Nothing's going to happen to her. And she's been really clever with that flow chart. She latched onto it right away.'

Simmy was increasingly aware that she was into the countdown to Mother's Day, as well as enjoying the renewed intimacy with Christopher. There was enough going on in her emotions already, without making space for Tanya Harkness, Anita Olsen or Debbie Kennedy. It had been the same for a week now – too many conflicting demands on her feelings. And she had failed to include her worrisome father in the list. 'Oh, Lord!' she said aloud. 'I'm supposed to go to Beck View after work. Should I go there first, and then to answer Moxon's questions? Or do him first? When do I get a chance to have some time to myself?'

'When you're dead,' Bonnie flashed back. 'People aren't designed to be by themselves. Be thankful so many people want you. You wouldn't like the opposite problem at all, believe me.'

'I know. But there can be too much of a good thing. I'll phone my mother and tell her I won't be there till a bit later. She'll be expecting me just after five. And I'll have to fib about the reason. I can't tell them I've got dragged into another murder.'

'Don't they know?'

'Not a thing. They're in blissful ignorance, and I want to keep it like that.'

'Well, good luck with that,' said Bonnie.

Before she could reply, Simmy's prayer was answered. A woman came in, and gave Simmy a little wave of greeting from just inside the door. 'Who's she?' whispered Bonnie.

'Don't know,' Simmy mouthed back. Then she realised that she had seen the face before. A young woman, wearing a green jacket, with curly light-brown hair and a bold look. Somewhere only a few days ago – but her memory failed at that point.

The newcomer came closer 'Don't you remember me?' She smiled teasingly. 'In the queue at the fish and chip shop in Staveley, on Friday evening. You were talking to that woman from Crook, about what happened to Declan Kennedy. You said something about Matthew Olsen, and I told you he lives in Troutbeck.'

'Right,' said Simmy, with a warning glance at Bonnie not to say anything. 'It's all come back to me now.'

'Don't worry. I haven't come to talk about that. I just want some flowers for my gran, that's all.'

The relief was profound. 'Great!' Simmy enthused. 'What did you have in mind?'

'Something old-fashioned with plenty of scent. And can you deliver them to her tomorrow, do you think? It's her birthday, and she insists she doesn't want any presents. She's always been like that – very unselfish.'

Simmy threw herself into total commitment to giving the old lady the best of all possible birthday bouquets. 'So where does your granny live?' she asked, her pen poised to write down the address.

'Oh – Staveley,' came the reply, as if that was obvious. 'We all live in Staveley. My great-great-grandfather bought land there back in the dark ages, and we've stayed put ever since. Not that any of the land is still in the family, and plenty of cousins and so forth have gone off to America or Australia, but there's still about twenty of my close relatives within about fifteen miles of here. I'm related to your Melanie Todd, as it happens.'

Simmy laughed. 'As far as I can see, pretty well everybody's related to Melanie. So do you know Anita Olsen or Gillian Townsend as well? They're solicitors in Kendal, and Gillian's mother lives in Staveley. So does Anita.'

'Oh yes. Gillian's my dad's cousin,' came the astonishing reply. 'Gillian Percival, she was, before she married. The old lady was a Gordon originally. I'm Emily Gordon. And my gran's Catherine Gordon. You won't get far around here without bumping into one of the Gordons – in spite of it sounding Scots.'

'Your great-granddad came over the border, then?'

'Something like that,' nodded Emily. She then devoted five minutes to a careful selection of flowers for the bouquet. Finally, having paid, and chatted about lilies and tulips and scentless roses, she headed for the door, throwing over her shoulder, 'You don't want to believe anything that Olsen woman tells you. You do understand that, don't you?'

Simmy's attempt to follow this up was impeded by astonishment, and the young woman's hasty departure.

Moxon was welcoming when she turned up at the police station, which was only a short walk from her parents' house. But he was also gently impatient, ushering her into a small room, offering her a drink, setting up his equipment for recording her testimony.

'So, in your own words, could you tell us what took place on Saturday morning, from the point where Mrs Townsend came to the shop and asked you to accompany her.'

'Um . . . all right. Well, we drove through Bowness towards Crook, and turned off the road up a track to a farm.'

'Please name the farm for us,' said Moxon. The *us* referred to himself and a young male constable, sitting at the end of the table, who did not appear to have anything to do. And perhaps it extended to the entire Cumbrian police force, Simmy thought.

'I'm afraid I don't know its name,' she said. 'I could probably find it on a map. The farmer's called Jonah. He lives there with his sister Dorcas.'

'Okay. Please go on.'

'He was obviously expecting us, and he knew Gillian. He took us to a sort of shed or small barn down a track away from the farmyard. It had a stone wall separating it from the fields, and there were a lot of tyre marks around the entrance. There was a white van inside it.'

'Registration number?'

'No idea.'

He chewed his lip as if this was a frustration to him. 'And then what happened?'

'Gillian asked him some questions, without naming the owner of the van. It had scratches and dents at the front, and I could see that it might easily have been involved in an accident. One of the mirrors was broken.'

'Anything else?'

'No blood, if that's what you mean.'

'Did the farmer offer to testify against the owner of the van?'

'I don't think so. Not directly. He said he wasn't entirely sure of which day it had been last used. He doesn't take very much notice of its movements. There's a spare key to it hanging on a nail.'

'Surely he'd notice the owner's car there, instead of the van?' She merely looked at him, unable to answer. 'Sorry. That's not an appropriate question, is it. The car could have been left some distance away, I suppose.' He gave the constable a look, but made no attempt to stop the recorder or rewind it. 'Never mind. What else can you tell us?'

'Nothing, really. Gillian took me back to the shop, and that was it.'

'So when did it become clear to you that the van was owned by Matthew Olsen?'

'That was when Anita came to talk to me, later on in the day. But Bonnie already knew, because Debbie must have told her . . . No, no. Wait a minute. Bonnie didn't know anything about the van having dents or anything. And it was Matthew himself who mentioned it, I think. We all got together later on, and pooled everything we knew. The van was the most important factor by then.'

'When did Bonnie see Debbie?'

'When she and Ben went to Troutbeck on Saturday. Debbie took them to Matthew's house. They wanted to update them about Gillian wanting me as a witness, and acting as if she'd found evidence to prove Anita was innocent.'

'Slow down, please. This is important. Your young friends went to the home of Matthew Olsen on Saturday? Were they aware at that point that evidence was pointing at him?'

'No, not at all. I didn't know myself. I told you – Gillian

didn't give me a name. I didn't know until Anita came and told me in the afternoon.'

He stirred his own hair in a fever of impatience and puzzlement. 'We have to take this step by step. Bonnie and Ben somehow learnt that there was a white van on a farm in Crook belonging to Mr Olsen, but they didn't know the van was implicated in the death of Declan Kennedy. So why was it mentioned at all?'

'I have no idea. You'll have to ask them.'

'I will. And you knew there was a suspicious van, but not who it belonged to until informed by Mrs Olsen.'

'Yes.'

'So the only person who was in possession of the complete picture was Gillian Townsend, at least up to Saturday afternoon.'

'And Anita, probably. That is, she said she had a text from Gillian telling her the vehicle had been found and she was off the hook.'

'When?'

'Presumably soon after Gillian took me back to the shop. Sometime in the afternoon.'

'What did it say?'

'I can't remember exactly. She didn't show it to me. But it was enough to reassure her, and send her straight to Windermere to thank me for helping them.'

He left a heavy silence, looking hard at her, but evidently thinking fast. 'You've believed all along that Anita Olsen was innocent, haven't you?'

'Yes, I have,' she said boldly. 'The idea that she killed Declan is ludicrous. You only have to look at Gillian to see that. She's incandescent with outrage and horror at the very idea. She's dropped everything to find evidence that will clear her friend. And everyone's on her side.'

'And yet Debbie Kennedy is perfectly credible as well. Shocked, grief-stricken, paralysed – yes. But her mind still works well enough, and she's extremely lucid and consistent in her accusation against her mother. She supplied motive, as well, up to a point.'

'There can't be a motive strong enough for such a terrible act. Nobody could hate their own daughter as passionately as that.'

He took a long breath. 'I'm afraid you're wrong there,' he said. 'Not that I've ever seen it personally, but I've heard a number of stories that would turn your hair white.' He eyed Simmy's healthy brown tresses with a little smile.

'So what about Matthew? Isn't he a more credible suspect?'

Moxon blew out his cheeks. 'Why would he want to wreak such suffering on his sister? They've been close all their lives, watching out for each other, like babes in the wood. It makes no better sense to put him in the frame.'

A treacherous idea darted into Simmy's mind. If Anita really did hate her children, she might have found a perfect way to punish them both, if Matthew was convicted of Declan's murder. She shook her head vigorously. 'What if Matthew found out something that Declan had done or was planning to do, that would hurt Debbie? What if he was trying to save her from years of trouble and deceit?'

'Possible,' Moxon agreed judiciously. 'He certainly doesn't seem to have gone to any great lengths to cover his tracks.'

'I don't agree. The van wasn't damaged badly enough to attract attention. Wing mirrors get broken all the time. He might well have intended to fix up most of the broken bits himself. He could explain it away to anybody who asked. His mistake was to underestimate Gillian. Without her, I think he might well have got away with it. The police weren't planning to search every farm or business for suspicious vehicles, were they?'

'Thanks to the constraints of time and manpower, that was never going to happen, I admit. But an even more crucial issue is the timing. We questioned Mr Olsen a short time ago, and he tells us he was in Keswick on the evening in question.'

Simmy's heart thumped. Surely her Christopher was not going to be called upon for an alibi for a suspected murderer? 'In the van?' she asked faintly.

'No. In his car. He says he was in a pub up there from six to nine, with some mates, but he doesn't know their full names or addresses, and thinks it unlikely the pub staff will remember them.'

'Well, that's not very convincing, is it?' Another treacherous thought cropped up: Christopher might know the 'mates' and be able to supply contact details, since it was probable that they were connected to his auction house in some way. But why did she keep having ideas that supported the wrong side of the argument?

'We can try to check it out.'

'You're going to have to talk to Ben, aren't you? I thought he was going to be too busy to pay any attention to this business, but I should have known better. He's only spent an hour or so here and there on it, and already it looks as if he's got a whole lot of crucial information.' She felt a grudging satisfaction at the brilliance of her friend, even while regretting the interruption to his studies.

'I'm not sure yet. He knows nothing about the timing, and all his involvement, as far as I can see, has been at second-hand, well after the event. The best he can do is to produce one of his dossiers or flow charts or whatever.'

'And you should be able to come up with all that yourselves,' she said, rather sharply.

'We should and we will. That's the job. It's what we do.'

'Indeed,' she agreed, silently thinking that the cumbersome police machinery made a poor second to Ben's lightning processes.

The next stop was Beck View, where her parents were preparing for a mass invasion of eight people, including a toddler, filling every corner of the house. '*Eight?*' Simmy gasped. 'How is that possible?' There were only three guestrooms, one of them intended as a single.

Angie explained. 'Two of them are going in the green room. It's a four-foot bed, so two can fit. The baby goes in a cot, and there's a teenager who can have the emergency fold-out bed in with his parents. They seem happy enough.'

'Are they all one party?'

'Luckily, yes. They're coming for a big birthday do for their old grandmother. She'll be a hundred tomorrow, would you believe? I got the whole story last month, when they booked.'

'She must be somebody's *great*-grandmother, surely?'

'Great-great, to the toddler. There's about eighty other

284

relatives, staying all around Windermere and Bowness. They're having the party at the Belsfield. Must be costing them thousands.'

'Why haven't I heard about it before?' wondered Simmy, thinking she might have been able to offer to do some flowers if she'd known about the event.

Angie shrugged, and pointed to a large stack of ironing.

Chapter Twenty-Three

Ben and Bonnie had admitted Tanya into their deliberations with minimal resistance. Approaching the end of Year Nine, she had mutated overnight into a noteworthy individual, separating from her twin by a violent act of will. Natalie had become sucked into the world of Instagram and Facebook, with clothes, boys and music her priorities. Tanya, after years of resistance, had succumbed to the magic of maths and the glory of geography. She loved maps and geometry, in particular. She loved her mother's set squares and rulers, used for the architectural drawing that she spent hours on in the attic room that was her place of work. Her sister Zoe, balanced between two brothers and the twins, blessed with an average IQ and pretty features, was the first to voice the obvious. 'Tanya's turning out to be another Ben.' Not quite, corrected the others, but certainly she was developing in surprising ways.

It was six-thirty on Monday evening. Ben was taking

one of his breaks from studying, insisting he had not a minute more than an hour to spare. Tanya arranged the various flow charts, and Bonnie produced some notes of her own. 'Just things I've noticed,' she said modestly.

'Okay,' said Ben. 'I suggest we work through two different hypotheses. Firstly, assuming Anita Olsen is the killer, and then again with Matthew. Means, motive and opportunity, evidence, witnesses – the usual stuff.'

With impressive enthusiasm, both girls threw themselves into the project, scribbling down ideas, connections, clues, characters and generally brainstorming with gusto. After twenty minutes, Ben called a halt. 'It's Gillian Townsend who's at the heart of it all,' he announced. 'Everything hinges on her, look.' He displayed the diagram he'd constructed, with arrows and lines and different-coloured ink. 'Compared to her, Debbie's not doing a thing.'

'She's online a lot,' Bonnie reminded him.

'Which is a poor substitute for real action. The Townsend lady got out there and found the actual vehicle that killed the man. At least, we presume she got the right one. The police must know by now if it is. The thing is, she knows everybody from Troutbeck to Kendal, and probably beyond that. There's nothing like local knowledge.'

All three smiled complacently – they had local knowledge themselves. The Harknesses had been born in Bowness, and Bonnie lived with Corinne who possessed a legendary grasp of every layer of Windermere society.

'Matthew didn't do it,' said Bonnie. 'That's obvious from the way he was on Saturday. People must have known he kept the van on that farm. Anyone could have taken it for half an hour, and put it back again.'

'How would they get into it?' asked Tanya. 'Did he leave it unlocked, with the key in the ignition?'

'Excellent question,' beamed Ben. 'My guess is that he wouldn't bother to lock it, given where it was. Could be the farmer needed to move it now and then, for one thing. I bet you the keys were kept in it, or beside it on a hook. Something like that.'

'Okay.' His sister was thoroughly fired up. 'But would people *know* that? If someone else went and borrowed the van, they'd have to have every detail worked out first. And how would they get there? Where would they leave their own car or bike or whatever?'

'We don't know Crook all that well, do we?' said Ben. 'All I can remember is that church tower in a field by itself, and a scattering of houses near the pub. Not many places to hide a car.'

'Except another farmyard,' Bonnie suggested. 'There's a few farms along that road. Simmy took flowers to a place at pretty much the same time as Declan was killed.'

Ben blinked. 'Did she? Nobody told me that. You're saying she could easily have witnessed the whole thing? That's bizarre.'

'Except obviously she didn't. She didn't see anything at all.'

Ben tapped his teeth with a pen. 'Did Anita Olsen know Simmy was going to Crook?'

Bonnie had to think. 'She might have heard her say so when she was on the phone to Gillian. That was the start of the whole thing. Gillian called about the party, and Simmy went round to Staveley after taking the flowers to Crook. It was a nice simple round trip. Except she went home after that.'

'It's bad, the way we've been in different camps. Nobody knows what the others know. That hasn't happened before. It's inefficient.'

'We couldn't help it,' Bonnie assured him. 'Simmy wasn't going to listen to all that stuff against Anita.'

'But she's never even met Matthew. If she had, she'd see he couldn't have killed anybody, either.'

'Ben – that's not like you. You have to assume he *could*, the same as anybody else could. Even Debbie,' she added softly.

'What? Is that what you think?'

'I think it's no worse than believing Debbie's mother did it. Statistically, wives must kill husbands more often than mothers-in-law do.'

Tanya giggled. 'That sounds funny. Sorry.' She ducked her head. 'Sorry,' she said again.

Ben became businesslike. 'Have we got all the relevant people here? Gillian's mother, Declan's father, the man on the farm in Crook . . . it's not a very long list.'

'Can't think of anyone else,' said Bonnie. 'But there could be a dozen more who had reason to hate Declan and want him dead.'

Ben shook his head. 'I doubt it. Whoever did it was super-clever, knew about Declan's movements, and is capable of keeping an amazingly clear head. That all points straight at Anita Olsen.'

'But it might also describe someone else entirely,' said Tanya, with a frown. 'If you look at it objectively, it could be either of them.'

Bonnie and Ben both started to speak, and then both fell silent. They gazed at Ben's diagram, made one or two comments, added one or two question marks, and then sat back. 'She's right,' said Ben. 'We haven't actually got anywhere, have we? And Gillian Townsend still holds all the cards.'

'And you've got to get back to your revision,' said Bonnie.

'Yes, I have.' He packed up the sheets of paper and coloured pens, then turned to his laptop with a sigh. 'Sorry, girls. Time to throw you both out. Go and make yourself some tea, Bon, and tell my mum I'm back on schedule.'

'Okay,' said Bonnie, and after giving him a friendly kiss, she ushered Tanya ahead of her and down the stairs.

At the same time, Simmy was doing her best not to think about anybody in Staveley or Kendal or Crook. She worked steadily through the pile of ironing, and then changed several duvet covers, bottom sheets and pillow cases. She replaced towels and toilet rolls. She poured breakfast cereals into Tupperware containers, and found two clean tablecloths to replace ones showing stains from that morning. It was, in effect, hotel work, with the relentless pursuit of perfect cleanliness that customers demanded. There was an essential wastefulness to it that she knew her mother deplored. Washing things that were really not dirty was probably the single most destructive thing that Western mankind was inflicting on the wretched planet. Hot water, soap powder, electric dryers – the whole notion was absurd, and there was an irony to the way Angie Straw had become so immersed in it. Her guests might have to use the same sheets and towels for two or even three days, but still at the end of it, the stuff wasn't really dirty.

'There,' she said, at seven fifteen. 'It's all ready for the next lot now. Is it all right if I go home?'

'Whatever you want,' said Angie, looking as tired as Simmy felt. 'Thanks, love. But have some tea first. Are you rushing back for anything?'

'Not really. Some washing and clearing up. I'm tired, that's all.'

'It's all go, isn't it?' said Angie vaguely, as she made tea. Russell was dozing by the Rayburn with his feet on a stool and the dog on his outstretched legs. His wife and daughter exchanged looks of impatience, which Simmy realised was unusual. Ordinarily, she'd take her father's part if there was criticism coming his way. 'All right for some,' said Angie.

'He can't help it,' Simmy ventured half-heartedly. 'But you won't be able to carry on like this indefinitely, will you?'

'What do you suggest?' Angie's voice was suddenly shrill. 'Are you another one who thinks we should sell up and move to a bungalow on some ghastly estate somewhere? Or you think we're in need of a warden and panic buttons, do you?'

'I'm not discussing it now. Don't shout at me. I'm doing my best.'

'Yes . . . Well . . .'

'We'll have a proper sit-down and talk it all through,' Simmy promised. 'But not until after Mother's Day, okay? I can't cope with anything else until then.'

'I'll look forward to that, then,' said Angie bitterly.

She was back at home, drinking a warming mug of tea when somebody knocked on the door. It was dark outside, and the familiar feeling of apprehension gripped her as she went to answer it. How many ancient tales of trouble and horror began with a night-time knock?

A man stood there, his face only faintly familiar. 'Hello? So sorry to startle you. I did try you a bit earlier, but you were out. I'm Matthew Olsen.'

Matthew Olsen was the owner of the van that had killed Declan Kennedy. That meant he was very likely to be a murderer. She closed the door to within a few inches, but couldn't bring herself to slam it in his face. 'I can't let you in,' she said. 'I'm sure you understand why.'

'I won't hurt you, I promise. I'm a very soft chap. Ask anybody.'

'I've seen you in the shop. You live near here, don't you?'

'Just down the hill. I wondered if you'd remember me. We had a little chat about scampi-flavoured crisps not long ago, if you recall.'

'So we did. But I still can't let you in.'

'Yes you can. Leave the door open. Keep your phone in your hand. Or call someone now and tell them I'm here. What do you think I'm going to do?'

'I know. But . . .' She remembered at least two previous occasions where she had stupidly walked into obviously dangerous situations, without a thought for her own welfare. *Too dumb to live* echoed in her head. 'But they say you killed Declan,' she blurted.

'They don't, actually. The only person saying that is your friend Gillian Townsend. I don't blame you, but I think you owe it to me to listen to the truth.'

The door seemed to open wider of its own accord. This man was *nice*, she realised sadly. Every bit as nice as Debbie, or Gillian or Anita or old Mrs Percival. The only person

292

who hadn't sounded nice in the whole case was Declan's politician dad.

Matthew took a cautious step. 'It's cold out here,' he said. Then, 'Oh, look! There's Pat from Nuthatch Spinney.' He waved exaggeratedly at a small silver-coloured car driving past. 'She's seen me here. She'd be a great witness if anything happened.'

'I'd still be just as dead,' said Simmy incautiously.

'I absolutely *swear* that I'm not going to kill you.'

'Yes, but you would say that, wouldn't you?'

'This is very silly, you know. Even if I had killed Declan – which I definitely did not – that doesn't mean I'm here to kill you. What's the logic in that?'

'I know. But . . .' Two conflicting value systems were clashing inside her head. Her innate wish to trust everyone, to take them at face value and believe the best of them was warring with all the po-faced warnings and security alerts and sensible edicts that came from almost everybody in authority, from schoolteachers to police officers, via media presenters and ordinary housewives. Everybody told you to trust no one. Everybody thought she was a fool to get herself into vulnerable situations so willingly and so repeatedly. Everybody, that is, except her mother, and Bonnie, and Ben, and Corinne. All those she most loved, in fact. 'You're right. This is silly. Come on in, then.'

'I should also mention that I do a bit of work for your . . . friend, Christopher Henderson,' he said as he followed her into the living room. 'Although I only made the connection yesterday. I'd seen him up here once or twice, but didn't know he was visiting you.'

Simmy waved at him to sit on the sofa, and took a chair

for herself. She was trying to organise her thoughts, and making a poor job of it. 'Have the police questioned you?' she asked, cutting through any tendency to chit-chat.

'They have. They made no secret of the fact that I am top of the list of potential killers of my sister's husband. A man I liked very much, I might add, and who died horribly while I was in Keswick.'

'I've been helping – if that's the right word – Gillian and your mother, as you probably know.' Who knew what continued to present an impenetrable tangle, largely thanks to Ben and Bonnie. Despite their claim to be sharing everything, Simmy knew there were details on both sides that remained undisclosed. 'And my friends have been meeting you and Debbie. It's been a bit like a pretend trial, with us on opposing sides.'

'You make it sound like a game.'

'I do, don't I? But we know it's not. The detective inspector has a good idea what's going on, and he'd put a stop to anything that caused actual harm. He values Ben's input, usually. He is very clever, you know. Ben, I mean. I suppose Moxon's no fool, either.'

'And who does your friendly DI think killed Dec, then?'

She shook her head. 'Good question. But I really couldn't answer it. Can you prove you were in Keswick?'

'More or less, although it all depends on what time the whole thing happened.'

'I saw your van. It's got quite a lot of damage.'

'So I see. I hadn't been near it until last night, when I heard it was under the spotlight.'

'You haven't used it for over a week?'

He shook his head. 'There's been no need. I've been

doing a big clearance job for an old chap at the top end of the village, and used his truck – as well as trying to keep my sister afloat. She's been almost a full-time occupation this past week, as you might imagine.'

'And you *really* think your own mother killed Declan, do you?'

He met her eyes and took a long breath. 'I really do,' he said solemnly. 'And I'm very sorry to say that I think you've impeded the course of justice by taking her side. I don't mean that aggressively' – he put out a hand towards her, making stroking motions – 'I just have to make it clear to you that she is more than capable of such a thing, despite how she might seem.'

'But *why?* Why would she?'

'Vengeance. Declan's caused her a lot of annoyance over the years, estranged her from Debbie and me, and turned his very influential father against her and Gillian. And probably more that I don't know about.'

Simmy drew back into her chair. 'Those aren't good enough reasons to commit such a cruel and careful murder. If it *was* her, she'd have had to plan it down to the finest detail. The van, the timing, the convincing everybody she was somewhere else. I can't actually see how it could even be feasible.'

'That's where your young friends come in. Debbie and I have a good idea, but we don't know the whole thing. And now they've got me in their sights as the likely killer, they're not going to tell us anything more. Even if Debbie's the next of kin to the victim, they can see how close she and I are, so they've clammed up.'

'So why have you come to see me?' She smiled tightly.

'I should have asked you that at the start, shouldn't I?'

'I wanted to persuade you to stop taking my mother's side. I know you mean well, and Gillian's incredibly effective at making people like her, and all that. I understand how they got to you. But I have to tell you that you've been used.'

She closed her eyes for a few seconds, trying to recapture that first meeting, over a week ago. 'I don't see how,' she said eventually. 'And how do you know what happened?'

'I don't suppose I should tell you, but it wouldn't take long for you to guess. Who else was there? Who knows Gillian and my mother better than anybody? And who do you think has the most terrible divided loyalties?'

'Mrs Percival,' Simmy realised. 'Gillian's mother. Although I don't see why her loyalties should be divided.'

'Ah – so nobody's told you, then? She's godmother to Debbie's older girl. Not just a token role, either. She's made it a major commitment, ever since Lorraine was born.'

'But – does that mean she managed to remain on good terms with Declan? Debbie did say she'd visited last weekend, now I think about it. Now, of course, I can see it couldn't really have been anybody else.'

'Right.'

'So what about Gillian?' She floundered, trying to articulate her revulsion at the many implications of the charge against Anita, particularly where her friend and partner was concerned.

'Gillian's a tragic figure,' he said. 'She's an only child, with no kids of her own. She's been in poor health much of her life, with various peculiar immunity issues. The

296

Crohn's disease is just the last in a long list. She's a martyr, I suppose. Except that people always seem to like her more than they usually like a martyr. Maybe I should call her a stoic.'

'Do *you* like her?'

His face hardened 'Not if she's been involved in killing my brother-in-law.'

'But she *hasn't*. It just isn't possible.'

'I don't think it would have been feasible without her.'

Simmy lifted her chin in triumph. 'Then you've got it all completely wrong. If it wasn't you and it wasn't Anita, then it was somebody else. What about Declan's father?'

'What about him? You think he killed his own son? His *only* son, come to that.' He made a scoffing sound. 'He's at least as devastated as Debbie and the girls.'

'Well, we don't seem to be getting anywhere, do we?'

'We might yet. At least I haven't taken a knife to you, have I? You might have a few second thoughts about me, now you've got to know me a bit.'

'My head's full of questions. Why did Declan go off as he did, not telling his wife where he was going? Who knew where he was? Who knew about your van? Who had a key for it? What was Declan really like?'

'We told your friends most of that stuff.'

'Well, they didn't tell me. All I know is how Declan kept nagging and nagging for a job with Anita and Gillian, after they'd told him loud and clear there wasn't a chance. He sounds a bit of a fool, actually.'

'That wasn't him. It was the old man, who never could take no for an answer. He's like an old-fashioned Mafia boss. Pretty much of a dinosaur, you'd think. But plenty of small towns still have a character like him, usually head of the council.'

But Simmy could no longer duck the burning, dragging, horrifying fact of a man and woman accusing their own mother of murder. 'But she's your *mother*,' she wailed, almost choking with the force of that single fact. 'How can you say and think such things about her?'

He went pale and clasped his hands between his knees. 'I know. I understand how it must look. We tried to explain to the boy and his girlfriend. She was never a real mother to us. We missed out on the bonding, or whatever it is. But somehow we seem to have missed all that family duty stuff as well. You probably know people, the same as I do, who were parked with minders or nannies or whatever, and scarcely knew their parents, but still behave quite normally as adults. I mean, they still speak to the old folk and celebrate Mother's Day and get together at Christmas. The social expectations are strong enough to make them go through the motions. But that didn't happen with me and Deb. I can't really say why. Possibly because our mother never seemed to want or need us to be like that. It all comes from her, you see. That's the whole point. All we ever do is react to her.'

'But Gillian loves her, doesn't she? *She's* not evil or wicked and you and Debbie haven't turned out so badly.'

He lifted an eyebrow, suggesting something close to offence. 'How can you possibly say that? You have no idea what we're like.'

She quailed. 'Sorry. But you did say you were a softie and not tempted to murder me.' She had hoped to make him smile at that, but in vain.

His head dropped forward and he mumbled, 'It's worse than that. I'm completely pathetic.'

Simmy recalled Christopher's comment about Matthew being good with old ladies. The psychology was not hard to comprehend. 'I'm sure that's not true,' she said.

It was approaching half past eight, and she wondered what happened next. Should she offer him a drink? Did she want to give him any hint of encouragement to build a friendship? He was, after all, a neighbour. His house was probably only three hundred yards from hers. Something threatening stirred when she realised that.

He said nothing, as she got up from her chair. 'I don't think there's any more to be said, is there?' She tried to sound brisk. A new thought occurred. 'Have you been helping in Keswick today? Getting things ready for next week's sale?'

'I did go, yeah, but I wasn't much use. They wanted some stuff fetched from Carlisle, but I couldn't go because the cops have got my van. For all I know, I'll never get it back.'

'Oh. Of course. Do they compensate you for loss of work?'

He looked up, and this time there was a faint smile. 'What do you think?'

'I think it's rather unlikely.'

'Right. So do I. But you want me to go. Okay.' He got out of the sofa with an effort. 'Another five minutes and I'd probably have gone to sleep here. It's been a very tiring week.'

'I can imagine. Thanks for coming,' she added, feeling foolish. 'I mean – it was good to meet you properly. You've given me a lot to think about.' *Not that that's a good thing*, she thought crossly.

'Just – stop sticking up for my mother, okay? It's not helping.'

So that was what he had come to say. In a nutshell. In a repeat of the scene on the doorstep, she experienced a violent inner conflict. Resistance to being told what to do fought with a dawning suspicion that she might have been wrong all along. 'I didn't do anything, really,' she said. 'Nothing that made any difference, anyway. You don't have to worry about me. I'm just a florist.'

Finally, he laughed. 'Yes, Simmy Brown, that's right. You're just a quiet ordinary little florist. God help us.'

She saw him out with the inner conflict still raging.

She was left with her attention focused on events in Staveley. Sticking up for Anita and Gillian had seemed entirely natural at the time. She had met them, listened to their party plans, admired Mrs Percival's lovely house, and worried with them about the missing Declan. After that, what choice did she have? Despite efforts to remain neutral and uninvolved, they had drawn her in with the sticky tentacles of normal human sympathy, until she was placed in painful opposition to Ben and Bonnie, and in the process made the object of DI Moxon's pity – again.

And now she still had a while to kill before she could decently go to bed. She wanted to phone Ben, Gillian, Debbie, and even Moxon – more or less in that order, although Moxon could quickly be deleted from the list. He had nothing to offer her, the way she was feeling. She wanted everyone to be happy, she realised. Sentimental, unrealistic idiot that she was – none of the people she'd met deserved the pain and misery that had overwhelmed them.

And the face that came most vividly into focus for her was that of poor Gillian Townsend, working so hard on behalf of her friend.

But Gillian had a perfectly good husband to watch out for her. She and Anita had a strong and healthy friendship based on decades of daily contact at work. Gillian even had an impressively capable mother, whose house was kept beautifully and who clearly had a kind heart. None of them really needed Simmy Brown any more, not even Gillian. She had probably never really needed her very much – it was just an additional string to her bow to have the support of someone so transparently innocent and reasonably objective about the whole business. The same feeling that had assailed her over recent days came again – a contradictory set of emotions that said *thank goodness I'm not fully involved* as well as *how dare they all think I'm too insignificant to worry about?* Her place was so often on the sidelines that she had to acknowledge that she deliberately put herself there. And yet, she wanted it all to come right, and yes, for everybody to be happy.

But they had not been happy before, had they? Debbie and Matthew had hated their mother for years. Debbie had sought solace, apparently, in family life with husband and daughters, but Matthew struck her as rather lost. No proper job, no discernible partner. Chances were he rented the Troutbeck house from some long-time acquaintance who owed him a favour. Matthew Olsen was a clear candidate for police interest – anyone could see that.

And Anita? No hint of a reciprocal loathing towards her children had been evident, despite what Debbie and

Matthew both insisted was the case. As Simmy saw it, her children's hostility made Anita sad and possibly guilty, but she didn't hate them back. It remained inconceivable that she would wilfully cause her daughter such utter heartbreak that would arise from the death of Declan. Simmy's mind stubbornly baulked at the notion, as it had been doing all week.

And just as depressing was the realisation that there were little or no grounds for hoping that the whole business might be almost over. Gillian's discovery of the van had seemed conclusive at the time, but here they were, three days later and still no announcement of any arrest or charge. She should know, she told herself, by this time, that nothing worked that quickly. Except that sometimes it *did*. At least, it had been resolved in her own mind, when Ben and Bonnie had worked it out, and Simmy had added useful contributions, and the malefactor had been confronted – often recklessly, but never mistakenly. This time, the three of them could not agree about any of the elements that mattered.

She had the television on, but was paying it no attention. Her mobile was lying beside her, on the arm of her chair, inviting her to make one of the calls that might improve her mood. Perhaps she should call a friend – someone from an earlier phase of her life, who knew nothing about Staveley and dead cyclists. There was Kathy, who had stayed with her a while ago, only to become unpleasantly involved in a murder in Coniston. They had parted distractedly, both very shaken by events and unsure of the effects on their friendship. They had exchanged old-fashioned letters at Christmas, full of news and optimism, but there had been a distinct absence of personal connection, from both sides. Kathy was part of Simmy's earlier life, and the harsh fact was that Simmy had no inclination to think back over those years.

Was that irresponsible of her, she wondered. Or worse – cowardly and self-deceiving? Or simply the way things had to be, with the fresh start already evolving into something much more settled and permanent? It was nearly two years since she'd moved to the Lakes. Kathy represented things she no longer wanted at the forefront of her mind. Even the poor little baby was best packed away, with love and grief and helplessness all in the box with her. You could not meaningfully love the pathetic scrap who had never seen the light of day. She had lived as part of Simmy's body; would always have a claim to that special bond, but it was no more than that.

She should have known better than to entertain such thoughts, she told herself later. She knew how powerful telepathy could be, conjuring or connecting with someone else's thought waves. It might not be scientific, but she, like most people, knew how real it was, from direct experience. When her landline rang, at ten minutes to nine, some part of her knew instantly who it was.

His mother had not needed to give him her number. He had needed it during their divorce proceedings. He knew where she lived, and where she worked, and her parents' details would be in a not-so-old address book still in his possession. Tony was always going to be able to find her if he wanted to.

She was struck dumb. 'Simmy? Are you there? Say something,' he urged.

'Erggh,' she managed. 'I was just thinking about you.'

'Listen. I'm sorry to call like this, but there are things I've got to tell you. Is that okay?'

'Yes.'

'Well, I'm not sure where to start. Listen,' he said again. 'I've been having psychotherapy. Heavy stuff, I can tell you. I've been going for three months now, and it's just coming a bit more clear. We were both so useless at dealing with what happened. Don't you think? And you know what next week is, of course.'

'Tony . . .'

'I know. I shouldn't be doing this to you. I don't know where you are emotionally. And I don't know exactly what you've been hearing about me. It's mostly true. I went insane. Literally. That poor woman. I should never have pressed charges against her. She didn't have much option but to take direct action, given the way I was chasing after her. Anyway, that's settled now. I can't tell you how much better I feel. But then I started wondering about you, and next week, and how we never really tied up the loose ends. I know it's jargon, but the only word for it is *closure*. I want closure, Simmy. And I can only get it from you.'

'Tony . . . I'm in the middle of other stuff now. I don't think I do need the same thing as you. I mean – I understand what you're saying. I really think I must have been reading your mind, over the past hour or so.' She recounted haltingly her imaginary packing away of their lost daughter, thinking she had never come close to talking to him in such a way before.

'That's exactly what I've been trying to do,' he told her excitedly. 'That's good, isn't it?'

'I suppose so. You sound good about it, anyway. But it's not something that's between us any more. We're apart now, permanently. We have to get on as individuals, not a couple. That's been true for a long time already.' Irritation was creeping through her, overtaking the sympathy and goodwill she knew she ought to be feeling. How could he be so *wheedling*, so intent on getting a response from her? 'You'll be fine now,' she said, briskly. 'Next thing I hear you'll have a new wife and we'll all live happily ever after.'

'Okay.' She could hear the disappointment and frustration in the single word. 'All right, then. But I'll be thinking of you later this month, all the same. And I wish you well, Simmy. I truly and honestly do.'

'Thanks. You too. Bye now.' She put the phone down gently, holding back the avalanche of unwelcome emotion until she was in the living room again. Then she burst out in a single cry of 'Shit!' It felt immensely transgressive. Simmy Brown never used a bad word. Or almost never.

She had spent the past weeks trying her best to forget that baby Edith had died on Mother's Day. Her father's collapse had given her hope that both parents would let the day go by unremarked. Nobody else knew about it. Not Melanie or Bonnie or Ben had a clue as to precisely why she shrank so cravenly from the wholesale celebrations of motherhood and all that went with it.

She had persuaded herself that the extreme busyness that a florist experienced on that day was in fact a clever way of avoiding any personal associations. She would be rushing to and fro, shouting at Bonnie, furious at obstructive drivers, intent on producing perfect bouquets again and again. It hadn't happened deliberately, but she had come to appreciate the skill of her unconscious. And now Tony had wrecked it, by his well-intentioned solicitude. She very nearly said another naughty word, which would have been preferable to sinking into tears as she did instead.

Chapter Twenty-Four

The phone rang shortly after nine, and she answered it thinking it was Christopher. Or possibly Ben. Instead, a woman's voice burst hysterically into her ear. 'Simmy? This is going to sound stupid, but my mother insists on my calling you. Can you come over here right away? I know it's late, but please come. Everything's fallen apart, and we need somebody calm and sensible to help us deal with it.'

'Gillian? Is that you? Why – what's happened?'

'Just come. Please!'

'What about your husband? And Anita? What do you want me to *do*?'

'Robin's no good. And Anita—' There was a wail of anguish that cut right through Simmy. Without any words or articulate thought, she knew in that moment what was coming. And she knew she had no choice but to be there and hear it all spoken out loud. *Somebody calm and sensible*, Gillian had said. It wasn't so very unreasonable, even if she resisted the flattering implications. Somebody uninvolved, objective, but also sympathetic. In a similar situation, she might have called for somebody like her to bear witness to unfolding events.

'All right,' she said. 'You're at home, are you?'

'No, no. I'm in Staveley. With my mother. You have to come. She says you must.'

At least that's closer, Simmy thought stupidly. She could be there in ten minutes, if she used the little road through Moorhowe. 'I'm not sure I can remember exactly where it is,' she said.

'Yes, you can. Turn right past the bus stop, and right again. Oh . . .' The voice faltered and died. 'You can find it,' she choked.

Simmy said nothing more. She remembered a footbridge over a waterway, crossed by a bridge too small for cars. And a maze of little streets, with a big house at the top of one of them. She had taken little notice of precisely how it was reached, merely following Gillian and Anita. But she had retraced her steps afterwards, back to her car, and although it was dark, she thought she might recognise enough to get her there again.

Closure, Tony had said. That's what she wanted now, she supposed, in the matter of the Olsens and Kennedys. She wanted to know, from the primary sources, just who and when and how – and overwhelmingly *why*?

But if Gillian was with her mother, why did she need Simmy? Barbara Percival was a capable, fully functioning woman, who had shown every sign of being able to console a distraught daughter. The sense of coming full circle grew increasingly strong as she approached the village.

But there was no prospect this time of a colourful party in the handsome old house. Nothing pleasant was waiting for her there. So why was she putting herself through it so willingly? Was she, in fact, walking blindly into another perilous situation, summoned by a weeping woman who might even now turn out to be a killer? Had her common sense deserted her yet again?

She sat in the car, parked once more across the road from the chip shop. *Be sensible*, she ordered herself. Could she trust Gillian Townsend? Who else might be there in that house, acting in some unguessed-at conspiracy that spelt serious danger for Simmy? The one sure thing was that there was a killer in their midst. A clever, deliberate killer, who planned meticulously and covered his or her tracks to perfection. It could be Gillian herself. It could even be her aged mother. Anybody who could drive was eligible.

Moxon was the obvious safety net, backup person. His number was in her phone. He was probably at home, but still awake, especially if the Kennedy murder was coming to a head, which she very much suspected it was. But she shuddered at the thought of him crashing in on an all-female gathering where there were sure to be tears and worse. On the basis of nothing more than Gillian's phone call, Simmy somehow knew there were no men involved. Matthew Olsen would not be there, even if there was a chance that his sister was. Ben would be better in some ways, but if danger threatened, then he could not be allowed to get close.

So who could she call? Who was capable of providing an effective level of protection against an unknown and unlikely peril? The absence of a suitable name made her feel lonely and vulnerable. The people she most trusted in this whole business were the two who were waiting for her in the house. Gillian and her mother were not to be feared. She had wasted time worrying, just as she had with Matthew. Nobody was going to hurt her. They had no reason to. All they wanted was to gain her understanding and support, in the face of the unthinkable.

She left the car and crossed the little bridge. What had Gillian said? 'Right past the bus stop and right again.' No mention of the bridge, but that was in effect a right turn – on foot. By car, it was altogether less obvious. But she was remembering landmarks, and was on the right course almost instantly. A woman walking a dog smiled and greeted her. A man just going into his house gave her a little wave. *Good,* she thought. *They'll be able to say I was here if there's a search for me.* The idea was enough to make her laugh – which would surely make her even more memorable.

The big house was quickly visible at the top of a small road. There was no mistaking it, and with a deep breath, she hurried to the front door and rang the bell.

Three ravaged female faces met her when she went into the living room. The person who had opened the door was an unfamiliar young woman who introduced herself as Megan, one of Gillian's junior staff. 'She asked me to drive her here,' she explained. 'I'll be in the conservatory if you want me. I'm not getting involved in any of this stuff.'

The surprise was Anita, huddled awkwardly on an upright chair, turned away from the room. *Of course, she lives in Staveley,* Simmy reminded herself. A crisis centring on her would naturally take place in the village – but not in this house, surely?

Mrs Percival stood up to greet her. 'Thank you for coming,' she said. 'This must seem profoundly strange to you. I'm not sure I can explain it, but we all regard you as a necessary witness. Without you, or somebody like you, we don't seem able to get anywhere.' She glanced towards the conservatory with an angry look, which Simmy interpreted as being directed at the young Megan, who might have fulfilled the role.

There was nothing she could find to say, so she merely nodded and took a seat on a chair matching Anita's. Mrs Percival still held the floor. 'You see, I want to make it plain that Declan's death is my responsibility. I caused it through my own blinkered stupidity. It's all down to me, you understand, that we're here together now. Debbie convinced me of the truth, and I couldn't just leave it to the police. I needed to take things into my own hands, but then it all felt so . . . well . . . *dangerous.*'

Gillian, half lying, half sitting on the sofa, gave a cry of distress. 'No,' she choked. 'None of this is true. Anita came right away when Mother asked her. If it was true, she would not have done that, would she?'

Simmy inspected her. 'You look really ill,' she said. 'Shouldn't you be in hospital?' The woman's face was grey, her hands were clasped tightly over her abdomen, and her knees were drawn up.

'That's my fault as well,' claimed the old lady.

Simmy began to think she might be going a trifle too far in her self-accusations. 'How?' she asked.

Without warning, Anita Olsen got to her feet. 'She's right, the old bitch. She's the one who ought to be dead – but that would only have made everything worse. She's right that she's been stupid and blinkered, ignoring everything that was right under her nose. She still doesn't see what she's done. Not properly.'

Barbara Percival's chin rose sharply. 'I have to disagree. How could I be expected to understand how truly monstrous a woman can be? A woman I've known for half my adult life, my daughter's closest friend? But now I see it all perfectly clearly. I know what I did, and I know what you did. And you did it to many more people than just Declan Kennedy. Look at your friend now. Think of the others.' She turned from glaring at Anita to appealing to Simmy. 'It was my will, you see. That's what tipped the balance.'

'I'm afraid I don't see at all,' said Simmy.

'She was leaving this house to my children,' said Anita, through clenched teeth. 'What do you think about that? Came and made the thing in my office, made me go through it with her, bold as brass, as if it had nothing to do with me except for the legalities.'

The room fell silent, apart from muffled gasps from Gillian. Simmy's mind was full of tangles and inconsistencies. 'I still don't see,' she said, after half a minute. 'What *did* it have to do with you?'

Anita turned red with fury. 'She was usurping my role! Surely that's obvious. They're *my* children, not hers. How dare she! And what about Gillian? Doesn't she deserve to inherit it?'

The old lady's voice rose to a shout. 'Gillian was perfectly happy about it. She's got everything she needs, including a devoted husband. Everything except her health, of course.'

Gillian lifted her head. 'She means I'm not likely to outlive her,' she said. 'This disease is going to kill me in another few years. There's no point in leaving anything to me.'

'No!' shouted Anita. 'You're going to be all right.'

Simmy remembered Matthew's words of the previous evening: *Gillian's a tragic figure*. The truth of it was starkly evident now. Gillian was sick in every way – physically, emotionally and possibly mentally. 'You really believed Anita was innocent, didn't you?' she said.

Gillian nodded wordlessly.

'Of course she did. She believes the best of everyone,' said Anita, with a sad smile. 'That's what made it so easy for me. She was always going to get me off.' She turned to glare at the old lady. 'Until you started interfering,' she snarled. Then her shoulders slumped. 'I had no idea of the toll it would take on me. I thought I could simply lie my way out of it, and carry on a normal life. That's not the way it works in the real world. I'm actually *glad* it's all come to a head. You can't imagine the relief. And I dare say I can still play the system well enough to avoid the worst set of consequences.'

Mrs Percival was still standing, and now moved closer to Anita, the two face to face like cats. 'Well, isn't that lovely? You feel relief, and everybody else is in utter despair. I usurped your role, because you abandoned it from the start. What were *you* going to ever do for them? Debbie's been struggling for money for years, and Matthew's barely able to manage to live a normal life. Who was going to help them, if I didn't?'

'They wouldn't let me,' grated Anita.

'At least they can see the truth of the matter. They've never had any illusions about you. They knew from the first moment who'd killed Declan, and it wasn't difficult to convince me they were right.'

Another wail from Gillian, filled with anguish, darkened the mood even further. 'You betrayed your only friend,' Mrs Percival accused. 'This sweet, brave, loyal friend, who believed you to be worthy of her affection, and you kicked muck in her face. You used her, exploited her, and now you'll watch her suffer and probably die even sooner than she would have, because of what you've done to her.'

'But why did you kill *Declan*?' Simmy burst out, still sorting the bits of the puzzle and failing to get a proper picture. 'What good would *that* do?'

'I couldn't just let them all live in this house together without me, could I? What would people say?' And she looked around the room, as if for validation. 'And I couldn't kill Debbie, could I? She's my daughter. Even Matthew, useless creature that he is, is flesh of my flesh.'

Both Gillian and her mother stared in disbelief at this. A sudden likeness made their relationship obvious. Both jaws dropped, both pairs of eyes widened.

'But how does Declan's death affect their inheriting the house?' Simmy asked, still entirely bemused.

'Because without him, Debbie and the girls would be sure to come to live with me. It's only a little way away. We'd all have been a family together at last.'

'In your dreams!' said Barbara Percival. 'You've gone totally mad if that's what you think. And what about poor Matthew? The way you planned it, he'd have spent most of his life in prison. Is that really what you wanted?'

There was no response to this. Simmy, watching the woman closely, saw more deeply into the cornered killer, and was already moving towards the conservatory when the crisis peaked. 'Megan!' she shouted. 'Call the police.'

Anita was at the mantelpiece, seizing the first of a row of china ornaments. Simmy recognised an identical jug to one broken by her father a few days ago, as it flew across the room, bounced off a low glass coffee table and landed miraculously intact on the thick carpet. 'Stop it!' she yelled. 'Calm down.'

But Anita was mad. She must have been mad for years, Simmy concluded. Megan came to the door leading from the conservatory, phone in her hand. One glance was enough to get her thumb moving, and she was rapidly giving directions to a call-handler. More china began to fly, at least one piece crashing into a bookcase and shattering noisily.

'Help me,' Simmy ordered both Barbara and Megan. The three closed in warily, Megan still holding the phone. Not one of them had the courage to lay hands on the wild woman, until she grabbed a heavy ormolu clock. 'No!' shrieked Barbara. 'That was my grandmother's.' And she seized Anita's arm in both hands, and clung to it like a bull terrier.

It was Gillian who spoke into the oddly quiet struggle. 'Put it down, Neet,' she said. 'You're just making everything worse. Nobody's going to let you make a plea of insanity, so stop playacting.'

It was spectacularly successful. Anita relinquished the clock into Simmy's waiting hands and then stumbled back to her original seat. 'You killed Declan because you didn't want people to see what a hopelessly bad mother you are and always have been,' Gillian went on. 'You thought you'd finally force Debbie to turn to you, like a real daughter at last, if she didn't have him always reminding her how much she dislikes you. That's as loathsome a motive as I've ever heard. The jury's going to hate you. The press will, too. You're damned, my love, and it serves you right.'

'But surely there must be more to it than that,' said Simmy. 'All that planning . . . and throwing the guilt onto Matthew . . . are you sure she isn't mad?'

'Not in a legal sense. Deluded, certainly, if she thought she'd ever get Debbie to live with her. She and her girls regarded me and my mother as much closer family than Anita. And we went along with it. Anita did her best not to see that, I realise now. And I can't imagine how she could be so *deliberate* about it all.' The pain washed through her again and she finished on a whimper that turned into a scream. 'Oh, God! It's on the sofa. Sorry, Mum.' A sour smell filled the room, as Simmy realised with horror what had happened.

'Darling!' said Barbara. 'We have to get you to hospital. You should have gone last night.'

'In a minute. I don't suppose Megan asked for an ambulance, did you?'

Megan had retreated again, looking earnestly out of the window, on the pretext of watching for the police. She shook her head.

'But how did you do it?' Simmy, mindful of the grilling she would undergo from Ben and Bonnie, was anxious to get the details. 'The van, and everything. And *when*?'

Anita was turned away, as before. She showed no sign of having heard the question.

Gillian was writhing, trying to move away from the

316

soiled part of the sofa, disgust at herself clear on her face. But she also looked slightly less sick. 'She walked,' she said. 'As soon as you left us on that Friday, she walked across the fields to Crook, took the van, found Declan and killed him. Then she returned the van and walked home again.'

'Okay,' said Simmy slowly. 'But how did she know where he'd be?'

'She texted him,' said Barbara. 'Saying he was needed because Debbie or one of the children was ill – some such pretext as that. And then took his phone away after she'd run him down in her son's van.'

Simmy was still struggling with feelings of disgust and disbelief. 'Oh,' she said.

Gillian made another determined effort. 'That must have been it - so there'd be no evidence. She'll have destroyed it, but of course the phone company will have a record. The police told Debbie they'd found a record of a text sent from Anita to Declan on Friday, but they couldn't see the actual wording of it. They didn't see it as relevant, especially when Anita gave them some explanation for it. Debbie thought it was suspicious from the start. She and Matthew between them can explain the whole picture. But of course nobody believed them.' Her face was grey, her body rigid. 'Least of all me,' she whispered.

'But Ben and Bonnie did,' said Simmy. 'And I think DI Moxon did as well.'

'Here they are,' said Megan. 'The police are here.'

Simmy texted Ben when she got home.

Debbie was right in every detail. A tragic business. Don't want to talk about it until tomorrow.

Then she went to bed, crashing into an exhausted traumatised sleep. Not until next morning did she phone Christopher and give him a summary of events.

'I'm coming over this evening,' he promised. 'I can hear how much you need some TLC.'

At six o'clock he was at the door, and cuddling her against him as she talked, making murmured comments, but asking no questions. Finally, he said, 'I'm glad Matt's in the clear, anyway. He's a good man.'

'It's sickening, though, don't you think? That a woman could be so depraved and deluded and devious, for absolutely no good reason – it shakes your faith in the world.'

'Sounds to me as if she did have her reasons, going back to when she first had a child. Some people just shouldn't do it. It brings misery all round.'

'You don't mean us, do you? Are you thinking we shouldn't have a child?'

He hugged her even closer. 'No, I don't mean us. We're going to have at least two, starting today.'

She laughed. 'We should have started months ago, if we're to manage two.'

'Twins. We'll have twins.'

'Good idea. And at least I can promise I'll be a better mother than Anita Olsen was.'

REBECCA TOPE is the author of three bestselling crime series, set in the stunning Cotswolds, Lake District and West Country. She lives on a smallholding in rural Herefordshire, where she enjoys the silence and plants a lot of trees, but also manages to travel the world and enjoy civilisation from time to time. Most of her varied experiences and activities find their way into her books, sooner or later.

rebeccatope.com